"Tell me what your grand scheme is, then! What is the purpose of all this deception?"

Sebastian's fists slammed on the tabletop behind her, making her start. "Make me understand why you would lower yourself to a man who's not worthy of you. Why are you hiding your intelligence, Kate? No—" He held up a hand when she opened her mouth. "I'm not a featherbrain like Seagrave. I know you are smart and skilled, despite your obvious attempts to conceal your knowledge. You helped me rebuild that wall and fixed that boiler by yourself. Do you love Seagrave that much that you would pretend to be unintelligent just so you could marry him?"

Her eyes grew wide and her lower lip trembled. "N-no."

"Then tell me why!" His frustration made his entire body tense up like a wound coil. Because the truth he didn't want to say aloud was ready to burst out: that he would move heaven and earth and give his very soul to the devil to stop her from marrying Seagrave.

The muscles in her throat bobbed as she swallowed hard. "It's not what you think."

D0829747

Author Note

The industrial revolution and the robber barons who "built the world" have always fascinated me. Since history books are already filled with the achievements of these men, allow me to name some of the women who have contributed to the development of modern railroad and transportation:

Catherine Gibbon—inventor of the Gibbon Double Girder Lap-Joint Track, which made tracks safer and easier to maintain.

Eliza Murfey—developed an oil lubricant used on train axles to prevent derailment.

Mary Riggin—patented the first crossing gate in 1890 after seeing an accident at a grade crossing.

Mary Walton—cleaned up both air and noise pollution by inventing a device that reduced smog from factory smokestacks (which was later used on locomotive engines) and a sound dampening system to reduce engine noise.

Thank you, ladies, for making the world a safer and less polluted place.

PAULIA BELGADO

May the Best Duke Win

HARLEQUIN®
HISTORICAL™

Recycling programs
for this product may
not exist in your area.

ISBN-13: 978-1-335-72340-6

May the Best Duke Win

Copyright © 2022 by Paulia Belgado

All rights reserved. No part of this book may be used or reproduced in
any manner whatsoever without written permission except in the case of
brief quotations embodied in critical articles and reviews.

This is a work of fiction. Names, characters, places and incidents
are either the product of the author's imagination or are used fictitiously.
Any resemblance to actual persons, living or dead, businesses,
companies, events or locales is entirely coincidental.

For questions and comments about the quality of this book,
please contact us at CustomerService@Harlequin.com.

Harlequin Enterprises ULC
22 Adelaide St. West, 41st Floor
Toronto, Ontario M5H 4E3, Canada
www.Harlequin.com

Printed in U.S.A.

Born and raised in the Philippines, **Paulia Belgado** has worn many hats over the years, from office assistant, flyer distributor, singer, nanny and farm worker. Now she's proud to add romance author to that list. After decades of dreaming of seeing her name on the shelves next to her favorite romance authors, she finally found the courage (and time—thanks, 2020!) to write her first book. Paulia lives in Malaysia with her husband, Jason, Jessie the poodle, and an embarrassing amount of pens and stationery art supplies. Follow her on Twitter, @pauliabelgado, or on Facebook.com/pauliabelgado.

Books by Paulia Belgado

May the Best Duke Win
is Paulia Belgado's debut for Harlequin Historical.

Look out for more books from Paulia Belgado
coming soon.

Visit the Author Profile page
at Harlequin.com.

To my parents, Mercy and Danny.

Thank you for your love,
support and sacrifice.

I love you both.

Chapter One

London, 1842

If Kate Mason could understand men as well as she did steam engines, life would be so much simpler.

Treat a piece of machinery well, and it would run smoothly. With a little bit of fuel, water, and heat, engines could do marvellous things, like pump water from underground or move hundreds of people across miles and miles of track. And if they broke down and turned temperamental, you just needed to look inside and simply fix or replace the missing part. Truly, there was no mechanical problem that Kate couldn't solve.

But men—what made them tick, how their minds functioned, and what fuelled them—were a mystery to her.

Take her father, for example.

Kate wished she could just look inside his head and figure out how he worked. That way, his words this morning wouldn't be catching her by surprise.

'By now you must have realised why I brought you to England, Kathryn.' Her father's hawklike gaze pinned her. 'You must find a husband so we can begin building a Mason locomotives factory here. Marriage to an influential lord will also ensure we can gain the necessary rights to acquire the land needed for our railway lines.'

Kate should have suspected something when her father—despite dragging her three thousand, four hundred and fifty-nine miles from New York to London—would not tell her more details about the new locomotives factory they were building, nor take her to his meetings with solicitors, bankers, even the architects and builders. When they'd arrived in London a few days ago he'd simply deposited her in their suite at The Ritz, in the care of another American family they had travelled with, and had not spoken to her until today as they'd sat down to breakfast.

But, then again, that was how industrialist and business magnate Arthur Mason had grown his fortune from practically nothing into the empire it was today: by being completely ruthless and never revealing his true intentions until it was too late.

Kate, however, would not give up so easily. Taking a sip of tea from the delicate china cup, she composed herself. 'But, Father, you never mentioned anything about marriage. I thought you said you needed me to oversee the building and operation of Mason Railroad & Locomotives here in England.'

There had even been a hint that she might be able to build an engine of her own design once the facility was up and running.

'Did I?' her father challenged. 'I don't recall any such thing. Did I say those exact words?'

And that was when Kate knew Arthur Mason had outmanoeuvred her.

Ever since he had first brought up the idea of going 'across the pond' to take advantage of England's booming railway industry, her father had dangled the prospect of her managing a factory of her own. *'I need you to start the factory, Kathryn',* he had said. *'Your Pap would have wanted you there.'*

And appealing to the memory of her grandfather had worked. There was no one in the world she had loved more. Right after his wife had died after giving birth to Kate, Arthur had left West Virginia to seek his fortune in New York, leaving her in the care of his father. Henry 'Pap' Mason had taught her everything he knew about engines from his days working in the coal mines. Eventually, when she was about seven years old, Arthur had sent for them and established Mason Railroad & Locomotives so his father could put his talents to good use.

Growing up, she had worked side by side with Pap, even helping him with his greatest creation—the Andersen steam engine. It had been one of the most efficient engines of its time, and it was because of the Andersen they'd been able to build farther west and north than any other railroad company, their rails stretching past Illinois as well as into Canada. It was unfortunate that Pap had died four years ago, before he'd been able to see his invention make Mason R&L a true success.

Despite the fact that Kate had helped with the building of the New York factory, the design of the Andersen, and managed operations after his death, all had ultimately been Pap's accomplishments, his pride and joy. So when her father had planted the seeds of going to England she had thought this was her opportunity to prove herself—that this would be her legacy. In fact, she'd even allowed herself to start thinking about her own engine design.

She now realised she had been mistaken. Or rather, misled and outwitted.

'You're twenty-one years old,' her father continued, now barely looking at her as he unfolded the newspaper beside his plate. 'Leaving you alone with only your grandfather for company growing up was one of the worst mistakes of my life. If your mother were alive she would have taken care of this years ago, and you would be wed and bred by now.'

Her father's coarse words shocked her, and yet she shouldn't have been surprised. Despite his vast fortune and great success, Arthur Mason did not make any secret of the one disappointment in his life—that his only offspring was female. And no matter how hard Kate had worked with Pap, and how efficiently she had run the factory after his death, in Arthur's eyes she would only ever be a woman.

'The sooner you are married off, the sooner we can build. And then you can begin producing sons. Healthy, strapping boys who can one day take over from me.'

Kate's heart plummeted in her chest. She knew, of course, that as a woman she had very limited choices in life. But to have her father state the obvious so bluntly nonetheless struck her like a knife to the gut.

After skimming the headlines, he sent her an ominous stare. 'We will be attending a ball with the DeVrieses tonight, and hopefully by morning you will have secured some offers for your hand.'

Little did she know those words were sealing her fate.

Sebastian Wakefield, Duke of Mabury, stared down at the cards in his hand as if contemplating his next move.

'Your Grace?' the dealer asked. 'Do you stand or choose another?'

He placed the cards face down on the table. 'Another, if you please.'

Beside him, Viscount Derry let out a snort. 'Overly confident tonight, aren't you, Mabury?'

Sebastian nodded to the dealer as he accepted the card, glancing at it briefly. With his expression barely changing, he flicked his gaze to Derry. 'There is confidence, and then there is skill.'

The young pup didn't know the difference, and never would if the way he'd been playing in the last hour was any indication. Or even in the last four years he'd been a member of Brooks's. Indeed, Derry was known as an easy mark amongst the more seasoned card players in the club.

The dealer cleared his throat. 'Your Grace?'

'I stand.'

'Thank you. Now, gentlemen, if you please, reveal your cards.'

Without a trace of emotion on his face Sebastian turned his cards over—the jack of hearts, five of spades, and six of diamonds. Twenty-one.

'Devil take you, Mabury!' Derry exclaimed. 'How could you possibly win three rounds in a row and now get a twenty-one?'

The other players around the table grumbled unhappily but did not express their displeasure as vocally as the young Viscount.

Sebastian turned his freezing gaze on Derry. 'Are you accusing me of something, Lord Derry?'

'I—I'm merely pointing out the impossible,' Derry spluttered.

'His luck is extraordinary—especially at *vingt-un*.' Devon St James, Marquess of Ashbrooke, was the only one at the table who held no expression of disappointment, derision, or controlled fury on his face. In fact, he looked amused. 'Good game, Mabury.'

The glint in the Marquess's eyes said he knew Sebastian had been counting cards, and everyone else at the table was just too slow-witted to have realised it. It was something Sebastian had always been able to do—ever since he'd learned the game as a lad of twelve—and for the first few years he'd thought everyone else could do it. And as for Ashbrooke... Well, perhaps he was either bored or a glutton for punishment as he lost round after round.

Sebastian acknowledged the Marquess with a stiff nod before rising to his feet. 'If you'll excuse me, gentlemen? I am running late for my next appointment.'

'Appointment!' said Sir Harold Gibbet, the gentlemen beside him, with a glint in his eyes. 'I can guess what kind of "appointment" His Grace is off to.'

The other men chuckled and elbowed each other. 'Did you not get rid of your mistress months ago?' Derry asked. 'Have you not found a suitable replacement yet?'

'Maybe he's still in the process of taking applications,' Gibbet added.

'I don't recall you being so choosy,' Ashbrooke said. 'What was it we said during our university days? Any flirt in a skirt!'

A cold chill ran through Sebastian. 'I really must go.'

Ignoring the protests from the other men, he strode away from the table to the exit, and accepted his cloak from the waiting valet. He was about to cross the threshold when he heard someone call his name.

'Mabury! One moment!' Ashbrooke was just behind having followed him out. 'Where are you headed off to in such a hurry?' he asked, narrowing his gaze at him.

Sebastian stiffened, wondering if he should walk

away from the Marquess. However, experience told him that Ashbrooke would never let go of a subject until he got his answer. 'If you must know, I'm headed to the Houghton Ball.'

'The Houghton Ball?'

From the expression on the other man's face, one might have thought Sebastian had said, *I'm off to the gallows.* But, then again, to notorious rakes like Ashbrooke, such an event as the Houghton Ball would be the equivalent of death.

'Why ever would you go there?' the Marquess exclaimed. 'Have you finally decided to enter the marriage mart and leave our club?'

Sebastian frowned. 'I'm not giving up my membership at Brooks's.'

'I mean, leave our club of confirmed bachelors.' Ashbrooke let out an exasperated sigh. 'I truly was betting on you sticking around as long as I. In my case, that would hopefully mean they carry me out of Madame Claudette's at the grand old age of eighty, with a smile on my face and my little marquess—'

'Ashbrooke,' he warned. 'I am not looking for a wife.' *Never.* 'I'm simply meeting my mother at the ball. She asked me to escort her.'

'Ah.' Ashbrooke looked visibly relieved. 'Thank God. You're my only friend here, and I'd hate to lose you to the bonds of matrimony.'

'Your only friend?'

Years ago—in another lifetime—he might have considered Ashbrooke a friend. In fact, they'd once run in the same circles and indulged in the same vices. But not any more. Now Sebastian had no friends at all. Acquaintances, yes. Employees, servants, and tenants, definitely.

But he didn't count anyone as a friend. Not in the last five years, anyway.

'Yes. Friend. Confidant. Comrade. Call it what you will.' As if to prove his point, Ashbrooke clapped him on the shoulder.

'I couldn't call it anything. We are *not* friends. We haven't seen each other in years.'

'So?' Ashbrooke looked completely serious.

But, as Sebastian recalled, that was the kind of person he was—Ashbrooke could part ways with someone and not see them for a long time and then would just pick up where he'd left off.

'Good God, man,' he continued, exasperated. 'We've been playing and drinking together since our university days. Of course we'll always be friends.'

Sebastian did the only thing he could think of—he stared back. Ashbrooke was not the kind of friend he wanted these days.

'Anyway, old chap,' Ashbrooke said cheerily. 'How is the Dowager Duchess these days?'

Sebastian didn't know how to answer that question. 'The Dowager Duchess is…well.' That was the truth, he supposed. He cleared his throat. 'Now, if there is nothing else, I must leave now or I'll be late.'

Ashbrooke let out a bored sigh. 'Are you certain you'd rather go to that stuffy ball than stay? I know about a dozen other ways to spend an evening that would be more enjoyable.'

Sebastian knew exactly what those dozen ways were—which was why he was eager to decline. Five years ago he would not have thought twice about joining Ashbrooke. He might even have suggested it himself.

'I'm afraid I can't keep my mother waiting.'

'Of course…of course.' Ashbrooke's head bobbed

up and down. 'Please send my warmest regards to Her Grace, and make sure you avoid those marriage-minded mamas of the ton when they throw their daughters in your path.'

That almost made Sebastian smile. 'I will. Good evening, Ashbrooke.'

'Good evening, Mabury.'

He continued on his way out, towards the waiting carriage emblazoned with his ducal crest, its door held open by a footman. As he settled into the plush velvet seat and the carriage began to move he contemplated Ashbrooke's words.

With the Season in full swing, the Marquess was not incorrect. Many mothers of unmarried young ladies and misses would fix their gazes on him. Indeed, to members of the ton an eligible bachelor like him attending such a ball at this time of the year was akin to declaring his intentions to seek a wife. And that was why Sebastian hardly went to such affairs—not even before inheriting the Dukedom. He had not been eager to find a wife then, and he certainly wasn't looking for one now. *Or ever*, he added silently, bitterness coating his tongue.

And it was rare for his mother to attend any social event—at least since the death of Sebastian's father five years ago. In fact, if he recalled correctly, this was the first time she'd shown any sign of wanting to leave her home at all.

A strange tightness formed in his chest. Thankfully, the coach stopping distracted him, and as he peered outside he recognised the Earl of Houghton's home in Hanover Square. Damn, he was already late. He should have left earlier, but he'd miscalculated how long it would take him to get here. His mother would be cross with him, for sure. She was probably already inside.

Sebastian rushed up the steps into the house. A servant stopped him immediately and, having no patience tonight, he mumbled his name and title. The man had barely finished announcing his arrival before he rushed inside. He scanned the guests crowded into the ballroom for any sign of the Dowager Duchess, all the while ignoring the whispers beginning to grow around him.

'Mabury? Is that you?'

Sebastian's shoulders tensed and he turned around. 'Lady Caulfield,' he greeted the matronly woman who had approached him. 'Yes, it's me.'

Lady Caulfield peered up at him. 'My, my, I thought I had been transported back twenty years.' Her hand went to her chest. 'You look so much like your father. I thought you were him.'

Thankfully, the retort he wanted to hurl at the old crone got caught in the thickness coating his throat. Would he never get rid of the previous Duke of Mabury's long shadow? It was like the stench from something on his shoes he could never scrape off.

'If you'll excuse me, Lady Caulfield? I've just arrived and have yet to greet our host and hostess.'

With a quick nod, he walked away from her and found a quiet corner. Pausing, he unclenched his fists and his jaw, then continued to search the room for his mother.

Minutes ticked by, and despite his calm demeanour he became increasingly anxious as he found no sign of her. He ignored anyone trying to catch his gaze, lest they see it as an invitation to conversation—especially the bright-eyed mamas who, as Ashbrooke had predicted, looked ready to toss their daughters at his feet.

Perhaps his mother was resting in one of the retiring rooms somewhere. Or maybe she had been delayed and had yet to arrive. Or had planned to be fashionably late. In any case, the crowd made the ballroom stuffy and overheated, so he decided to head to the main reception room and wait for the Dowager Duchess to arrive.

A hush followed him as he wove through the crowd. And, try as he might, he could not shut his ears to the whispers around him.

'Mabury's here...'

'Dear God, he's the spitting image of his father...'

'And from what I heard, the similarities don't end there...'

'Well, we know how *he* turned out...'

'Five years,' Sebastian grumbled under his breath.

He'd stayed away for five years and the ton still hadn't forgotten about his father. Forgiven him, perhaps—because he did hold a coronet after all. But never forgotten.

Growing up, his father had been the ideal loving, doting parent, and Sebastian had returned his affection fiercely. He hadn't spent much time with his mother as Charles Wakefield had been his world and everything he'd needed. When he was young Charles had taught Sebastian how to ride and hunt. And as he'd got older there had been a different sort of hunting and riding that Sebastian had learned on his own. As a young man, he'd been a notorious rake and hadn't cared to hide it. He was the heir to a dukedom, after all.

Unbeknownst to him, his father had been pursuing his own pleasures. His world had shattered that day his father had died in a brothel fight. The father he'd adored had turned out to be a womaniser and a wastrel. The Mabury coffers had been drained and the estate in ruins. His love for his father had shrivelled and died.

And what had followed... Well...

Sebastian swallowed the lump forming in his throat. He would never do that to anyone. Could never subject another human being to that. Which was why he had vowed never to marry. No, the Wakefield line would end with him. *It was better that way.*

As he discreetly made his way to the other side of the ballroom, a high-pitched laugh caught his attention. 'How clever you are, my lord!' a nasal female voice said.

Sebastian halted and winced. It was hard to ignore it—surely everyone in the ballroom had heard it.

'That's them, isn't it?' said a man.

The stage whisper caught his attention, and he tuned his ears for more.

'Which ones? The Gardner sisters?'

'No, no,' the first man replied. 'The Americans.'

Americans? Here at the Houghton Ball?

His curiosity piqued, Sebastian turned his head, locating the two men who were just behind him, then following their gaze towards the corner of the room, where two young women stood surrounded by a gaggle of finely dressed gentlemen. He could clearly see the pretty face of the blonde one as she let out another godawful titter.

Sebastian was about to continue on his way when he noticed the woman next to her—and it was as if he had no choice but to continue staring.

The first thing he noticed were her dark locks, swept up artfully and gleaming like burnished mahogany under the light of the hundreds of candles in the ballroom. The same light made her creamy skin glow, adding an ethereal quality to her. She was not beautiful in the classical sense, yet there was something about her striking features that he could not ignore...not even from a short distance. He wondered what colour her eyes were.

'Rumour has it that the dark-haired one's father owns half of Manhattan Island.'

He stiffened as the two men behind him continued their conversation, but he was unable to stop himself from listening in.

'No wonder Newbery is circling her like a hawk looking for its next meal.'

'Hawk? More like a weasel.'

Sebastian scoffed to himself. That did sound like Newbery. The young lord was known to have run up his accounts at all the London clubs. And now he eyed the woman like the aforementioned rodent. A strange tightness gripped Sebastian's chest as she glanced over at Newbery, whose face lit up as he soaked up this minuscule bit of attention from her.

'I must admit she's quite pretty. Not as fashionably beautiful as the blonde. But she is…comely.'

Comely? Were these two men blind?

'Of course, there is the issue of her background…'

'Her dowry will more than make up for her lack of breeding and pedigree.'

'Yes, well…in Newbery's case, beggars should really be no choosers.'

They laughed in unison. And as the two men continued to gossip like a pair of old society matrons, Sebastian forced his gaze away from her. *Another American heiress on the hunt for a titled husband*, he huffed to himself.

Though he steered away from ton gossip, even he hadn't been able to escape the news about the Earl of Gablewood, who had been trapped by a rich American fur heiress two years ago. He wasn't surprised that more of these colonial princesses had now trickled into London's ballrooms and drawing rooms, hoping to lure in impoverished lords with their deep pockets.

Sebastian would never put himself in such a situation. Indeed, the very idea made his insides twist. After all, he'd spent the last five years undoing what his father had done and making up what that wastrel had lost.

And with the reminder of the old Duke his thoughts once again turned to his mother. So, as he'd attempted to do before he was distracted, he strode out to the main reception room, leaving all thoughts of the dark-haired beauty behind.

Once again, he stood to the side, scanning the arriving guests. Half an hour passed, and Sebastian knew he had to face the truth: His mother was not here and was clearly not coming to the ball after all.

Years of learning control—over his emotions, his actions, and reactions—allowed him to prevent the deep disappointment from showing on his face. He swallowed the lump in his throat and marched towards the exit. However, he stopped short when he saw the hostess herself, the Countess of Houghton, giving instructions to the butler who guarded the door.

Sebastian knew that if she saw him he would either have to explain to the Countess why he was leaving, or why his mother hadn't turned up. He had to make his escape—but to where?

It didn't matter where—only that he could wait somewhere until he could slip out unnoticed. And so, on a whim, he pivoted on his heel and headed towards the first door he laid eyes on.

Chapter Two

Because Arthur Mason willed it so, Kate was at the Houghton Ball that evening, dressed in her best ball-gown of blue silk and grey tulle, surrounded by a group of gentlemen who seemed as insipid and uninspiring as the tepid lemonade the hostess was serving.

'Lord Benton, you are so witty,' her blonde, blue-eyed companion tittered as she slapped the handsome young lord on his shoulder with her fan, then let out a high-pitched laugh that sounded like a cross between a goose's honk and a crying cow.

Kate didn't know how Caroline DeVries managed to smile for hours without her cheeks hurting. Or give false compliments to dim-witted men without utterly losing her mind.

But, then again, she shouldn't put anything past the vivacious young woman, who seemed completely set on bagging herself a lord. After all, that was the reason the DeVries family of Pittsburgh had come to London—to secure matches for their two daughters and elevate their standing in society.

Kate fought the urge to curl her fingers into fists. *I should have known it was no coincidence that we trav-*

elled with them. How obtuse she'd been, not realising her father's schemes.

From across the room, Arthur Mason's gaze landed on her with the force of a hammer on an anvil. He had warned her that he would not tolerate any attempt to dissuade the attentions of eligible gentlemen. And so, since Caroline attracted said gentlemen like bees to honey, she decided to stay by the younger woman's side—if only to appease her father.

When the conversation slowed down, Kate cleared her throat. 'Gentlemen, I fear I'm feeling fatigued and parched.'

'Shall I fetch you some lemonade, Miss Mason?' asked Mr George Moseby, who was in line for a viscountcy from a distant uncle.

'Oh, let me,' Lord Wembleton insisted. 'It would be my honour.'

Caroline spoke up. 'Kate, you do look quite flushed and…wilted.' The slightest sneer appeared on her lips. 'Perhaps you should have a rest inside one of the retiring rooms instead?'

Thank you, Caroline.

'A wonderful idea.' Turning on her slippered feet, Kate marched away from the group. However, she had no intention of going into one of the retiring rooms. What she needed was some privacy and some fresh air.

She tried to appear casual as she made her way across the ballroom through the throng of guests. Finally she reached her intended destination—a door on the far side of the room that would lead to the gardens outside. Just before the dancing had started, she'd heard Lord Houghton boast to a few of the guests that he had one of the most beautiful gardens in London, and then he had led them out through this door. Surely by now they would be gone, and Kate would be able to get a much-needed break from the stifling atmosphere of the house and have a few precious minutes alone.

As she stepped out into the gardens she took a deep breath. The crisp, late-winter air was just the balm she needed. Her tutor back in New York had warned her numerous times never to be caught alone anywhere during a ball, and certainly not unchaperoned with a gentleman. Of course Kate had focused on the 'never be caught' part. Besides, surely that rule wasn't strictly imposed. For how did anyone get any rest at these dreadful balls that could go on until the wee hours of the morning?

Kate continued down a stone-covered path. The full moon shone above, and only a few torches had been scattered about, but they were enough to guide her through the rows of hedges. She gasped in delight as she spied a large structure up ahead. Springing forward, she made her way to the centrepiece of the gardens—a glorious white marble fountain. Water sprang from the top and cascaded down to a second level before streaming out from the mouths of the carved lion heads decorating the third tier.

She drew closer—not only because she wanted to cool herself, but also to observe the fountain's mechanics. Taking off her left glove, she skidded her fingers over the surface of the water. She wondered if the fountain was powered by a mechanical pump or simply through hydro—

A prickle on the back of her neck made her halt. She was no longer alone.

Her instincts were proved correct as she turned around.

Indeed, there was someone in the gardens with her. A

male someone. Though she'd never seen him before—
or anyone quite like him.

He was dark-haired, and tall, but unlike many of the
more refined gentlemen of the ton he had broad shoulders that looked barely contained underneath the black
fabric of his coat. The moonlight illuminated sharply
handsome features and dark eyes—and those onyx orbs
were fixed on her. The look he was giving her was like
nothing she'd ever seen from any gentlemen before.

Many men looked at her with adoration, fascination,
even curiosity. But this man… Something about his gaze
made her throat go dry and a thrill crawl down the back
of her knees. An unknown emotion passed fleetingly
across his face, before a hint of a sneer made the corners of his mouth pull back. Kate felt the wave of con-
tempt from his arrogant stare.

Something about this scenario sparked a memory
in her, something in one of the books she'd recently
read. In her haste to pack for the voyage to England she
hadn't considered how tedious two weeks on a steamship
would be, and hadn't brought anything for entertain-
ment except for her diary and a few well-worn engineering books. She had had to make do with whatever
books had been in her suite, including a few volumes
of Shakespeare.

'"*Ill met by moonlight, proud Titania.*"'

'Does that make you the jealous Oberon?' he asked.

She blinked. 'I beg your pardon?'

'Shakespeare. *A Midsummer Night's Dream.* Act
Two.'

Despite the flatness of his tone, the deep timbre of
his voice brought on that strange feeling again. 'Yes,
I've read it. What about—?'

Oh, dear. He was either a mind-reader, or she had said

those words aloud. The heat of embarrassment crept up her neck, and she prayed he wouldn't notice the flush that must surely be evident on her face.

Silence stretched between them as seconds ticked by. He seemed unaware of the awkwardness, so she spoke again. 'Have we met before, sir?'

'I can't say we have.'

What was that supposed to mean? And why was she scrambling for more words to say to him? Her instincts screamed that this man was nothing like those foppish gentlemen back in the ballroom. There was an air of danger about him, as well as a kind of cunning that told her he was not one to be trifled with.

Which meant that if anyone should find them out here, unchaperoned... Well, her tutor's warning suddenly rang clear in her mind.

'I should make haste and head inside. Since we have not been properly introduced.' Her reputation would be in tatters if anyone found out. 'I shall trust in your discretion, sir.'

Picking up her skirts, she was about to slide past him when he spoke again. 'Yet it was not I who was splashing about in a fountain like some fairy sprite.'

A flash of temper made her stop and turn her head towards him. '"Splashing about"? You make it sound like I was cavorting inside the fountain with water up to my knees!'

She knew one should never mention body parts in polite company—but, blast it, something about this man made her forget about propriety.

His steely gaze caught hers. 'A young foreign miss alone in the gardens would give anyone the impression that she was, indeed, cavorting.'

She bit her tongue to stop herself from saying what

was really on her mind. 'And I suppose you are innocent? Do you make a habit of crawling about darkened
corners quoting Shakespeare to young women?'

'It was you who quoted Shakespeare.' The left corner of his mouth twitched. Almost like a smile, but one
that he caught before it had a chance to become fully
realised.

'I didn't mean to quote the Bard.' Kate bit the inside
of her cheek. 'And if I had, I would have picked something better. Like something from *Othello* or *Richard III*.'

'Something better?' A dark brow quirked up. 'Pretty
girls and handsome Athenians falling in love—what
more could a young woman ask for in a story?'

'Please...' she huffed. 'None of those people in that
play were truly in love—except perhaps for poor Pyramus and Thisbe.' She grinned at the memory of the an-
tics of Bottom and his friends in Act Five. 'Everyone
was "in love" with those who appeared attractive to
them, without much thought to personality or character. Or just with the aid of magic. That's not real love.'

'And do you believe in love?'

'I—' She stopped, her mouth hanging open for one
second before she clamped it shut. The superficiality
of the love between the characters in the play had been
obvious to her. But love in real life...? Did she believe
in such a thing? How did one even begin to understand
such a concept? It was not something she could examine and take apart and put back together again. And
since that was not possible she could not give a defini-
tive answer as to whether she believed in love or not.

His magnetic eyes held hers once again. Another
pulse of a thrill shot through her, starting somewhere
in her stomach and spreading up to her chest.

'Of course you do,' he stated, before she could put

words together to form a sentence. 'A young eligible miss like yourself is always on the lookout for a good match.'

'And you, sir?' she shot back. 'You aren't at this ball looking for a match?'

'No,' he replied flatly. 'I shall never marry.'

'But what about heirs?' Kate inhaled a sharp breath. What in the world had possessed her to ask such a question of a stranger?

'What about them?' The dark eyes turned flinty.

Did he mean he didn't need them? Or want them? *Why should I care?*

But Kate could not help herself. That hard, determined expression on his face only made her itch to know more. 'You're a man. Don't all men have the urge to… uh…go forth and multiply?' Heat tingled up her cheeks, warming them despite the cool evening air.

A giggle and the sound of footsteps made them both go still. Oh, dear Lord, someone would find them here. While she had known it was risky to come out to the gardens alone, the reality that she really could be compromised struck her like lightning. If she were to be ruined, then no aristocratic lord would have her. What her father would do if that happened, she didn't know, but the thought of it filled her chest with dread.

She glanced around, searching for a way out even as the whispers and footsteps grew louder. Fear and panic drove her to do something she would never dream of doing. Pushing at her companion's chest, she cornered him behind one of the hedges. Her breath caught in her throat as his form caged her body.

Dear God, he was a stranger. She had no idea who he was…what he was doing here. If anyone found them, her reputation would be ruined. He was unknown to her.

This man who held her in what anyone would surmise was an embrace—albeit one she'd initiated—in darkened gardens on a moonlit night.

Kate would bet no other young woman would have such a ruination as she.

'Stay still,' he whispered, his lips hovering just above her temple. 'We will wait for them to leave.'

He was so close to her...not quite touching...but she could feel the warmth of his body even through the layers of clothing between them.

She closed her eyes, biting her lip to stop herself from crying out or laughing at the absurdity of this whole situation. Hopefully, things would get better from here on.

'Lord Newbery, please...' came a breathy female voice.

'Please what, sweet? Please stop? Or please continue?' a male voice asked, followed by a whimper and the unmistakable sigh of pleasure.

Oh, dear, things weren't getting better. Not even by an inch. No, they were now on their way to disaster.

Panic rose in her as her instinct screamed at her to flee. But any noise or disturbance would surely alert the amorous couple.

Looks like I have no choice.

'My lord...you must stop.'

'You're so beautiful, Caroline. I can't help it.'

Caroline?

'But you must!' The woman giggled in a nasal tone. 'Please, my lord.'

That was definitely Caroline DeVries.

'One more, darling. Please...'

'Well...since you asked...' The unmistakable sound of passionate, wet mouths meeting followed.

Oh, for heaven's sake!

With a resigned sigh, Kate leaned her head against her stranger's shoulder.

Her stranger? It was an absurd thought, but then again here she was, trapped between a hedge and his chest. The scent of his cologne tickled her nose. Not that it was unpleasant. It was…unnerving, to say the least. She'd never been this close to any man, after all. Not in this way.

'My lord, I must insist… My mother will be looking for me by now.'

'I… Of course, Caroline.' Newbery cleared his throat. 'I know a separate exit that will lead me to the front. You take the door that leads back to the ballroom.'

'You are so wise, my lord.'

There were a few more whispers that Kate didn't quite catch, followed by two separate sets of footsteps fading in opposite directions.

Kate let out a relieved breath. Finally, the couple was gone. Bracing her hands on his chest, she gave the man a soft push. However, he didn't budge.

She frowned, then pushed a little harder.

He remained in position, unmoving.

'Sir?' she said softly. 'The coast, as they say, is clear.' When still he didn't respond, she lifted her gaze to meet his. 'Sir…?'

Dark onyx eyes were fixed on her, and now that the fear of being caught had dissipated a different kind of sensation filled her. One that reminded her of how close they remained, even though their bodies didn't touch. Her lips parted as her dress suddenly felt too constricting, as if her corset had laced itself tighter.

The sudden loss of his warmth told her he had moved away from her. Taking in a sharp breath, she opened her eyes.

A myriad of expressions was crossing his handsome face. He looked as if he had been possessed by some other consciousness and was only now returning to his senses. That arrogant mask soon settled back on his face. Shock and shame at their closeness filled her, making her cheeks flame as if someone had set a match to them.

And for the first time in her life Kate did something she'd never thought she'd do when faced with a conundrum—she turned and ran in the opposite direction.

When Kate saw her father at breakfast the next morning, he minced no words with her.

'You will go to the DeVries suite as soon as you are finished with breakfast,' he stated. 'Since it seems you've no gentlemen callers, no gifts, nor letters or cards, I can only assume your hasty exit during the ball has warded off any potential suitors. So Mrs DeVries and I have secured the services of a well-regarded chaperone—the Honourable Harriet Merton.'

'A chaperone?' she echoed.

Arthur continued as if she had not spoken. 'We have written to her and told her of our requirements, and she has agreed to teach you and the DeVries girls about English etiquette and society. Miss Merton has the right connections to ensure you secure a match with a lord. From now on you will spend every moment of your time with Miss Merton, learning everything you need to know about moving amongst the upper class. Besides, seeing as young Caroline is attracting the right kind of suitors, perhaps some of her charm and influence will rub off on you.'

Taking a delicate sip of her tea, Kate calmed herself

before speaking. 'Father, surely there is another way to get the factory built and establish the railway company?'

'No one wants to deal with unknown Americans,' Arthur stated. 'And they think our knowledge and machines are inferior.'

'Inferior?' The cup clattered loudly on the saucer as Kate set it down. 'Have they never heard of the Andersen?' she fumed. 'Perhaps we should go back to America and continue expanding westward instead. With a brand-new locomotive design we'll be able to scale the mountainous terrain and—'

'Westward?' Arthur sneered. 'And what would expanding the rail out west do? What's out there anyway? Just dirt and rocks and sand. No, with the current upturn in the English railway industry I must get in now, or lose this opportunity to increase our holdings.'

'Of course all you care about is money,' she huffed. 'What about progress and—?'

'Are you trying to defy me, Kathryn?' The air in the room grew thick as Arthur Mason shot her a frigid stare.

'Father, all I'm saying is—'

'If you do not find an English husband in the next few weeks, then I'll consider this whole trip a lost investment.' His voice remained cool, but the force behind his words was unmistakable. 'And you know I do not like it when my investments don't return a profit.'

It stung that Arthur Mason saw her—his only child—as just another number in his ledger, but Kate supposed she shouldn't have expected otherwise.

'Finding a husband—and a titled one—isn't like going to the market and picking up fresh vegetables.'

'Do not be impertinent with me, young lady,' he warned. 'You will find a husband, or we will go back to New York and you will be married to a man of my choosing. And you can bet that, whoever it will be, he won't allow you to set foot in any factory or engine room again.'

Shock made her clamp her mouth shut. Arthur never made empty threats—especially when it came to business. 'If that is all, I would like to be excused.' She would not cry in front of him. Not over this.

His nose wrinkled, but the victory on his face was evident. Then again, Kate had never really stood a chance.

'You may go.'

As she stood up, the butler strode in to announce a visitor. 'Mr Malvery is here, Mr Mason.'

As if her morning could get any worse. Waiting just outside was another man she wished never to cross paths with again. Her second cousin—Jacob Malvery. He had been sent to London a few weeks ahead of their arrival, and Kate counted herself lucky that she hadn't seen him since New York. Of course, she had known her luck was bound to run out sooner or later.

Her father folded his hands together. 'Ah, just in time. Send him in.'

Jacob was a sycophantic, odious toad who hung on her father's every word. His greatest crime, however, was calling himself an engineer. Some years ago he had come to Mason R&L to apprentice under Pap, but from the first day it had become obvious that Jacob had exaggerated his own abilities.

Pap had thrown him out of the factory a mere three days later, when he had nearly caused an explosion. Her father had then put him to work somewhere his skills would be more appreciated—in the boardroom of Mason R&L, negotiating with government officials and landowners to help pave the way for the expansion of their rail lines.

'Good morning, Arthur,' Jacob fawned as he entered.

His suit looked brand-new—probably from one of the fine tailors on Savile Row. Kate heard others refer to him as handsome, with his wavy blond hair and bright green eyes, but then again, she knew what was behind that smile.

'And I must be the luckiest man on earth! The lovely Kate is here as well. How are you today, Cousin?'

Kate gave him a perfunctory nod. 'Cousin Jacob,' she managed to say without choking.

His eyes ran up and down her figure. 'Leaving already?'

'I'm afraid so.' She rounded the table, making her way to the side opposite him. 'I can't keep Mrs DeVries waiting.'

'Ah, how unfortunate for me.'

Her father waved him over to sit on his right side, then turned to her. 'Remember what we talked about, Kathryn,' he said, and then looked at Jacob meaningfully. 'Jacob will be joining us for dinner tonight.'

This time she did not miss the telling glance her father sent her, nor the weight of implication in his words. Jacob would be the man of Arthur's choosing if she did not find an English lord to wed.

She swallowed the bile rising in her throat. 'I shall see you both then.'

Whirling around, she trudged out of the dining area of their suite. Once she was certain she was far away enough, she balled her hands into fists and let out a soft, unladylike shriek.

Damn that scheming, vile man!

If he couldn't get a return on his investment then Arthur Mason would find another way she could be useful— namely, keeping his fortune in the family. And since he didn't have a coveted son, the only way to do that was to marry his only child off to an heir of his choosing.

The thought made Kate want to lose the breakfast she had hardly touched.

While he might be an incompetent engineer, Jacob was as sly and ambitious as her father. Jacob had always boasted about wanting to see his name immortalised on buildings and locomotives. If Jacob were ever in charge of Mason R&L he would turn it into some kind of monument to his legacy, and all Pap's work would be gone like dead ash from burning coal.

Pap didn't work himself to the bone just to have that taken away from him. I would rather never step foot in any factory again than let that egomaniac take over.

Somehow she had to find a way out of this. If Pap were here he would tell her to buck up, use her head, and find a solution.

No, she would not run away from her predicament. For now, she was merely making a tactical retreat, so she could sit down and figure out how to solve her Marriage Problem. While it seemed hopeless now, she was not one to give up. Hell's bells, she could figure out what was wrong with an engine just by listening to it. There was no hurdle too big for her—not if she put her mind to work. But to do that she would have to be just as sneaky and underhand as Arthur Mason.

Heading out, Kate made her way to the DeVries suite, just one floor below. She was not looking forward to spending the day with the insufferable Caroline and her equally insufferable mother, but at least she would be around Maddie, the elder of the two DeVries daughters. Maddie was more like her father, Cornelius DeVries, and father and daughter were just as close as Kate and

Pap had been. In fact, the two men had been the reason she and Maddie had become friends.

A few years ago, she and Pap had travelled to Pennsylvania to visit the iron forges, in order to source materials for their engines and tracks. Eventually they had settled on the DeVries Furnace and Iron Company as her grandfather had got on well with the owner, Cornelius DeVries.

Cornelius was an eccentric and boisterous businessman, and perhaps Pap had seen himself in the other man. Or maybe seen him as the son he'd wished Arthur had been. Pap had been particularly impressed that Cornelius, having no sons of his own, had encouraged his own daughter's interest in metallurgy. Just as Kate had grown up by Pap's side, Maddie had been learning the science of forging at her father's knee.

It was too bad Maddie hadn't been there at the Houghton Ball. According to her mother, she'd been feeling ill. Kate, however, could guess why Maddie hadn't attended. Though she thought Maddie more beautiful than Caroline—both in her heart and her looks—the elder DeVries daughter had always felt self-conscious about her 'unfashionable' stature.

The maid who answered Kate's knock led her to the luxurious sitting room, where Maddie and Caroline were already waiting.

She gave Caroline a perfunctory nod before turning to her friend. 'Maddie, good morning. I'm sorry to have missed you at the ball. I hope you are feeling better?'

'I am, thank you.' Maddie got to her feet and gave her a warm embrace.

Once released from the hug, Kate looked up to meet her friend's gaze. And, truly, she did look up, for while Maddie, too, had received the same stunning looks from their Dutch heritage as Caroline had, she was also the unfortunate recipient of another of their qualities—their towering height. Even in her flat satin slippers Maddie stood nearly six feet tall, a fact much bemoaned by their mother.

As if to compensate, Eliza DeVries dressed her elder daughter in pastels and other light colours, which made Maddie look even more comical—like an overgrown doll. Today, she wore a light blue frock edged with an inordinate amount of white lace, making Kate wonder if it had been designed by a cake maker.

'Caroline? Madeline?' Eliza DeVries called as she breezed into the sitting room. Some might describe her as beautiful, and indeed she was, with her delicate face, flaxen hair, and slim figure. However, Kate didn't care much for the woman's character. Instead of being satisfied with their vast wealth, Eliza was obsessed with seeking a higher status for her family, and hell-bent on using her daughters to achieve this goal.

'And, Kate, you're already here. Good.' Eliza DeVries turned to the woman who strode in behind her. 'Welcome, Miss Merton. May I present Miss Kate Mason, Arthur's daughter, and my own two daughters, Caroline and Madeline. Ladies, this is the Honourable Miss Harriet Merton.'

'How do you do?' Miss Merton's bright blue eyes sparkled as she smiled at them warmly. 'I am so glad to be here and to meet you young ladies.'

Kate hadn't been sure what Miss Harriet Merton would be like, but she certainly hadn't expected this. In fact, she'd rather imagined a stodgy old maid who would slap their hands with her cane if they so much as slouched, not this sweet and charming woman before them. Harriet Merton looked to be a few years younger than Eliza, and though she wore a spinster's lace cap, her bright yellow morning gown and light blue shawl matched her sunny disposition.

'Why don't I call for tea?' Eliza began, then nodded to the young maid standing in the corner. After exchanging a few more pleasantries, they all settled down. 'Miss Merton, allow me to thank you once again for answering our letters. Your assistance in navigating the Season will be utterly welcome and much needed.'

'I must admit I was intrigued when I read your letter, and Mr Mason's.' Miss Merton glanced over at Caroline. 'Caroline, you're just as beautiful as your mother says. And Madeline and Kate,' she said, turning to where the two of them sat together on the sofa. 'Mrs DeVries and Mr Mason were quite…fervent in their descriptions of you both.'

Kate bit her tongue. She could only imagine her father's commentary about her. 'I'm sure he was most detailed.'

There was a gleam in Miss Merton's eyes that Kate did not miss. 'Yes, well… I must admit you all intrigue me. Over the years I've been asked to chaperone and guide many a young miss as she travails the Season, but I've never met any Americans.'

'And what have you heard about us?' Kate bit out, which earned her a reproachful look from Eliza.

'Nothing terrible, I assure you,' Miss Merton said with a laugh. 'Only that you American girls can be quite…spirited. Not a bad thing, mind you. But here in England things are very different.'

'Indeed they are,' Eliza piped in. 'Which is why we need your help. We have been in London for over a fortnight, and yet we have not met any respectable gentlemen. I was told we needed to be seen at the right places, so we used my husband's and Arthur's connections to secure an invitation to the Houghton Ball. Maddie was feeling ill, so she did not attend, but Caroline and Kate were surrounded by a host of gentlemen throughout the evening. And yet not one has sent a gift or come calling. They're both heiresses with sizeable dowries!'

'Mrs DeVries,' Miss Merton began gently. 'To those who did not grow up in England the rules of the English aristocracy can be quite confusing. And sometimes… er…wealth is not always the solution.'

Caroline seemed perturbed. 'What about Cecilia Lefebvre?'

Miss Merton frowned. 'Who?'

'You know,' Caroline said, exasperated. 'Her father made a fortune in the fur trade in Canada. The Lefebvres were unwelcome in many of New York's society parlours and ballrooms. That is until she went to London and came back as the Countess of Gablewood. When she returned to New York with her Earl, everyone fell over themselves trying to get into their good graces.'

'Ah, yes, I've heard of the Countess…' Miss Merton wrinkled her nose. 'I'm afraid she's more of the exception, rather than the rule.'

Eliza pursed her lips. 'Then what must we do if their dowries aren't enough?'

'I'm not saying they are not enough,' Miss Merton clarified. 'But surely you do not want to attract fortune-hunters and scoundrels? There are other methods of finding a good, respectable husband.'

'I don't care if he's good or respectable, as long as he has a title,' Caroline declared. 'I'll go as low as a viscount, but I'm setting my sights on being a duchess.'

'I should like someone gentle and caring,' Maddie added. 'A man who would be a loving father to our children.'

'So, what do you think, Miss Merton?' Eliza said. 'Will you help us?'

Miss Merton laughed. 'Of course, Mrs DeVries. I made up my mind when I read your letters.'

'You did?'

'Yes,' she said with a nod. 'In fact, I am about to tell you one effective way of navigating the Season—and that is with a sponsor. The stamp of approval from an influential patron could lead to many more opportunities for the girls.'

'A sponsor?' Eliza's eyes grew wide. 'Where would we get such a person? And how much would one cost?'

'If a sponsor can help me land a lord, then surely Papa will pay for one,' Caroline added.

'Oh, dear girl, I'm afraid one cannot pay for such a service.' Miss Merton shook her head. 'But I have already written to a potential sponsor. The widow of a distant cousin of mine, who happens to be a dowager duchess.'

'A duchess?' Eliza's eyes gleamed with excitement, and Caroline covered her hand with her mouth.

'Yes, when I read about you young misses I knew she would be the perfect sponsor' When Miss Merton mentioned 'misses', however, her eyes darted over to Kate and Maddie. 'And, well… The reason I came here right away was to give you some good news. Her Grace the Dowager Duchess of Mabury has agreed to meet you and discuss the possibility of becoming your sponsor for the Season.'

This time Caroline could not hold on to her delight as she let out a gleeful shriek. 'A duchess sponsoring me? This is fantastic news!'

'Oh, dear.' Eliza fanned herself with her hand. 'This is…quite astonishing, Miss Merton. Now I know why you came so highly recommended. I cannot thank you enough.'

'Do not thank me yet, Mrs DeVries,' Miss Merton warned. 'I'm sure you will understand that as her own reputation is at stake Her Grace will want to meet the girls first, before officially agreeing to sponsor them. And so she has invited us all to stay at the ducal estate, Highfield Park in Surrey, for a few days, to assess the ladies'…er…dispositions and suitability.'

Eliza's head bobbed up and down like a cork in water. 'Of course. Whatever she wants.'

'I was actually quite surprised that Her Grace responded right away.' A strained look briefly passed across Miss Merton's face. 'Since her husband died she has not been seen in society. It's quite tragic, actually…'

'What happened?' Maddie asked, leaning forward.

'Madeline!' Eliza warned. 'We do not gossip about people we don't know. Especially not someone who is being so kind as to open her doors to us. Apologies, Miss Merton. We will start preparing immediately.'

Kate stifled the urge to groan aloud at the thought of spending a few days in some lofty English estate. She did not have time to perform like a show pony for an aristocratic society matron. Not when her grandfather's legacy was at stake.

She chewed at her lip. If this was an engineering problem, how would she solve it?

'Not every obstacle is a setback,' Pap had used to say. *'You might find a way to turn it into an opportunity.'*

Right now, however, an English lord sounded much more appealing than Jacob taking over Mason R&L— even if it did mean she might never work on her own engine. While the thought deflated her, just imagining the words *Malvery R&L* emblazoned on the side of an Andersen engine filled her with so much rage she couldn't think straight. It was the lesser of two evils. If nothing else, she could use this opportunity to delay her marriage to Jacob and give her more time to think of a solution to her Marriage Problem.

Chapter Three

The moment his carriage left the crowded streets of London behind, Sebastian blew out a breath. But it wasn't because of the smog and stench of town. Well, perhaps that was part of it, but his disdain for London only grew the longer he stayed there. Usually, he did not linger in the city for long—three days at most, perhaps—but there had been urgent business he'd needed to attend to, which had delayed his departure. At least that was what he told himself.

With his mind idle, his thoughts drifted to the Houghton Ball and, more specifically, to the dark-haired beauty in the garden. How a short, innocent encounter with one girl—an American at that—had somehow burned itself into his memory, Sebastian did not know.

But he needed to forget about her. Forget about those mesmerising eyes the colour of cornflowers and the creamy, soft pale skin of her neck. Forget about how she'd smelled of fresh powder and lemons and the warmth of her body. Though he had not got the chance to find out in detail, he just knew that her curves would fit perfectly into his and—

Devil take me!

Leaning on the side of the plush seat of his coach, he massaged his temple with his thumb and forefinger. *I should have left London earlier.* As he had lingered in town he'd found himself looking over his shoulder or glancing outside his carriage every so often, wondering if he'd see her on the street, coming out of some shop or tea room.

Perhaps now that he had left London those memories of her would fade away and completely disappear. Once he breathed in the sweet air of the country he would stop thinking about the warmth of her body or the weight of her head on his shoulder. And what a pretty head it had been. He remembered glancing at her from across the ballroom and thinking her beautiful, but up close, under the bright full moon, she had been exquisite.

Of course it had turned out that head of hers wasn't empty or—worse—filled with fluff. Hidden beneath those gorgeous layers was a woman who had a mind of her own, and damned if that wasn't what had aroused him the most about her.

A jostle from the carriage wheels going over a stone or a stray tree branch knocked him out of his reverie.

The tightness in his chest loosened even more as they drove further and further away from the soot and grime of the city. One good thing about his thoughts being filled with the mystery woman was that he'd hardly had time to think about his mother's failure to arrive at the Houghton Ball. But, then again, he should be used to it by now. He'd been disappointed many times before, and why he had thought this time would be different, he didn't know.

'The ride over seemed too long, Sebastian.'
'I tried, darling, I did.'

'I just couldn't bring myself to get out of bed.'

So many excuses. Perhaps one of these days he'd eventually be done with her and he'd stick to the vow he made each time she didn't show up: to leave her to her languishing and never attempt to see her again.

Still, she was his mother, and he loved her dearly. How he longed to see her as she'd used to be, before the ugliness of the events of five years ago had drained her of joy. Before his father had destroyed Sebastian's love and faith in him. In everything.

His mind drifted back to the mysterious woman in the garden. He should have left the moment he'd discovered her, but he'd found himself intrigued, even answering her questions. She'd been right about the ball being the place to look for a match. But, as he'd told her, he was never marrying or siring an heir. He had a distant cousin who lived in Hertfordshire. He would leave the title and the estate to him. Sebastian would be the last of the Wakefields to hold the title Duke of Mabury.

When he'd been alive, Charles Wakefield had doted on his only son and heir. Sebastian had been made to feel like the most important person in the world. But little had he known that once he had arrived Charles had no longer needed anyone else—especially his wife. She'd given him the heir he needed, so he'd been free to do as he pleased. To carouse and frolic all over London. It was how things were done in their circles after all. It was what Charles's father had done and probably what Sebastian would have done if he had married.

But the cycle would end with him. That was the vow he'd made to his mother that day that had changed his life, though she might not have heard him say the words.

The coach slowing told Sebastian that they were nearly at Highfield Park, and a few minutes later it halted. A uniformed footman held the door open and he breathed in the fresh air, his boots crunching on the gravel as he alighted. As he made his way to the front door he stopped. *Something was not quite right.* Turning his head, he saw that only half his household staff were lined up to greet him.

He frowned. Not that he cared much for ceremony, but his butler certainly did. The staid and decorous Eames, who had been the butler at Highfield Park ever since Sebastian could remember, took pride in ensuring that the house ran with military-like precision, with the staff acting like his little soldiers and doing his bidding. Indeed, Eames only had to give a wayward servant one glacial stare or the lift of a thick eyebrow to put them in their place.

Today, however, the usually reliable Eames was not even amongst those here now to welcome him home.

'Higgins,' he said to the head footman, who was at the end of the receiving line. 'Was someone sent ahead to tell Eames of my arrival?'

'Yes, Your Grace.'

'Then where is he? And the rest of the staff?'

The man's jaw ticked. 'The others and Eames are… er…occupied at the moment, Your Grace.'

'Occupied? Do you mean sick?' Eames must be deathly ill, because not even the plague would stop the butler from getting out of bed in the morning.

'No, Your Grace. Eames is busy getting the house in order.'

'What do you mean? I've only been gone a little over a week. What could possibly have gone out of order in that time?'

Higgins's brows drew together. 'Your Grace, I thought you knew…'

'Knew what?' he said, his patience running thin.

'Your Grace, she—that is your—'

The door suddenly swinging open interrupted Higgins. 'Who in the world is—?' It was Eames, whose eyes bulged like a day-old fish's eyes the moment his gaze landed on Sebastian. 'Your Grace!' His face turned red. 'Your Grace, I have only just received word of your arrival! Forgive me for not ensuring you were properly welcomed back.' He bowed his head deeply. 'I take full responsibility.'

'You are forgiven, Eames. But tell me—where is the rest of the staff?' Glancing inside the house, he saw two maids scurry by, their baskets filled with fresh linen, while a footman nearly collided with them as he carried an enormous silver candlestick. 'And what in heaven's name is going on?'

'Your Grace… Were you not…informed?'

'Of what?'

'Of the Dowager Duchess's arrival.'

Sebastian opened his mouth, then quickly clamped it shut lest it remained hanging open for all his servants to see—well, half of them. Composing himself, he managed to say, 'It seems Her Grace's visit has caught all of us by surprise.'

Eames straightened his shoulders and his usual cool, efficient mask slipped into place. 'So it seems, Your Grace.' He cleared his throat. 'The Dowager Duchess did ask that you meet her in her private sitting room as soon as you are able. Would you like to refresh yourself beforehand?'

Sebastian ignored Eames and instead strode directly inside. He didn't know what had possessed him, but something inside him had to know if his mother really was here. Because surely this had to be a cruel joke of some kind. Miranda, Dowager Duchess of Mabury, had not stepped foot into Highfield Park in years. Not since she'd left five years ago.

A knot formed in his chest as he made his way to the Duchess's private sitting room on the east side of the manor. Ignoring the tremor in his hand as he reached for the doorknob, he turned it. His hopes for a quiet arrival were dashed, however, by the loud creaking sound of the hinge.

'Oh, dear, we really should get one of the footmen to oil that.'

The familiar crisp voice sounded like hers. And the figure in profile standing by the window looked like hers. Yes, the beautiful face that turned to him was indeed that of his mother. Still, every instinct learned from the last five years prevented him from believing it was actually her. For one thing, this woman was fully dressed in a lovely purple morning gown, her hair pinned up meticulously, her back straight as an arrow. In the few times he'd visited his mother in the last five years she had either been abed in her night rail or slumped in a chair by the fireplace, her hair in disarray.

He swallowed the lump forming in his throat and stepped inside. 'Mother?'

'Sebastian.' Turning forty-five degrees on her heel, she strode to him, her steps light as air. 'Darling, what a wonderful coincidence that we have arrived at nearly the same time. I was hoping I wouldn't have to wait too long for you.'

He searched her face. While the lines of strain around her eyes and the paleness of her skin would have worried anyone else, to Sebastian they at least looked familiar. This told him she was not a spectre of his imagination.

'Mother. I'm glad to see you here.'

A million questions went through his mind. What was she doing here? Why hadn't she shown up at the ball? How had she managed to get herself out of bed this time? And was she going to stay?

'You look as if you've seen a ghost.' A slip of a smile curled her lips. 'I hope you do not mind me coming unannounced?'

'Of course not—you are always welcome here,' he blurted. His mind still reeled at the fact that she stood before him.

'Come, let us sit.'

She dragged him to the sofa and sat him down as if he were a boy in short pants again. And he let her— because, frankly, he was agog to know what had lured his mother out of her hermit-like state.

'You must be surprised at my turning up all of a sudden,' she began, as if reading his mind. 'Are you cross with me about not coming to the Houghton Ball?'

Yes. And all those other times, as well, he wanted to say, but bit his tongue. 'Of course not, Mother. I'm sure you had good reason.' And she needn't explain because he'd already heard all her excuses before. 'But what are you doing here?'

She folded her hands in her lap. 'Did you mean what you said? About my being welcome here?'

Like most ducal estates, Highfield Park had a dower house about a mile from the main manor, but following his father's death his mother had instead opted to move to one of their smaller estates in Hertfordshire, which had been part of her original dowry. Sebastian had buried the hurt that she didn't want to live near him, because he most of all understood *why*. No matter how much he tried, or how hard he worked, the shadow of his father was there—and Sebastian's face was a constant reminder of what her husband had done to her.

'*You two are like two peas in a pod,*' his mother would always joke in those early years. '*You'd think he was the one that bore you.*'

Indeed, when he looked in the mirror he could see that the only thing he'd inherited from his mother were her eyes. They had been so alike Sebastian would wake up in a pool of sweat some nights, after the same nightmare plagued him: he would be looking in a mirror, and instead of his own reflection he would see Charles Wakefield with a knife in his chest.

'Sebastian?'

He nodded at her. 'Of course, Mother. Stay as long as you please.'

'Excellent.' A wider smile lit up her face, reminding him of a wilted flower slowly coming to life after being given water. 'I hope you don't mind…but there is a reason I wanted to come here.'

'You don't need a reason to come here.'

'Yes, well…' She fiddled with a bit of lace on her gown. 'It's not just for myself, you see.'

'Bring as many staff as you like to make your stay comfortable.'

Eames would probably grumble in private at having to accommodate more servants downstairs, but the loyal butler would find a way.

'No, darling, not servants. I'd like to invite some guests to stay.'

'You mean entertain?' A spark of hope flashed in his chest. The Dowager Duchess of Mabury had not mingled with society in years. However, his instinct extinguished that hope, fearing disappointment once again.

'Not exactly.' Her lips pursed. 'Sebastian, I shall be

sponsoring some young ladies for the Season, and I would like to host them here.'

'Here? Why not at your home in Hertfordshire? Or the London townhouse?'

'My house is not equipped for guests, and I believe they might do better out here in the country. It will allow them some breathing room before being plunged straight into society. And it will give me a chance to make a list of suitable gentlemen to invite to meet them.' Dark eyes met his own. 'You don't mind, do you, Sebastian?'

Mind that his peace would be disturbed by a bunch of giggling young women? That his home would be invaded by marriage-minded misses? That at every turn he'd run into girls twittering about nonsense like gowns and gossip? Of course he minded.

Yet there was something that made him pause. Despite the gauntness of her face, he saw a fleeting glint of life in his mother's eyes as she spoke of these young misses. 'Of course I don't mind,' he blurted, before he could stop himself. 'Highfield Park is always open to you, and you may invite as many people as you see fit.'

Perhaps it was too late now, but Sebastian hoped he would not regret it.

'Thank you, darling.'

'I do have one condition,' he added.

'Of course. Anything you say. What is your condition?'

'That you don't include me in your list of "suitable gentlemen".'

'Darling—'

'I mean it, Mother,' he said firmly. 'The doors of Highfield Park will be open to your guests for as long as you like, and I shall play the perfect host, but I refuse to be the subject of any matchmaking schemes.'

'As you wish, Sebastian,' she assured him.

'All right.' He smoothed a hand down his coat. 'When are these young ladies arriving?'

'Today.'

'Today?' A pulse throbbed in his temple. Why did he already have the feeling he would regret this?

'Yes, they should be on their way as we speak.' She bit at her lower lip. 'I know it's rather impulsive of me, but I thought with the Season already started we don't have much time.'

Sebastian supposed it would make no difference if they arrived today or next month. At the very least, the sooner these ladies were matched, the sooner he could have his peace and solitude back.

'I'll make sure Eames knows about our guests.'

'No need, darling, I've already informed him. He knows what to do.'

'No wonder Eames was running around like a hen trying to gather her chicks.' And it seemed his mother had already known he would say yes—not that he would deny her anything.

She placed her hands over his. 'Thank you, Sebastian.' That spark of life remained in her eyes and seemed to brighten. This time, he let the hope in his chest flare for just a moment.

He stiffened when she leaned over to kiss his cheek—not because he minded, but because it was something she hadn't done since he was a young boy. The small gesture of affection and the scent of her lavender perfume stirred up memories that he had locked away.

Clearing his throat, he said, 'Since you seem to have things in hand, I shall take my leave and see to some matters that need my attention.'

'Of course.'

'If you will excuse me...?'

As he walked out of the sitting room it still seemed quite unbelievable to him that his mother really was here. That if he turned around and went back into the room she wouldn't be gone like a puff of smoke. How many times had he wished for this in the past five years? That one day she would wake up and remember that the world outside still existed. That her son still existed.

Those thoughts were turning dangerous, so Sebastian put them out of his mind. Instead, he headed to his bedroom to change out of his travelling clothes. He'd been away far too long, and he needed to attend to his estate. When he'd inherited the Dukedom, along with it had come all the responsibilities of a failing estate. However, while many of his peers would have found a way to raise cash by selling off what they could, Sebastian had taken to the work head-on.

Yes, the estate had needed work. But, more importantly, Sebastian had discovered that he'd needed the gruelling activity too. To keep him busy. And to keep him from turning into the one thing he hated most. Now, after just a few short years, the estate was richer than it had ever been. Still, no matter how hard he worked, he couldn't help but feel it wasn't enough. That he was still failing. And that his nightmare would come true.

After a quick meal, and a change into riding breeches, a loose linen shirt, top boots, and a light jacket, Sebastian made his way outside to the stables, where his horse, Thunder, was already saddled and ready. While the cacophony and chaos in the house had considerably lessened, Sebastian was glad to escape for a few hours, before his home was descended upon by silly, fluff-headed girls. An afternoon outside in the sun, sur-

rounded by greenery, would prepare him for a long, tedious evening of playing the perfect host.

Hours passed by as he went about his business. Finally, after visiting one of the water meadows, to ensure
his improvements were being done properly, he went
to meet one of the newer tenants—a man by the name
of Fellowes—and checked to see how he and his family were getting along. By then the sun was sinking in
the west, which meant he'd have to make his way back
to the house. No doubt his mother's guests would be
well settled in by now. Though the thought of having
to sneak around like a burglar in his own home did not
sound appealing, Sebastian hoped to avoid encounter-
ing any of the simpering misses who had descended
upon the manor.

Bringing Thunder to a stop, he dismounted by a
stream to let the horse have a drink of water. Since the
manor was only about a mile away, Sebastian decided
to take the rest of the way on foot, gently guiding Thunder to walk beside him on the rough path and leading
him up a hill. It wasn't a terribly difficult climb, and
they'd done it a hundred times before. As he and Thunder ascended, however, the horse slowed and halted, as
if sensing something was amiss.

'My hat!' he heard a feminine voice cry.

A strong gust of wind blew by him, and something
smacked into his face. As he spat out what seemed to
be bits of lace from his mouth, he grabbed the offend-
ing item and tossed it to the ground. Sure enough, it
was a woman's bonnet.

Where the devil had that come from?

Looking up, he saw what must be the source of said
headwear as a slim, feminine figure trudged downhill,

coming faster and faster. If she wasn't careful she'd tumble and hurt herself.

'Slow down!' he shouted. 'You'll—'

Sure enough, the female slipped on a wet patch of grass, which made her land on her behind and slide down the rest of the way.

Damned fool!

Striding over to the girl, he stood over her and offered his hand. 'Madam, may I—?'

His breath caught in his throat, and for the second time that day he found himself questioning reality as a pair of familiar cornflower-blue eyes stared up at him. Surprise flashed across her face as he studied those mesmerising orbs.

'You,' he managed to choke out. 'What are you doing here?'

'What am *I* doing here?' Kate shot back. 'I should be asking you that question.'

She was certain she'd retorted right away. At least, she hoped so. Because she had spent an extraordinary amount of time staring up at the darkly handsome stranger.

Her stranger, to be precise.

How could he possibly be here?

But he was not the product of her imagination, nor some spirit conjured from her memory. No, he really was here. In the flesh, so to speak. And there was so much of him—as if he'd grown larger and taller from their last encounter over a week ago. His tall, well-worn Hessians encased powerful calves, while the tan-coloured buckskin trousers clung to muscled thighs. He wore no waistcoat and his white linen shirt hung loose and open at the throat, exposing a tantalising amount of golden skin.

How far did that tan extend?

As her gaze lifted higher she found herself mesmerised by those dark eyes. But the spell was broken when he cleared his throat, and heat immediately rushed up her neck and cheeks.

Realising her current state—dishevelled and lying on the ground like a wayward sack of grain—she scrambled to her feet and brushed off as much of the dirt from her dress as she could.

'Well?' she asked, picking a blade of grass from her sleeve. 'What have you got to say for yourself?'

'What have I—?' He blew out a strong breath. 'And why should *you* be the one asking the questions, madam?'

'It's *miss*.' She straightened her spine. 'And I happen to have been invited here. By the Dowager Duchess of Mabury herself.'

'Really?' An ebony brow lifted. 'And what does the Duke have to say about that?'

She trained her gaze on his again, but kept her expression haughty. Dear Lord, considering how he looked now, he had to be some kind of servant. That night in the gardens he'd been wearing a fine dark coat—but then again, he hadn't been inside the lavish Houghton home. Perhaps he was a coachman who had sneaked inside the garden.

'I imagine he'd have a lot to say about one of his workers speaking so impudently to a guest.'

The corner of his mouth quirked up. 'I'd like to hear what he has to say about one of these supposed guests traipsing about his land like a fairy sprite with no escort or chaperone. Or were you hoping to run into your very own Pyramus?'

If it were possible, her cheeks burned further at this reminder of their conversation from the night of the ball.

'And if I recall correctly,' he continued, 'it was not I who pushed us into one of the hedges in the gardens. Do you make a habit of accosting gentlemen after quoting them Shakespeare?'

She let out an indignant huff. 'I beg your pardon? Are you implying something, sir?'

'According to you, I am no gentleman, so there is no need for such formal language.'

Those bold obsidian eyes raked over her, travelling in a slow, lazy motion that was much too indecent. It set her pulse racing, and once again her dress felt constricting.

'But perhaps you are not seeking a gentleman.'

'Why, I never...!' Spying her trampled hat on the ground, she summoned up all her dignity and courage, marched to where the bonnet lay, and picked it up. Brushing off the dirt at the brim, she hastily secured it back on her head.

He patted his stallion's nose and retrieved an apple from his pocket and fed it to the giant black horse. 'Leaving so soon, miss?'

'Why, yes. The air around here seems to have taken an unbearable turn.'

Before he could say anything she turned on her heel and marched up the hill, concealing her shortness of breath as the slope turned steeper. Still, she could feel his gaze burning a hole in her back, and she shivered at the thought that he continued to stare at her so boldly. It wasn't until she had completely scaled the peak and was making her way down that she allowed herself to slow down and take short, shallow breaths.

Kate, you fool.

Once again, she'd put herself in a compromising position—and all because she'd wanted some fresh air after the long coach ride from London. The bumpy ride in the stuffy carriage had been unbearable, but mostly because she'd had to suffer the company of Caroline and Eliza DeVries. While Cornelius DeVries had napped, the two had gone on and on about the Dowager Duchess and their plans for capturing a lord. Neither woman had seemed to show any shame, even though Miss Merton had been with them.

Maddie, at least, had cringed every so often. And Miss Merton, bless her heart, had seemed to develop deafness... Or perhaps it was English politeness that had prevented her from reacting to the tactlessness of mother and daughter.

As they'd driven farther away from London the scenery had changed, and Kate had had to admit that the English countryside was divine—very different from its American cousin. There was a genteel, almost refined quality to it, unlike the wildness of American terrain. And when they had finally arrived at Highfield Park her breath had caught in her throat at the sight of the splendid three-storey mansion with an archway and four-columned entrance.

The manor was even more beautiful on the inside. She'd practically been able to see dollar signs in Eliza's and Caroline's eyes when they'd passed through the richly decorated corridors lined with paintings and sculptures as they were shown to their rooms. No one had asked about their hostess, but Miss Merton had told them they would all meet the Dowager Duchess in the drawing room, just before dinner. Eliza had rushed her daughters into their rooms to rest and refresh themselves before tonight, leaving Kate to fend for herself.

Not that Kate had minded—nor had she expected more. Her father had told her he couldn't be bothered to go along with them to Surrey, so he had left her in the care of the DeVrieses and Miss Merton, telling them to write to him once a suitable lord had offered for Kate. Though Eliza had fawned over her as they'd departed, and assured Arthur that his daughter would be in safe hands, Kate knew that she had only said that because of the DeVrieses' lucrative dealings with Arthur Mason. In private, Eliza treated her at best as little more than a stranger, and at worst as competition for her daughters.

No, Kate had not minded at all. However, seeing as the afternoon would be the last time she'd be able to have time alone, she hadn't been able to resist snatching that last piece of freedom. The sweet air had beckoned her and, while the inside of her bedroom was lavishly comfortable, she had been cooped up indoors for far too long, so she had headed outside.

Now she regretted her actions. And knowing that her handsome stranger was on this very estate had perturbed her. *No matter*, she told herself as she sneaked back into the house. She doubted she would ever see him again.

Chapter Four

Kate had done her best to forget the incident. After all, she was about to meet their mysterious hostess. After she'd taken a short nap, a maid had come into her room and helped her dress for the evening, and now she was headed downstairs to the drawing room.

The DeVrieses and Miss Merton were already there when she strode in.

'I should have worn the blue gown.' Caroline gave a disdainful glance to her butter-coloured satin dress with black lace edging. With her gleaming blonde hair brushed to perfection and pinned into curls, she looked elegant and worldly. 'I told you, Mother—it suits my eye colour better.'

'The yellow is fine, Caroline,' Eliza assured her. 'And you must save the blue gown for when there are unmarried gentlemen around. Maddie, will you stop fidgeting?'

'Sorry, Mother, but it itches.' Maddie tugged at her pink lace capelet trimmed with velvet ribbon. The sausage curls around her pretty face made her look even more ridiculously childlike. 'Is there anything else we need to know about the Dowager Duchess, Miss Merton?'

'I've already told you all I know,' Miss Merton said. 'It's been years since—'

Before she could continue the butler strode in. 'Her Grace the Dowager Duchess of Mabury.'

Everyone immediately got to their feet and faced the doorway. A reverent hush settled over the room.

When Miss Merton had first told them of the Dowager Duchess Kate had pictured a rather stiff, white-haired old matron. But the woman who glided into the room was not at all what she'd expected. The Dowager was of average height, and elegantly dressed in an amber gown that enhanced her slim figure. Her hair was rich and dark, pinned up to her head, though a few tendrils had been let down to soften the style. And, while her complexion held a trace of pallor, and shadows smudged the skin under her eyes, there was a warmth to her facial expression that made her appear youthful.

'Good evening. Welcome to Highfield Park,' the Dowager Duchess greeted them, her voice smooth as honey. 'I am so delighted that you've all accepted my invitation. I hope you've found your rooms to your liking, but if you have any requests please do approach Eames.' She nodded at the butler. 'Apologies… His Grace seems to be running late, but perhaps—'

'His Grace the Duke of Mabury,' the butler suddenly announced.

The air in the room shifted once more. There was that stillness again, but of a different sort. A tall figure strode inside, dressed in all-black formal wear.

'Good evening,' a voice greeted them, in a familiar low baritone that made Kate's heart crash into her ribcage.

Oh, no. Dear Lord, no.

As her stranger—the Duke, apparently—surveyed

the room, she groaned to herself as dread pooled in her chest.

Father in heaven, she began to pray. *If You open up the ground and swallow me up right this moment, I promise that the rest of my life shall be devoted to prayer, charitable acts, and service to You.*

But before the Good Lord could even ponder her request those dark eyes landed on her, their gazes colliding. She flinched inwardly, waiting for him to say something, but his expression remained unperturbed.

'Sebastian.' The Dowager Duchess walked over to him. 'Come, I must introduce you to our guests.'

Kate's body stiffened, her stomach turning to lead. Would he say something about their encounter at the ball? Or this afternoon, when she'd accused him of being a servant?

Kate, you idiot!

The Duke could send her packing from his estate before they'd even started dinner and she wouldn't blame him—she had behaved abhorrently earlier. Hopefully he would at least allow the DeVrieses to stay, if only for Maddie's sake.

'This is the Honourable Miss Harriet Merton...' the Dowager introduced their companion.

'Your Grace,' Miss Merton greeted him. 'It is an honour to finally make your acquaintance after all these years. Such an oversight, considering our connection.'

'Connection?' the Duke asked.

'Yes,' Miss Merton continued. 'Your father was a distant cousin of mine.'

'I see.' Mabury's face remained neutral. 'An oversight, indeed.'

The Dowager cleared her throat delicately. 'Miss

Merton, if you please?' she said, her eyes darting to the DeVrieses.

'Ah, yes.' Miss Merton clasped her hands together. 'Your Grace, may I introduce Mr and Mrs Cornelius DeVries of Pittsburgh?'

'An honour, Your Grace.' Cornelius took the hand the Duke offered. 'Thank you for hosting us here on your splendid estate.'

'I've never seen such a beautiful home,' Eliza added, her eyes glossing over with awe.

Mabury did not speak, but merely nodded.

'And these young ladies,' Miss Merton continued, 'are Miss Madeline DeVries, Miss Caroline DeVries and Miss Kate Mason.'

Kate took her time with her curtsey, keeping her head low and her gaze anywhere but on the Duke. Beside her, she could practically feel Caroline's giddiness as she struggled to hold in her excitement.

Oh, please, let this all be over soon.

'It is a pleasure to make your acquaintance,' he finally said. 'I believe it's time we began dinner.'

'Of course,' the Dowager Duchess agreed.

As Mabury offered his arm to his mother everyone else followed their hosts out of the parlour and into the adjoining dining room, where they sat around the table with the unmarried misses at the end. Maddie sent Kate a small smile, while Caroline fumed silently—perhaps because they were too far away to make conversation with the Duke.

Kate did not mind. In fact, she could have been seated in the next county and it still wouldn't be far away enough from him.

Each course that came seemed richer and finer than the one before it, all delivered by liveried footmen who lifted the silver dome from each plate with a precise flourish. Rich soups with truffle. Puréed roasted vegetables. Baked pheasant in a creamy, buttery sauce…

Kate couldn't enjoy any of the sumptuous offerings as her thoughts continued to circle back to her encounter with the Duke that afternoon, and mortification churned her stomach.

It was like waiting for the hammer to fall on an anvil. The night wasn't over yet, and there was still a chance for Mabury to reveal their acquaintance. Would he do it over dinner? Lord it over her? Keep her stewing and squirming in her seat until he had revealed what a horrible, ungrateful guest she was? Or, worse, would he tell everyone that she'd pushed him into the hedges at the Houghton Ball?

Conversation was muted, and the Duke only spoke when asked a question by his mother or Cornelius DeVries. The ladies' side of the table was practically silent—except for Caroline, who made comments every now and then.

'This is perhaps the best meal I've had in England,' she declared rather loudly in the middle of the fish course, turning her head towards the head of the table. 'Maybe in the world.'

'Indeed, it is wonderful, Your Grace,' Miss Merton said. 'I've heard you employ one of the finest French chefs.'

'Yes, Pierre is a marvel in the kitchen,' the Dowager Duchess answered.

After what seemed like eternity the dinner was concluded and the Dowager Duchess announced that there would be tea for the ladies in the blue sitting room while the two gentlemen would be heading to the Duke's private study for port and cigars. The men left the dining room first and the ladies followed behind them, and although Kate felt relief that she would be escaping Mabury's presence for the next part of the evening, the dread and anxiety in the pit of her stomach only continued to grow.

'Kate, where is your reticule?' Maddie asked as they trailed behind the other ladies headed to the library.

She looked down at her empty arm. 'Drat.' In her daze, she'd left it behind. 'Tell the others I've gone back to retrieve it.'

'But, Kate, you shouldn't just—'

'I shan't be long.'

Without another word, she pivoted on her heel and marched back into the dining room. In her haste, she dashed through the open doorway—and promptly collided with a solid object. She staggered, and would have fallen back if not for the firm grip on her arm that steadied her.

'I'm sorry! I—' Her throat went dry as sand when she looked up at that familiar onyx gaze. 'Y-Your Grace.'

Mabury quickly released her arm. 'Miss Mason.'

His expression remained restrained and polite—so different from his bold gaze this afternoon, which had sent warmth through her.

'I was just retrieving my reticule.' Bowing her head low, she sidestepped him, intending to rush to her seat and search for the wayward item. But on impulse, she stopped. 'Your Grace?'

'Yes?' He turned his head towards her.

Here goes nothing. Pap had always told her to tackle problems head-on.

'Your Grace, may I speak frankly? A-about this afternoon?'

'Miss Mason, I don't know what you are speaking of.'

Was he jesting? Or was she mistaken and she'd some-how twice run into his twin? She searched for humour in his eyes. 'You know…about—'

'Miss Mason.' His voice was like a sharp, cold knife. 'Perhaps it would be best for all concerned—especially considering propriety and decorum—if we do not speak of anything that happened before this moment.'

'But I— Oh!' It dawned on her that the Duke was saving her from embarrassment. *How gentlemanly.* Per-haps this was her stranger's altruistic and noble doppel-gänger. 'Of course, Your Grace.'

With a dismissive nod, he left the room.

As she stared after him Kate knew she should be grateful. Ecstatic, even. She had escaped embarrass-ment and disgrace without any repercussions.

But a tight ball knotted under her chest, growing as she formed one thought in her head: *she was noth-ing to him.*

The encounter that had plagued her thoughts and dreams had not affected him. Perhaps he didn't even remember it. The heat from his gaze this afternoon had been extinguished, only to be replaced by a cool de-meanour.

You're being irrational, she told herself.

Besides, catching the Duke's eye was not her pur-pose here. No, she had only one reason for coming here. Preventing her marriage to Jacob in order to save Pap's memory and legacy. And to do that she had to first obtain the Dowager Duchess's sponsorship—which meant expelling the handsome, dark-eyed Duke from her thoughts.

Chapter Five

Kate did not see the Duke of Mabury at breakfast the next day. When Miss Merton enquired about him at the table, the Dowager Duchess explained that her son was very busy running the estate and was usually up at dawn and out tending to business during the day.

Kate told herself she was very glad that she would not suffer his presence.

Caroline, of course, was disappointed. 'His Grace's charming company will be missed,' she said.

Kate knew the younger woman already had designs on the Duke, and not just because of his 'charming company'. He could have been old and decrepit and Caroline would have thrown herself at him just the same.

'Now, ladies,' the Dowager Duchess began, 'after breakfast, I'd like to invite you all for a stroll in the garden. I know it's early in the year, but I do love to see it before it fully blooms. Then we shall have a quick luncheon, and this afternoon you will have a choice of activities: shopping and tea in the village or a quiet afternoon in the library.'

'Shopping and tea sounds lovely, Your Grace,' Caroline burst out. 'Much more enjoyable than an afternoon in a room full of books.'

'We also have a telescope,' the Dowager Duchess mentioned.

'A *what*, now?' Eliza asked.

'A telescope, Mother,' Maddie said. 'A device to look at the stars.'

Eliza looked horrified. 'Heavens, why ever would you need such a thing?'

Maddie placed her hands in her lap. 'I should like to see that.'

'Then Maddie and I shall spend the afternoon in the library,' Kate declared. Tea and shopping with Caroline and Eliza sounded dreadful.

The Dowager's mouth pulled back into a smile, her twinkling dark eyes making her seem ten years younger. 'Excellent.'

As Her Grace had mentioned, the gardens were still in their early stages of growth, as winter had only just finished. It was still quite bare, but Kate could imagine just how beautiful it would be when in full bloom— especially with its variety of trees and plants, from crab apples to cherries, to gardenias and hydrangeas. An orangery had been built high at the top of the garden and the gardeners were busy rushing in and out of the brick and glass structure, tending to the numerous bulbs about to be transplanted throughout the garden and estate.

'It must be heavenly here in the spring and summer,' Eliza stated.

The Dowager Duchess stopped to nod at a gardener, who bowed to her as he walked by carrying a cherry tree seedling. 'The gardens will be splendid indeed, after all the work has been done.' She followed the gardener as he knelt in the earth and placed the seedling into the ground. 'The seeds must be planted in the autumn and cared for and maintained at a precise temperature throughout the winter, until they are ready to be planted. When I look out here,' she said, and gestured at their surroundings, 'I see the potential and know the hard work will all be worth it. Come,' she added, 'let us continue.'

After their tour, they once again headed to the dining room for luncheon, before retreating to their rooms to refresh themselves. Caroline and Eliza were excited about the prospect of tea and shopping, and discussed what they were going to wear for the excursion.

'Do you think we should change our plans and go with them?' Maddie asked as they walked down the long corridor towards their assigned bedrooms—which thankfully were next to each other. She lowered her voice. 'What if the Dowager Duchess thinks I am too much of a bluestocking to attract a husband?'

'One afternoon by ourselves won't hurt our chances.' Kate stopped outside her door. 'Besides, if Her Grace hasn't asked us to leave by now, then surely she considers us strong candidates.'

Maddie seemed to contemplate her words. 'You are pragmatic as usual, Kate. And I really should like to see this telescope.'

Kate, too, was intrigued. 'Well, I think I shall lie down and nap for an hour. See you at the library?'

Maddie nodded, her curls bouncing. 'I shall see you there.'

Precisely one hour later, Kate entered the library. Maddie was already there, standing by a cylindrical brass object perched on a three-legged stand and propped up by the window, peering into one end.

'Maddie?'

'There you are.' Maddie stepped back and turned to her. 'Oh, this device is such a marvel. Would you like to try it?'

'I would...thanks.' Kate took the same position as Maddie had, bending down to look into the eyepiece.

'I thought it would only work at night,' Maddie began. 'But even in the daytime you can see a great distance.'

Sure enough, the telescope did let her see quite far— past the gardens and the parkland to the nearest farm on the estate. As she moved the telescope around, however, the images blurred. She fiddled with the eyepiece until the scene sharpened.

What in the world...?

Kate continued to play with the eyepiece, wondering if it was the telescope or her eyes that were defective. But, no, she was quite certain of what she was seeing. Yes, it was Mabury himself, helping one of his tenants repair a stone wall. He was dressed much as he had been yesterday, except now his linen shirt was opened all the way to his slim waist, exposing his chest, which was covered with a mat of dark hair.

So he was tanned all the way down.

'Yes...um...it's a wonderful device.'

Warmth crept up her cheeks and a tightness pulled somewhere low in her belly. The Duke picked up a large slab of stone and hoisted it over his shoulder. Fascination kept her glued to the scene, but part of her was curious too—why would a duke lower himself to work with his tenants?

'Kate?'

The hand on her shoulder made her start and Kate shot upright. 'Yes?' she said, sheepish.

Maddie cocked her head to one side. 'Are you all right? You look flushed.'

'Wh-why, yes. I'm quite fine.'

'What did you see? It must have been captivating, seeing as you didn't hear me calling you the first few times. Can I see?'

'No!' Kate stepped in front of the telescope. 'I mean…uh…there was a…a beautiful blue jay on top of a tree.'

'Blue jay?' Maddie's brows drew together. 'I thought those were only in America?'

Drat! 'Are they?'

'I think so…let me see.'

'Er…let me check again.' Clearing her throat, she bowed down again to look through the telescope. She intended to move the scope away, before Maddie discovered what she was really looking at, but before she did, she couldn't resist one last peek at the Duke. 'It's…uh…'

She gasped as the view came into focus once more and she saw a portion of the wall collapse, barely missing the Duke.

'Oh, no!'

'What's wrong?'

Kate jumped back. 'I need to go.'

The Duke was unharmed, but what had caused the collapse? Perhaps there was something wrong with the way the wall was being built. Did they not have a mason to direct them?

'Go? Wherever to?'

Kate bit her lip. If there was something she couldn't resist, it was a problem that needed solving. 'I can't tell you yet.' Holding Maddie's hands in hers, she stared up into her friend's face. 'But I require your help.'

Maddie's head bobbed up and down, sending her sausage curls bouncing. 'Whatever you need.'

'If anyone asks, will you tell them I spent the rest of the day with you? Please?'

'Of course,' she replied, with no hesitation.

'Thank you.' Releasing Maddie's hands, she pivoted on her heel. 'I shan't be long.'

Chapter Six

'You can say it,' Sebastian muttered as he brushed dirt from his once spotless shirt.

'Say what, Your Grace?' asked John Lawrence as he handed Sebastian a clean cloth.

He took it and wiped the sweat from his brow. 'That you were right. We should have waited for the mason to come and mend your wall.' He nodded ruefully at the scattered pile of stones at his feet.

'Well, my wife kept complaining about the sheep comin' in and eating her herbs and such. And you know my Mary when she's cross.' John Lawrence chuckled. 'And far be it from me to say no to a duke—especially one who offers a hand.' He scratched at his chin. 'It did look like a simple job, Your Grace, pilin' stones on top of each other. Besides, I'm grateful for all your help. I don't think I ever seen a farmhand work as hard as you these last two days. Maybe when you're tired of doin' all your dukely duties you can come work for me, Your Grace.'

The corner of Sebastian's mouth quirked up. 'I'll consider your offer.'

John shook his head. 'Still don't know why you bothcrcd with us thcsc past years. You already paid for improvements on all the farms and fixed all the houses and things. The old Duke never bothered with us. Never even met us tenants.'

Sebastian froze, clenching his hand around the cloth at the mention of his father.

'Beggin' your pardon, Your Grace.' John took his hat off. 'Wasn't meaning no disrespect to your father. And I'm happy for the help.'

His shoulders relaxed. 'It's no bother at all, John.'

Most men of his rank went to fencing or boxing clubs to stay fit. Indeed, Sebastian had used to pursue such sport. But he couldn't even remember the last time he'd stepped into a ring or on a mat. Now he was in the best physical condition of his life, as back-breaking estate work allowed Sebastian to stay in top form. Some might say his tanned skin and hulking shoulders were unfashionable, but he had stopped caring about what the ton might say about him five years ago, and he wasn't about to start now.

When he'd first taken over the running of the estate, he'd discovered that physical activity helped distract him. After all, when the body was exhausted, the mind had no time to wallow in grief. Now he needed the physical activity. Craved it. Sought it out. It had become like a balm to him, preventing old wounds from opening.

Today, however, he hoped to tire himself so that he could sleep peacefully tonight—instead of lying awake in bed as he had the last two evenings, thinking about things he shouldn't be thinking about.

Like cornflower-blue eyes.

Hair like a mahogany waterfall.

The scent of fresh powder and lemons.

And because his mind had been consumed by those

thoughts he had dropped the last slab of stone on top of the wall, sending the rest of it tumbling down.

Damn it all to hell.

'You all right, Your Grace?' John asked.

'Yes.' Putting the cloth aside, he buttoned up his shirt. 'I suppose the wall will have to wait until the mason comes. Wouldn't want to muck it up any more than I already had.'

'I can push my cart up to stop those pesky sheep from comin' in. Let's take a rest, Your Grace. How 'bout some water to wash you off and refresh you?'

Sebastian blew out a breath and observed the dirt clinging to his clothes. His valet was used to seeing them in such a state after he'd been working outside, but some cool water sounded like a good idea. 'I shall come with you to the well.'

He followed John Lawrence to the rear of the house and helped him haul up a bucket of water from the well. He washed the dirt from his face, hands, and fingernails as best he could, but the rest of him would require a bath.

After cleaning up, Sebastian went over the list of things that needed to be done in the next few weeks, as well as the concerns of other tenants. Since John Lawrence worked on the farm closest to the estate and had been there the longest, he functioned as a go-between for Sebastian and the other families on small matters.

'All right, I'll see what I can do about procuring a few more ewes for Robert Talling,' Sebastian said as they concluded, adding the task to his running mental list of things to do. 'Now—' he nodded towards the direction of Highfield Park '—if you don't mind, John, I'll be on my way. Do send word if anything else needs repair.'

John nodded. 'Thank you, Your Grace.'

They made their way back to the front of the house, so Sebastian could retrieve his horse from where it was tied to a post. However, when they circled around the building Thunder was not alone. A figure was bent over the damaged section of the wall. A very feminine figure. Sebastian didn't know why, but from the way his body reacted he knew who it was.

Miss Kate Mason.

Hell's bells.

A shock ran through him—the very same sensation he'd felt when she'd appeared before him two days ago, on his own estate, like an apparition he had conjured up. He'd been amused at first, as he'd realised that she was one of his mother's guests while she'd had no idea who he was—even mistaking him for a servant or a farmer. He had even experienced a kind of satisfaction, seeing the horror on her face upon finding out his identity last night at dinner.

However, she'd somehow turned the tables on him—because being so near her, under the same roof, yet untouchable, had made him want her more. Made him wonder what those curves would feel like under him and how those lips tasted. Missing breakfast hadn't helped because she'd still consumed his thoughts.

He let out a huff. Whatever his body might feel about Miss Kate Mason, he took comfort in the knowledge that she was exactly as he had pegged her in the beginning: another crass dollar princess, looking to bag a titled English lord. That was the reason why he'd treated her so coldly—lest she set her cap on him.

John Lawrence cleared his throat. 'Beggin' your pardon, milady, but are you lost?'

Miss Mason whirled around, her eyes widening when they landed on Sebastian.

'What are you doing here, Miss Mason?' Sebastian thundered.

She flinched, but quickly composed herself. 'I was… taking a walk when I noticed your wall had collapsed.'

Sebastian narrowed his eyes at her. Though her tone sounded confident, he'd played enough cards in his life to know when someone was bluffing. And she was definitely bluffing. And doing it badly.

'Really? And how do you know it had collapsed?' he asked. 'Could it not be that we are in the midst of building it?'

Had she been spying on them? How long had she been here?

A blush deepened the colour in her cheeks. 'I…uh…' Glancing around, she poked a slippered foot at a stone by her feet. She picked it up with both hands, as if judging its shape and size, then marched towards the wall and placed it between two other stones near the bottom.

'Aha! A perfect match.' The stone did, indeed, fit snugly into the crevice. Brushing her hands down her skirts, she looked back at them. 'As I deduced, this wall must have collapsed. And, b-based on the state of your clothing, you were probably in the midst of repairing it.'

Sebastian chewed at the inside of his cheek. 'A lucky guess. In any case, Miss Mason, you should perhaps— What are you doing now?'

She had picked up another stone and was placing it on top of the previous one. 'There you go.' Gesturing towards the fallen stones, she asked, 'How in the world did this happen? Is there no stonemason around to help you with the repair?'

'I've sent for him, miss,' John interjected. 'But he won't be able to come for another couple of days. My wife got all in a temper with the sheep comin' in, and wanted it done right away. His Grace and I thought it would be a simple enough job to put it together.'

'Hmmm…' She tapped a finger on her chin. 'Stone-masonry requires knowledge and experience, but I suppose with careful observation and study one could easily work out how this wall was constructed.'

Crossing over to the other side, she bent lower to examine the intact section of the wall.

'The bottom is made of larger stones, which makes sense as that ensures a more stable foundation. Then it's built up in layers, with the middle filled with smaller pebbles and stones. Perhaps to prevent the stones from sliding apart?'

A finger poked at the layers.

'It seems you did one part correctly, but what happened to the rest?'

'His Grace dropped a long flat piece that was supposed to go in the middle,' said John. 'It must have… er…slipped,' he added, looking at Sebastian sheepishly. 'The rains must've made them too wet.'

'Ah, I see.' She crossed her arms over her chest and drummed her fingers. 'I think we should be able to fix this section for now—at least until the mason comes.'

'We?' Sebastian said in an incredulous tone. 'What do you mean "we"?'

'You don't expect me to pick up all the stones, do you, Your Grace?' she replied sweetly. 'Now…' She turned back to John. 'Let's have a further look, shall we?'

'Do you know about wall-building, miss?' asked John. 'Are you a mason?'

She shook her head. 'Only in name. My Pap—that's my grandfather—loved to tinker and build things. Having no formal education, he learned everything he knew from working in the coal mines in West Virginia.' She paused, the corners of her mouth turning up. 'He always had to figure everything out on his own, and one way he did that was by disassembling something to discover how it was made and then trying to replicate the process.'

There was something about the way she smiled—the way her entire face brightened and her eyes sparkled—that caused a twinge in Sebastian's chest.

John contemplated her words. 'Huh... My Mary likes to do something similar in the kitchen. One day we went to the fair and I bought her a mince pie. She loved it so much that she saved half of it, brought it home, and tried to identify every ingredient with each bite. Eventually she made one and it tasted just like the first pie.'

'Ah, if my Pap had been able to cook or bake he would have done the same thing. He loved pies.' Miss Mason laughed. 'Now, let's see what we can do about this wall so we can keep your Mary happy, shall we? Perhaps she'll make you more mince pies once we're done.'

Sebastian wasn't sure exactly what was happening, but one moment they were standing around, and the next Miss Mason was directing them like a general ordering his soldiers. As he and John Lawrence picked up stones for her she examined each one and placed them methodically in certain positions, occasionally checking to see if their construction corresponded with the undamaged portion of the wall. She also answered John's questions patiently, without brushing him off as if he were a child or a simpleton unable to understand the concept of wall-building.

'Place it closer to the centre, if you please, Mr Lawrence,' she instructed John, and he placed a flat slab of stone on top of the stack.

'Why can't we just pile 'em up on top of each other, miss?'

'Making the wall narrower as it gets to the top directs the weight towards the centre,' she explained.

'To prevent it from collapsing,' Sebastian added. 'Two opposing forces, pushing against each other.'

'Exactly, Your Grace.'

She lifted her head, and when that cornflower-blue gaze collided with his that twinge came back. This time Sebastian swore there was a sparkle in her eyes, but she quickly averted her face.

'I believe that one goes on next, Your Grace.'

She nodded at the long slab of stone by his foot—the same piece that he'd dropped, and which had caused the wall to collapse.

'If you don't mind.'

'Not at all.' He picked it up and balanced it on top of the pile, checking the other section of the wall to ensure they fitted the same way. 'Looks like a perfect match.'

She placed her palms on top. 'Seems stable enough.' Her lips twisted, seemingly in concentration, as she checked their work against the remaining wall. 'I believe we need one more layer of stones, and then a top piece to weigh everything down and keep it all together.' She pointed to the rounded stones on top of the wall. 'However, I think those might require specialised tools and skills, so you might have to wait for the mason to complete the task after all. Assuming we haven't botched it—in which case he'll have to start again.'

'I think it looks fine, miss,' said John. 'If nothing else, it'll stop those sheep from ruinin' Mary's herbs. Thank you so much for your help.'

'You're very welcome, sir. Well, I should be going,'

Miss Mason said quickly. 'I can't be late. Good day, Mr Lawrence... Your Grace.'

After a hurried curtsey, she turned and strode out towards the gate.

Sebastian stifled the urge to go after her, instead watching her retreating figure.

What in the world had just happened?

If he had been confused before, he was downright befuddled now. How could she know how to figure out the process of building a wall just by looking at it?

However, his mind drifted back to that first evening at the Houghton Ball, and he recalled how well-read she was for a young debutante. With wit and intelligence. His instinct told him that there was more under the surface. She was like a puzzle wanting to be solved. And his damned curious mind had always been drawn to mysteries.

'Oh, dear, I didn't think Her Grace would invite so many people,' Maddie said as her eyes scanned the room, sinking her teeth into her lower lip.

Once again, the Dowager Duchess had asked everyone to gather in the drawing room, but this time so that they could be acquainted with new guests before they sat down to dinner.

'So many?' Caroline sneered. 'I wouldn't call this many.' Her gaze narrowed on the people gathered around them. 'There's...what...? Eight people here? Three eligible gentlemen, and only one of them even remotely close to a title. Where are the dukes? The earls? I'd even settle for a baronet.'

Unfortunately, Kate had to agree with her. The clock was ticking, and each day that passed without her meeting an eligible lord brought her closer to an even drearier fate with Jacob as her husband—as she had been promptly reminded by the letter that had arrived that morning.

When the cream-coloured envelope with the familiar neat handwriting of her father's personal secretary had arrived in her room, her heart had plummeted in her chest.

> *Kathryn,*
>
> *I trust that you are settled into the Dowager Duchess of Mabury's home and can now concentrate on securing a match. I look forward to hearing from Miss Merton about the offers you have secured, so that I may review them for suitability.*
> *Signed,*
> *Father*

The cold, brusque note, which sounded as if he was corresponding with a trader rather than his own daughter, was typical of her father. Being used to it, she was not offended, but the meaning behind the words was not lost on her: she must find a titled husband soon.

That's what I'm trying to do, Father.

The Queen of England herself would dance a jig on London Bridge before Kate married Jacob. Hopefully tonight's party would bring her some prospects.

The Dowager Duchess had invited a few people who lived nearby, including a countess and her younger son, but so far no one suitable had arrived.

I'll marry the first lord who walks through the door.

She didn't care what he looked like, or how old he was, as long as he had a title.

At that precise moment the Duke of Mabury entered

through the doorway and Kate's heart leapt up into her throat.

Kate thoughts jolted back to yesterday, when they'd been building the wall. While he had barely spoken while she was there, it had been obvious that Mr Lawrence was used to having the Duke around. Indeed, they'd both acted casually around each other, as if the Duke working on Mr Lawrence's farm was an everyday occurrence. Which had told Kate it probably was.

She'd been surprised, and confused, for what landowner anywhere in the world took the time to help a tenant with such a menial task? None that she knew. They wouldn't even think of how they could help those they deemed beneath them.

Well, not *all* men.

'There's no such thing as an insignificant job,' Pap had always said when he'd talked of the factory. *'Everyone here contributes in some way.'*

Indeed, her grandfather had known the name of every person who worked for him—from the skilled mechanics who kept the equipment in shape to the boys who mopped up grease from the factory floor.

But that was the way Pap had been—tough, but caring and kind to those around him. Was the Duke the same?

The thought had made something flutter in Kate's chest, and she'd been so unnerved she'd quickly left and bolted back to Highfield Park.

'Finally he's arrived.' Caroline beamed, her eyes never leaving Mabury's tall, handsome form. 'Mother, should I have worn this dress tonight? I know it makes my eyes look bluer, but it's much more suitable for a ball.' She craned her head, trying to catch Mabury's gaze.

A different emotion gripped Kate, making her irra-

tionally cross at Caroline's covetous gaze at the Duke.
She supposed with Caroline's beauty she would indeed
make a fine duchess. However, the Duke barely acknowledged them, and instead crossed the room to be
at his mother's side. That tightness around her chest
loosened. *Poor Caroline.* She had no idea that Mabury
had no intention of ever marrying.

Caroline pouted. 'Mama, this is a waste of time. Perhaps coming here was a mistake. We could have attended a *real* ball if we were in London.'

'The Dowager Duchess has many other friends, I'm
sure,' Eliza soothed, trying to appease her daughter.
'Perhaps they didn't have time to make the trip. Or
maybe the Dowager is testing us.'

'T-testing us?' Maddie glanced around nervously.

'Yes!' Eliza's eyes gleamed as if she had stumbled
upon some great secret. 'That must be it.'

'I thought she'd already agreed to sponsor me,' Caroline grumbled. 'Why do I need to pass some test?'

'Her Grace couldn't possibly introduce us to the
upper echelons of society right away,' Eliza reasoned.
'Remember what Miss Merton said? It's not just about
how much money we have. We must prove to her that
we have what it takes to move in the right circles.'

Caroline seemed to contemplate her words. 'I suppose that makes sense...'

'It makes perfect sense,' Eliza stated. 'Come, I see
your father is speaking to Countess Farley and some of
the other guests. We should join them.'

The four women walked over to where Cornelius
DeVries stood chatting with the Countess and her son
William, Viscount Davenport, and Mr Robert Hughes,
the gentleman who owned the neighbouring estate.

'Eliza,' Cornelius greeted his wife as he made space

for the women to join them. 'I was just telling Lady Farley about our impressions of London.'

'Such a delightful, exciting city!' Eliza tittered. 'And the shops! So many fine things on display. I have to say Bond Street has become one of my favourite places in the world.'

'Yes, well, I'm sure you were all overwhelmed,' Lady Farley commented in a haughty tone. 'We are so much more civilised over here than in the colonies.'

Kate bit her tongue, so as not to tell Her Ladyship what was on her mind. That these snooty English really thought they were the centre of the world.

'Our very first venture into one of the glove shops left me utterly confused,' Caroline said. 'The pricing is so different... I told the shop manager I simply don't have the head for numbers.' Caroline placed a hand over her forehead. 'Dollars...pounds... I can't quite make sense of it all.'

'You should have let your father take care of it,' suggested Viscount Davenport, gesturing towards Cornelius. 'He's a fine businessman, or so I've heard.'

'Ladies simply do not have the capacity for numbers or ledgers,' Mr Hughes agreed.

'You're both so wise,' Caroline fawned. 'I shall not attempt to bargain next time.'

Kate gnashed her teeth before smiling sweetly at the two gentlemen. 'Indeed, so wise,' she said, hiding her indignation as best she could.

If they'd been back in the factory in New York, she would have shown them just how much capacity she had with numbers. Pap himself had relied on her calculations while he'd designed the Andersen.

'We ladies desperately need men to take care of those

things while we concentrate on shopping and household management.'

Mr Hughes raised a glass to her. 'Here, here, Miss Mason.'

'Thank you,' she said, lifting her glass in mockery.

Caroline cleared her throat, bringing the attention back to her. 'If only you had been there, Mr Hughes.' She fluttered her eyelashes coquettishly. 'I'm sure you could have made sense of it all. With you running such a large estate, I'm sure it would have been an easy transaction.'

Mr Hughes's eyes lit up. 'Indeed, Miss DeVries.'

'My number skills are just as sharp,' interjected Viscount Davenport. The young man had been eyeing Caroline ever since he'd arrived, and it was obvious to everyone that he was smitten. 'I'm sure I could have taken care of it for you.'

With both men's attention diverted to her, Caroline became animated. Kate wanted to throw her hands up in exasperation. As usual, Caroline droned on without really saying anything of substance. Yet these men couldn't see past the—

That's it.

Her mind began to fill with all sorts of ideas.

Could she…?

Would it work…?

Did she dare?

Of course!

Kate gulped in a large breath of air. Who knew that it would be Caroline who provided her with the solution to her Marriage Problem?

Maddie cocked her head to one side. 'Kate, what's wrong?'

'I'm…fine.'

Why she'd never thought of it before, Kate didn't

know, but it was clear to her now that Caroline knew exactly how to attract the male species. Men were naturally drawn to her—and not just because of her beauty. No, it was because she made them feel clever and capable.

So Kate came to the conclusion that those of the male sex preferred not only a meek and obedient woman, but one preferably less intelligent than themselves.

Damned male superiority.

She'd known about that all her life. Except for Pap, every man she had ever encountered in the factory had underestimated her intelligence and brushed her aside. That had only made her want to prove them wrong, which she so often had, and many of them now grudgingly deferred to her. However, it seemed that in order to attract the right mate she must act significantly more witless than him. If she wanted to catch a husband then she had to hide her intelligence and be completely and utterly vacuous.

The thought made her shudder.

But it would only be temporary.

Just until she'd secured her match and removed herself from the clutches of her father and Jacob.

As Caroline continued to entrance the men, Kate couldn't help but sneak a glance across the room to where Mabury stood by his mother's side. She was once again reminded of yesterday, but this time a bolt of heat struck her as a different image popped up in her mind— that of golden skin and a muscled chest, with that shirt undone down to his waist.

Stop thinking about him.

She had, after all, more important matters to attend to—like using her newfound knowledge to find a husband.

He could be your husband, a small voice inside her replied.

The Duke?

Yes.

Kate huffed as she remembered his words back in the garden. *'I shall never marry.'* She couldn't very well drag the man to the altar and force him to be her husband. Besides, she had nothing to offer him. He was titled, and richer than a king, so had no need of an American heiress's dowry.

The very thought made that small voice evaporate. If only the same would happen to her unseemly thoughts of the Duke—especially of his shirtsleeves rolled to his elbows and his forearms flexing as he lifted those stones.

Kate attempted to swallow, but her throat had gone dry. Realising her glass was empty, she spied a footman with a lemonade jug by the door and slipped away from the group. Before she could ask for a refill, however, a latecomer strode in and nearly collided with her.

'Apologies, my lady!' the stranger cried as he steadied himself. 'Oh, dear, are you all right?'

Kate, thankfully, regained her balance quickly. 'No, it's my fault. I shouldn't have been standing in the doorway.'

'I'm terribly late, and I was rushing in, so the fault is mine.' He ran his hands through his blond hair and gave her a sheepish smile.

'If you insist, then apology accepted.'

Kate couldn't help but grin back. The man was quite good-looking, in a delicate way, as if his features had been chiselled by an Italian sculptor. He also had the loveliest light brown eyes she had ever seen. They reminded her of a puppy's.

'Edward—I mean, Your Grace—welcome,' the Dowager Duchess greeted him as she came to join them.

'Your Grace.' He bowed deeply to the Dowager.

'Please do accept my apologies for my tardiness. I had to attend to some business on the estate.'

'We haven't started dinner, so it's no trouble at all. I had thought maybe you'd changed your mind.'

'I wouldn't dream of it, Your Grace—especially since I am one of the first people invited to Highfield Park now that you have returned.'

The Dowager Duchess's lips pulled into a tight line. 'Yes, of course…' She cleared her throat delicately. 'Oh, excuse my rudeness. Have you met Miss Mason? She's one of my guests.'

'We have bumped into each other, but I'm afraid we haven't been introduced.'

'Then allow me.' The Dowager gestured to Kate. 'Your Grace, may I introduce Miss Kate Mason of New York? Miss Mason, this is His Grace the Duke of Seagrave.'

Kate curtseyed. 'How do you, Your Grace?'

'I'm well, thank you. Lovely to meet you, Miss Mason.'

The corners of the Dowager Duchess's mouth tugged up. 'Oh, dear… I was on my way to ask Eames about dinner. Would you think it rude of me to leave you, Your Grace? Perhaps Miss Mason can keep you company?'

'Not at all rude,' he said. 'Your skills as a hostess and attention to detail are impeccable as always.'

'All right, then, if you will excuse me…?' The Dowager Duchess gave Kate a knowing glance before she headed out of the drawing room.

'So… Miss Mason…you're American,' Seagrave began. 'Tell me, what brings you to England? And how are you liking it here?'

Kate stifled the urge to be honest, and before she could give her standard answer she remembered her earlier thoughts. *Meek and obedient. Completely and utterly vacuous.* She had to do it—if only as a means to an end.

Could Seagrave be the one to rescue her from a dreadful marriage to her second cousin and save her grandfather's legacy?

If he wasn't, she could at least practise…

'Oh, London is just so lovely. Especially all the shops on Bond Street,' she began, pitching her voice higher, as she'd often noticed Caroline do when she was around any male. 'And as for why I've come here…my father has business in England, so I came along.'

'Business? What kind of business?'

She shrugged. 'Oh, I don't know… Building and selling things… I'm not really sure I understand it all.' Lord, it pained her to sound so foolish, but she had no choice. 'I could try to explain it…'

'Don't trouble yourself on my account, Miss Mason,' he said. 'But do tell me more about what you think of England so far. And Surrey? I hope life in the country isn't too dull?'

'Not at all, Your Grace.' She batted her eyelashes at him, the way she'd seen Caroline do countless times. 'Everything here is so…uh…green and fresh.'

'Ah, yes. It's the trees and the grass and the clear air, you see,' he explained, as if she were a child. 'London doesn't have a lot of greenery.'

Really? I hadn't noticed.

Kate forced a smile to her face. 'How right you are, Your Grace.'

Oh, dear, this was going to be a long evening. However, if things went right tonight it would not be a loss.

Chapter Seven

'I think they're getting along quite well.'

Sebastian turned his head at the sound of his mother's voice. 'I beg your pardon?'

'Them.' The Dowager Duchess took his arm and then nodded to Miss Mason and her companion. 'Miss Mason and the Duke of Seagrave. They've been deep in conversation since I introduced them.'

'Ah.' No wonder the man looked familiar. *Lord Edward Philipps.* They'd been at Eton at around the same time, and from what Sebastian could recall Lord Edward hadn't been much of a student, so he could hardly believe the man to be deep in conversation about anything. Deep as a saucer, perhaps. 'I didn't realise the old Duke had passed on.'

'About a year ago, from what I've heard.'

'Really? I'm surprised he hung on that long. The old man was ancient—and that was when I was a boy.'

He had outlived two wives, then gone for his third trip down the aisle a few years ago with some young chit. Apparently, the old Duke had been quite loose with the purse strings with her and the estate was now nearly bankrupt.

His mother took his arm. 'Shall we go in to dinner?'

Sebastian nodded and led his mother to the dining room, with the guests lining up behind them. To his surprise, his mother had decided on an informal seating arrangement for this evening. He remained at the head of the table, but the Dowager Duchess sat at the opposite end, while men and women sat interspersed. Unfortunately, Caroline DeVries sat only two places from him. But that wasn't what truly irked him. No, it was the fact that Miss Mason sat next to Seagrave, and the two of them were carrying on whatever conversation they'd been having earlier.

'Your Grace,' Caroline began, as she craned her neck around Lord Clive Sheffield, the gentleman to her left. 'Your chef has truly outdone himself this evening. This is the best food I've had yet.'

Sebastian looked down at his bowl of creamy asparagus soup. It was half empty, so he had had some of it, but he couldn't remember what it had tasted like. 'Yes, the soup is divine,' he lied.

Seemingly encouraged, Caroline continued. 'You are such a generous host, Your Grace. And I've heard your London home is just as beautiful as Highfield Park.' Her smile turned sickly-sweet. 'Perhaps one day I— we—will be lucky enough to see it.'

He highly doubted it.

'Perhaps.' Taking his wine glass, he brought it to his lips and took his time sipping.

'Sooner rather than later, I hope.' Her eyelashes fluttered coquettishly.

Downing his wine, Sebastian motioned to the footman to refill his glass and watched Seagrave fawn over Miss Mason. She was seemingly basking in his attention. While they did make conversation with other people in their vicinity throughout the meal, they would always eventually gravitate towards each other again, which irritated Sebastian. The Dowager caught his eye, but said nothing and merely sent him a cryptic look.

Once the blasted dinner was over, it was time to entertain in the drawing room. Usually Sebastian surrounded himself with the gentlemen, as they drank their port and conversed about politics or business, but this time he hovered near his mother as she mingled amongst the guests, waiting patiently until she finally reached Seagrave, Miss Mason, and Miss Madeline DeVries. The Duke was talking animatedly as the two ladies listened.

'I hope you are enjoying your tea, ladies?' The Dowager enquired. 'And you your port, Your Grace?'

'Most excellent.' Seagrave took a sip from his glass. 'Mabury, your cellar's selection is superb.'

'Eames deserves all the compliments as he selects the wines,' he replied. 'It seems you've found yourself in lovely company this evening.'

'Ah, yes—how truly lucky I am to be surrounded by such beauty.' He smiled at the ladies. 'And they don't even seem to mind that I chatter on about Stonewin Crest. Though I'm afraid talk about the estate probably seems dull to them,' he replied.

'It doesn't seem dull at all,' said Miss DeVries. 'It's so different from where I grew up, and hearing about farming and livestock and how it all comes together is interesting—right, Kate?'

'I suppose…' Miss Mason let out an exaggerated sigh. 'But talking about soil, plots and crops and animals…it all sounds like dirty and grimy work.'

Dirty and grimy? Just yesterday she'd been examining stones with her bare hands and helping him build a wall. He fixed his gaze on her, attempting to catch her eye, but she seemed intent on avoiding his stare.

'I would much rather hear about your townhouse in London, Your Grace,' she continued, batting her eyelashes at Seagrave. 'How far is it from Bond Street?'

Sebastian's instincts flared. They told him that something here was not quite right. Miss Mason was acting more like Caroline DeVries by the minute.

'Not too far, but I'm afraid at this time of year my stepmother is in residence,' Seagrave answered.

'You don't mind?' she asked.

'Not at all. I prefer Stonewin Crest—especially since all my prized horses are there.'

Miss Mason clapped her hands together. 'You love horses, Your Grace? Do tell me more!'

Seagrave chuckled. 'If you insist...'

Sebastian stifled the urge to yawn as Seagrave prattled on about his thoroughbreds and his prized Arabian stallion. While he enjoyed a good discussion on horseflesh, he was certain that no one liked hearing *that* much about it. But what truly irritated him was the way Miss Mason's eyes never left Seagrave's face as he rambled on, nodding and smiling as if she were listening to the most fascinating lecture in the world.

'Are you sure you want to hear more, Miss Mason?' Seagrave asked eventually.

'Oh, yes,' she replied in a high-pitched tone. 'Please go on.'

Why in the world was she acting like some empty-headed fool? There was something going on...

'Seagrave,' Sebastian interrupted. 'I've heard that a company from Bristol has approached you about mining for minerals on your estate.'

'Mining?' Miss Mason piped in.

Seagrave chuckled. 'Ah, yes. Nothing that would interest you, Miss Mason. I'm afraid it's just minerals used in factories and such—not emeralds or diamonds or anything pretty.'

She opened her mouth, then snapped it shut. 'Of course.'

Madeline DeVries spoke up. 'I should like to hear more, Your Grace.'

'You would?' Seagrave asked, quizzical.

Her head bobbed up and down with excitement. 'My father owns an iron forge back in Pittsburgh,' she began. 'And I work with him as a metallurgist.'

'A meta-what?' Seagrave exclaimed.

'Someone who works with metals,' Sebastian explained.

'You...*work*?' Seagrave looked at Madeline DeVries as if she had grown a second head.

She nodded. 'Why, yes. My father taught me everything he knows about smelting and ironworks.' She turned to Miss Mason. 'Much like Kate, who learned from her—'

'Maddie!' Miss Mason burst out. 'Oh, you are so very clever and sweet.' She cleared her throat. 'But His Grace is correct. Minerals sounds like a boring topic. Could we talk about something else?'

Sebastian ignored her. 'If you decide to have them survey your land, Seagrave, you should be prepared.'

'Really? For what?'

'For all the digging machines they'll be carting around.' He directed his gaze at Miss Mason, then spoke slowly and deliberately. 'Machines are large contraptions made of iron that can perform the work of several men.'

'Really?' she replied without missing a beat. 'How... quaint.'

Sebastian continued. 'Anyway, they'll bring boring machines—steam-powered monstrosities that make a lot of noise—to tunnel into the ground.' He did not miss how Miss Mason's nostrils flared when he said 'monstrosities'. 'They'll disturb your peace. If you ask me, industrial machinery is a nuisance to the senses.'

'Indeed,' Seagrave agreed, raising his port glass.

Miss Mason merely huffed, but her cheeks had gone red.

Sensing her frustration, he continued. 'Do you have something to say, Miss Mason?' he asked as he casually took a sip of his wine. 'Any deep thoughts on boring machines?'

The barest hint of outrage flashed across her face, but she managed to control it. She placed her finger on her chin and seemed to contemplate his question. 'Not at all, Your Grace. All this talk of minerals and machines sounds *boring* to me.'

She let out a laugh and Seagrave followed along, his eyes looking at her adoringly, like a puppy's. Miss Madeline DeVries, on the other hand, only looked at her friend in confusion. If Miss Mason was a terrible bluffer, Madeline DeVries was even worse. And now he knew something was definitely afoot with Miss Kate Mason.

Sebastian finished off the last of his port. 'If you'll excuse me... I require a refill.' Turning on his heel, he marched away.

Spying an empty glass, the footman holding the bottle of port immediately rushed forward. As he stared at the ruby liquid pouring into his glass Sebastian's mind ran the gamut of explanations for Miss Mason's odd behaviour. After taking a hearty sip, he glanced back at her and Seagrave, who was once again taking over the conversation. Miss Mason seemed entranced with whatever it was Seagrave was nattering about.

Perhaps he should ignore Miss Kate Mason from now on. Stay away from her. Yes, that would be the best. Let Seagrave have her. Forget about the chit and let go.

But for the life of him, he just couldn't.

Chapter Eight

To the rest of the world, His Grace the Duke of Seagrave was the perfect suitor.

'Miss Mason, you're looking lovely today,' he said as they stepped out into the garden. 'Like Aphrodite, whose face launched a thousand ships.'

Kate bit her lip. *Actually, it was Helen of Troy.*

'You are too kind, Your Grace.' She tugged at Seagrave's arm. 'My lord, why don't we head this way?' She nodded to the right.

'Of course, Miss Mason. It looks like they've finished planting the lavender.'

Kate allowed him to lead her and ignored the strain on her cheek muscles as she fought to keep a smile pasted on her face and prevent the frustration building inside her from seeping out.

Yes, Seagrave was perfect.

Perfectly stupid.

Which made it much harder for Kate to act more dim-witted than him. But other than that he was the right candidate for her husband. Why, if she could, she would propose to him this very moment, even if it was only their third meeting.

After that first dinner he had called upon her the following morning. Well, her and all the other ladies and the Dowager Duchess. After that, the Dowager had invited him once again to Highfield Park, to visit the gardens and take afternoon tea the next day.

Kate thought him quite fashionably handsome, especially today, in his dove-grey coat and trousers, his fine blond hair tousled in the wind and those puppy-like eyes. Truly, he was good-looking—which was not a bad thing at all. She supposed if she were to have a stupid husband he might as well be pleasing to look upon.

Yes, he was exactly what she needed. Not only was he titled, but from what Miss Merton had told Kate after she'd enquired about the Duke's family, he also needed money. Apparently, his stepmother, the current Dowager Duchess, had spent every shilling the old Duke had left upon his death and the estate was now on the brink of insolvency. Being a duke was costly, after all, plus his prized horses must cost a fortune to keep. A bride with a rich dowry would help replenish the Seagrave coffers and keep the creditors at bay.

Now she only had to ensnare him.

Glancing around, she saw Maddie, Caroline, and Miss Merton exploring various parts of the garden. This was the first time she and Seagrave had been truly alone, but it was considered proper as they were outdoors and her chaperone and companions were still in the vicinity. This was her chance.

'My lord…' she began, entreating him with her gaze. 'Do tell me stories of your childhood days at Stonewin Crest. What was your favourite thing to do on the estate?'

'I'm glad you ask, Miss Mason, because— Oh, Mabury. What a coincidence, running into you.'

Kate's head snapped forward.

Oh, dash it all.

Sure enough, there he was, the Duke of Mabury himself, approaching them from the opposite end of the path. Dressed in form-fitting riding clothes and wiping a sheen of sweat from his brow with a handkerchief, he had obviously just come in from a ride, or perhaps from working with Mr Lawrence. She wondered for just a moment if he'd had his clothes on the entire time.

Stop thinking of that!

Oh, no, this would not do at all.

Mabury's dark gaze landed on her briefly, then turned to Seagrave. 'Yes, such a coincidence—considering this is *my* garden. So, Seagrave,' he continued as he put the handkerchief back into his pocket, 'this is your third visit this week?'

'Yes, Her Grace is extremely kind to allow me to visit Miss Mason and the other ladies.'

An eyebrow rose. 'Indeed, she is.'

'Would you like to join us for a walk amongst the lavender, Your Grace?' Seagrave asked.

'I'm sure he is much too busy for such activities.' Kate tightened her grip on Seagrave's arm. 'Aren't you, Your Grace?'

Her heart thumped in her chest as she raised her head to meet Mabury's eyes. Dear Lord, why did this man elicit such a response from her? How she wished he would just leave, so she could continue with her quest to bag Seagrave.

'It's been a while since I've strolled in the gardens. It would be such a waste of all the effort my gardeners have put in if I never see their hard work.'

'Excellent.' Seagrave shuffled sideways to give space to the Duke. Kate had no choice but to let him drag her to the left, which meant Mabury was now directly on her right side.

'Actually…' he began. 'It's chilly this morning. Why don't we go to the orangery?'

'A capital idea,' said Seagrave. 'I'm afraid Stonewin Crest doesn't have its own orangery, though I've visited one at a distant uncle's estate.'

They walked further up the gardens, towards the glass and brick structure. As they stepped inside, the pungent smell of greenery hung in the humid air like a heavy blanket. Exotic plants and seedlings crowded the sides and hung from baskets above as they followed a path marked by colourful tiles on the floor and flanked by intricate ironwork gates.

'What is that smell and that racket?' Seagrave asked.

'Engine oil,' Kate said automatically. 'And that's the sound of a boiler.'

Seagrave's head snapped towards her. 'I beg your pardon? Engine oil and boilers?'

'Ah, how clever you are, Miss Mason,' Mabury piped in, the corners of his lips tugging up.

Seagrave's expression soured, especially since Mabury had exaggerated the word 'clever'.

Drat!

'I mean… I think that's what it is,' she added quickly. 'I have overheard the servants in our house talking about boilers and engines and…things.'

Oh, Lord. Her grandfather would be turning in his grave if he heard her.

I'm doing this for you, Pap.

'I don't recall my uncle's orangery being so noisy and pungent?' Seagrave continued.

'Perhaps it was an older structure, which relied on brick or straw for insulation and heated with open fires or stoves. Highfield Park's orangery was installed a few years ago and uses a boiler to keep the temperature at the correct level.'

Seagrave lifted his chin and sniffed the air. 'There is an unusual heaviness in the air. What is it?'

Mabury's dark gaze flickered to her.

This time, Kate bit her tongue, preventing herself from answering.

'It's the steam,' Mabury explained. 'As Miss Mason correctly deduced, there is a boiler underneath us.'

'A lucky guess,' she piped in. 'Very, very lucky.'

'I could tell you more about how it works,' he said. 'But I would be very afraid of boring Miss Mason.'

Kate pressed her lips together. 'I'm sure the topic will be too complicated for me.'

Mabury flashed her a perfect set of pearly white teeth. 'Ah, yes, such things tend to go right over such pretty little heads like yours, Miss Mason.'

'But perhaps His Grace would like to know more?' She looked up to Seagrave.

The expression on his face said otherwise, but politeness made him say, 'Of course.'

'As you wish, Seagrave.' He turned to Kate. 'But I'll do my best to make the explanation easy for the female mind. Should you find it difficult to follow, I will not be offended if you choose to admire the flowers while we gentlemen continue our discussion.'

'How magnanimous of you, Your Grace.'

Mabury's condescension irked her today, as it had a few nights ago, during that dinner when Seagrave had first come to Highfield Park. It was as if he was a different person from the man she had thought him to be when they had repaired the wall together. Now he was acting like a pompous fop.

But why in the world was Mabury speaking to her as if she was an idiot? Did he—?

Wait.

That condescending tone.

Those pauses in his speech.

And that delighted smug look.

Mabury was not patronising her.

He was deliberately needling her.

The scoundrel.

He was trying to ruin her plans for some reason. Perhaps he'd sensed her deception and didn't want his fellow peer to fall for her.

I shouldn't have helped him build that wall, she thought ruefully.

Narrowing her gaze, she focused her loathing at him for trying to expose her to Seagrave.

Not that it helped, because Mabury continued. 'An orangery is called thus because it is meant to keep citrus fruits warm, but it can be used for almost any type of flora. This is where we house most of our plants during harsh weather, as the temperature here is the same year-round,' he explained as they continued their walk. 'The boiler underneath us creates steam and is released through these vents.' He stopped to point the tip of a boot at an ironwork grate on the floor next to the tiled path.

'How clever,' Seagrave mumbled. 'How does the steam reach the vents?'

'Good question.' Mabury's dark gaze was trained on Kate, as if he were waiting for her to speak.

Kate bit her lip, refusing to answer. *I have to stay on guard from now on, until Seagrave proposes.* She was determined now, more than ever, to have him as a husband. *Think of Pap*, she reminded herself.

'Well?' Seagrave prodded, but he was not looking at her at all.

'Pipes,' the Duke continued. 'Pipes bring the steam up to the vents.' He once again turned to Kate. 'Pipes are long, cylindrical—'

'I know what pipes are,' she snapped. Realising her mistake, she quickly batted her eyelashes and smiled until the corners of her mouth reached her ears. 'Thank you, Your Grace.'

Amusement crossed his face. 'You're very welcome, Miss Mason. Well, that's about as much as I know about the orangery,' Mabury confessed. 'But, Seagrave, why don't we talk more about those mineral rights you spoke of? We can discuss it over some port.'

'That would be excellent, Your Grace. And— Oh.' He glanced at Kate. 'Miss Mason, forgive me. I know I said I would have tea with you and the other ladies...'

'Oh, not at all, Your Grace.' What was she supposed to say? She couldn't very well stamp her feet and beg him to stay like some petulant child. 'It sounds as if you've much to talk about with His Grace. I should go to Miss Merton anyway. She's probably looking for me.'

He tipped his hat to her as he released her arm. 'Thank you, Miss Mason. I shall call upon you again this week.'

'That would be lovely, Your Grace.' She curtseyed. 'If you'll excuse me?'

Lifting her head, she looked up at Mabury. This time there was no amusement. Instead, the force of his stare seemed to knock the air from her lungs, but she managed to keep her composure.

'Miss Mason,' he said with a short nod.

Turning on her heel, she made her way out of the orangery. *Blast it all!* Why was he trying to expose her to

Seagrave? Maybe he didn't like that fact that an American like her was going to marry a peer—and a duke to boot. Well, it didn't matter. She just had to make sure he didn't get in her way.

That dratted man. And to think that just the other day she'd thought him to be like Pap, working with Mr Lawrence on his farm.

'Never give anyone work you wouldn't do yourself,' Pap had always said.

Of course, the Duke could be both a kind landowner to his tenants and act like a cad to women. After all, he'd vowed never to marry. Perhaps he just didn't think much of the female sex. But his actions towards others and those less fortunate were admirable to say the least.

Stop thinking of him as admirable.

Actually, what she had to do was stop thinking of him, period. And make sure he didn't get in the way of her plan to marry Seagrave.

Just because he doesn't want to get married, it doesn't mean the rest of us can't.

Seagrave was in need of a wealthy wife, and she needed a way to save Pap's legacy.

Slowing her steps, she took in a deep, calming breath of the fragrant air. *Think of Seagrave instead.* He was the solution to her Marriage Problem, after all.

Chapter Nine

Thankfully, Kate wouldn't have to wait too long to see Seagrave again, as the Dowager Duchess had announced she was hosting a musicale at Highfield Park the following day, and had invited over two dozen guests, including Seagrave.

Kate decided that she needed more time alone with him, to indicate her interest in his attentions. But how would she accomplish that? Kate had never been alone with a man before.

Yes, you have.

Her mind drifted back to the night of the Houghton Ball. To Mabury and the garden and the hedges. Heat spread all over her body, as it always did when she allowed herself to recall the incident. It was as if it had just happened, and the scent and feel of him were burned into her head.

Think, Kate.

But not about being alone with the Duke.

Surely she couldn't just overtly tell Seagrave to meet her somewhere private? No, that wouldn't do at all. She would have to find other ways of telling him she wished to have a moment alone with him.

* * *

On the evening of the musicale, after her maid, Anna, had brushed and styled her hair and helped her into a peach-coloured satin gown with a low neckline, Kate made her way down to the ballroom, which had been converted into a performance area, with chairs lined up in neat rows. The grand piano had been set in front, as well as seven chairs for the other musicians. Many of the guests milled about, and she walked over to where she spied Seagrave talking to Miss Merton, Mabury, and another man Kate had never seen before.

'Miss Mason,' Seagrave greeted her as she curtseyed. 'How lovely you look this evening.'

'Thank you, Your Grace.' She turned to Mabury and curtseyed again. 'Good evening, Your Grace.'

The Duke acknowledged her with a nod. 'Miss Mason.'

Miss Merton cleared her throat. 'If I may, my lord?' she said to the Duke's companion. 'May I present Miss Kate Mason of New York? Miss Mason, this is Devon St James, Marquess of Ashbrooke.'

She bowed her head. 'A pleasure, my lord.'

'The pleasure is all mine,' the Marquess replied, a hint of amusement in his tone.

Kate allowed herself to look up at him, lifting her gaze from his collar to his face, and was met with the most extraordinary blue eyes—like twin sapphires, glittering with promise. The rest of him was just as striking—stylishly cut blond hair, a straight, aquiline nose, cheekbones that could cut diamonds. His firm lips were set into a smile that held just the right amount of cynicism and made him appear both charming and worldly at the same time.

Miss Merton cleared her throat and embarrassment heated Kate's cheeks at how she was gawking at the handsome Marquess. To his credit, Ashbrooke didn't say a word, but the glint of mirth in his eyes said he had noticed her appraisal. She averted her gaze, but found herself eye to eye with Mabury's dark stare instead. A different kind of heat rushed through her.

'Are you a fan of music, my lord?' she asked Ashbrooke, trying to distract herself.

'Music?' He laughed. 'I suppose I am fond of many kinds of…art.'

Mabury stiffened beside him. 'Ashbrooke is my guest tonight. I invited him here.'

'Or rather, I finagled an invitation from him.' Those sapphire eyes twinkled. 'Especially since I'd heard Highfield Park has once again opened its doors to visitors. I had to see it for myself.'

'And are you satisfied with what you've seen so far?' Kate asked.

He eyed her boldly. 'Indeed.'

'I think we're about to begin.' Miss Merton gestured to the front of the ballroom, where the musicians had taken their places.

'Miss Mason, Miss Merton…' Seagrave began. 'If it would please you, it would be an honour if you would sit by my side during the performance.'

Miss Merton opened her fan and pressed it to her chest. 'Of course, Your Grace, we would love to.'

'Thank you for your indulgence, Miss Merton.' He turned to the gentlemen. 'Mabury… Ashbrooke.'

As Seagrave led them to the second row of chairs, Kate did her best to put Mabury out of her mind—especially since she had started to form an idea on how to get the Duke alone.

According to the Dowager Duchess, there would be a twenty-minute intermission in the middle of the programme, and refreshments would be served in the adjoining room. With so many people streaming out of the ballroom it would be easy enough to slip outside to the terrace for some fresh air. While she wasn't trying to be found in a compromising position with him, surely a few minutes alone wouldn't be so bad? Especially if they weren't caught. After all, she hadn't been the only one to be alone with a man that night at the Houghton Ball and still have her reputation intact. And if Caroline DeVries could manage it, then why couldn't she?

Kate could hardly concentrate on the orchestra as they began their programme. Anticipation stretched her like the bowstrings on the violins. When they'd finished the first *concerto*, she leaned over to Seagrave, who sat between her and Miss Merton. 'That was an amazing piece, wasn't it, Your Grace?'

'Yes, I do enjoy Beethoven very much.'

It had been Mozart, but she stopped herself from correcting him. 'Yes. Lovely. But I don't think I've been in such close quarters with other people in a long time. Being out here in the countryside, I mean.'

'Ah, of course,' he replied. 'I suppose not being in the crush of London has made you forget what it's like to be in a crowded ballroom.'

Before Kate could reply, the conductor raised his baton and the musicians moved on to their next piece. Settling back into her chair, she focused her attention on the music. Halfway through, a strange feeling crept over her—as if someone were watching her. She tamped down the urge to look around her. Besides, she was near the front of the room, so of course there would be people staring at her back.

Near the end of the final piece of the first half, Kate let out an exaggerated sigh.

'Are you quite all right, Miss Mason?' Seagrave asked. 'I'm afraid the air in here hasn't improved.'

'Indeed, it's got warmer. Perhaps the Dowager Duchess should have the footmen open some windows.'

'Or better yet…' She moved her head closer to his ear. 'Perhaps I might go out for a minute or two to refresh myself on the terrace during the intermission.' Shifting her leg, she let the satin of her skirt brush against his thigh.

He patted her hand. 'A capital idea, Miss Mason.'

Kate nearly exclaimed in joy at her success in conveying her message, but thankfully the orchestra struck its final notes and the conductor put his baton down, prompting the audience to break into applause.

'That was truly entertaining,' Miss Merton declared as they stood up and joined the other guests filing out of the ballroom. 'Her Grace has impeccable taste in music.'

'Truly,' Seagrave agreed. 'Shall we head to the next room?'

Kate smiled up slyly at him. 'Of course, Your Grace. But first I should like to make a detour to *refresh* myself.' Surely Seagrave did not miss how she emphasised the word refresh.

'The parlour has been set up as the ladies' retiring room. But don't be too long, dear,' Miss Merton reminded her. 'We only have twenty minutes.'

'I shan't, Miss Merton.'

With one last glance at Seagrave, she broke away from them, walking in the direction of the ladies' retiring room. However, once she was safely away from her chaperone she made an about-face and crept back towards the glass doors that lead out to the terrace.

Slipping outside, Kate shivered as the cool night air caressed her bare shoulders. *I should have brought a shawl.* But it was too late now. She hurried away to the edge of the terrace and wrapped her arms around herself as she stared up at the moon. What a perfectly romantic setting it was. And perhaps this would be the night that would finally help her solve her Marriage Problem and save Pap's legacy.

The sound of the door latch clicking open told her that Seagrave had been able to sneak away. 'Your Grace.' She gripped the railing with her gloved fingers. 'I'm so glad you could join me for some fresh air.' When he didn't reply at once, she pushed away from the balustrade and turned to face Seagrave. 'Did you—?'

Her heart leapt into her throat. It was not Seagrave standing by the door.

'You!' she croaked, staggering back against the cold marble of the railing. What in God's name was Mabury doing here?

A dark eyebrow lifted sardonically. 'Not what—or rather, who—you were expecting?'

No, decidedly not.

'I d-don't know what you mean, Y-Your Grace.' The tremor in her voice annoyed her. 'I was merely trying to escape the stuffiness inside.'

'And you were hoping for Seagrave to join you?' It was not a question, but rather a statement.

'I do not know what you're referring to, Your Grace,' she began.

Blast it. He was going to ruin her plan to be alone with Seagrave. He could arrive at any moment! It would be a disaster.

'But I find the air out here colder than I expected and would like to return inside.'

'Then by all means go.' He waved his hand towards the door.

'You're blocking the only exit, Your Grace.' She ground

her teeth. 'Perhaps, for the sake of propriety, you should go back inside first, and I shall follow in a few minutes.'

Eyes black as midnight gleamed with challenge. 'You talk of propriety, Miss Mason? But this is not the first time you've found yourself alone with a man. One might think there is a pattern emerging here. Or perhaps it is more of a habit?'

'I beg your pardon?' Her fingernails dug into her palms. 'Are you insinuating that I'm some kind of… of…lightskirt?'

He took several steps forward, his strides so long that it took mere moments to reach her. 'Well…here you are again…alone in the moonlight. With me.'

The timbre of his voice sent heat coiling in her. But if she were honest that had been building since the moment she'd realised he was near. Heavens, this would be not just be a disaster but a full-on catastrophe if she didn't stop it now.

'And so what if I am here alone with you again? It doesn't mean anything.' She had to leave. Yet her feet would not move. 'Nothing's happened thus far, and nothing will. I never allow myself to get lost in passion.'

That last word triggered something between them— like the initial spark to a flame. It hung in the air, swirling like the heat generated in a firebox.

He took a step towards her. 'You're trembling.'

'I'm n-not,' she denied.

'Of course you're not.' His gaze burned into her. 'You never get lost in passion.'

His face drew nearer to her, his head tipping to the right. Her body tensed and she sucked in a breath, trying desperately to fill her lungs before the inevitable came.

Oh, Lord, he was going to kiss her.

And she wanted him to.

'Your Grace...'

Oh, dear, her tone didn't sound as if she was protesting. At all. In fact, it sounded almost...needy.

Not to mention the fact that her hands had somehow found their way to his shoulders and were clutching him tight, pulling him closer.

The world around her slowed down as his mouth descended on hers. After the initial shock of its touch wore off she melted into the kiss. His warm lips moved over hers eagerly, and she found herself responding, matching his growing intensity.

In that moment she could pinpoint exactly where the heat had built up in her. Not in her lower belly...no. Much lower. It was between her thighs, in her most private place, where she throbbed and ached. Her clothes once again felt too tight. Her nipples had hardened into points that scraped against her silk chemise, the delicious abrasion fuelling her even more. His hands had somehow moved to her hips, and now were trailing up the back of her dress until they reached the neckline. Warm gloved fingers delved inside, and her skin tingled from the heat radiating from underneath the kidskin.

The sensation made her gasp, and in that brief moment, as her lips opened, he drew her lower lip between his own, sipping on it. She crushed herself to him, wanting to be near him and hating all the layers of clothes between them. Her body was ablaze with a fiery desire she'd never felt before.

Then, in an instant, he pulled his mouth away, and that fire burning between them cooled as they stared at each other, both of them wide-eyed with shock.

Good Lord, what had they done?

Chapter Ten

Sebastian knew he had just made his second mistake of the night.

His first? Inviting Ashbrooke to this damned affair.

He had gone to London early that morning to conduct some business that needed his personal attention at his bank. Afterwards, he'd stopped for lunch at Brooks's, and of course out of every acquaintance he knew he'd *had* to run into Devon St James. Despite trying to tell the Marquess politely that he wanted to eat alone, Ashbrooke had pestered Sebastian throughout his meal, until somehow he'd finagled an invitation to tonight's musicale.

He hadn't expected the Marquess to come. But he had arrived on the dot, dressed in his usual finery, looking handsome and sinful as Lucifer himself. And, of course, with his damned keen eye for observation combined with a tenacious nature, he'd sniffed out Sebastian's unwilling attraction to Miss Kate Mason.

'Aren't they cosy?' Ashbrooke had remarked as they'd sat two rows behind Seagrave and Miss Mason. 'Careful, Mabury.'

'Careful of what?'

'Some might say you're acting like a jealous lover with the way you're looking at Seagrave.'

'And how exactly *am* I looking at Seagrave?'

'As if you want to throttle him. And then drag him out and shoot him. Then skin him—'

'The music's starting,' he had said, hoping to shut up the Marquess.

Sebastian had thought that was it, but throughout the entire performance his blood had boiled as he'd watched their heads gravitate towards one another, seen them whispering like naughty children.

'My, she does look lovely as a peach. And just as ripe for the picking,' Ashbrooke had drawled. 'And she definitely said "terrace".'

'I beg your pardon?'

He'd tapped a finger on his mouth. 'I can read lips. A useful trick.' A slow, lazy smile had spread across the Marquess's face. 'Seems our two lovers are planning a moonlit rendezvous.'

Yes, it was Ashbrooke's damn fault. Sebastian could have continued with the evening—hell, with his life— not knowing that Miss Mason and Seagrave were in each other's embrace.

But, no, the Marquess had had to needle him with that information, thus causing him to be in the situation he found himself now. Under the moonlight, on the terrace, with the last woman in the world he should be desiring.

You could have turned around and gone back inside.

Yes, he could have stopped himself from making this mistake. But at that time he hadn't wanted to.

And now he would be paying for it.

Sebastian swallowed hard as he reluctantly released her soft and pliant body. 'Forgive me,' he murmured.

'I forget myself. Of course I shan't speak to anyone of this.'

Pivoting on his heel, he marched away from her as he attempted to rein in his desire. Now he knew how Orpheus had felt, fighting the urge to look back at his Eurydice.

The ballroom felt even more suffocating after having been outside, but Sebastian welcomed the smell of sweat and perfume in the air. The musicians had returned and were once again setting up. He strode out to the adjoining room, weaving through the crush of people towards the nearest footman to grab a glass of wine and down it in one gulp.

What had possessed him to kiss her? It was one thing to desire her and another to act on it.

I've wanted women before, he told himself.

A tumble or two—and not necessarily with the same woman—often took care of that itch. That kiss hadn't even been half as provocative as it might have been. Indeed, her inexperience had been apparent. But damned if that hadn't made him hungry for more. To see the full potential of her desire blossom under him.

Bloody hell.

'Sebastian?'

His mother's soothing tone cooled his inner turmoil as she came up behind him. 'Mother.' He placed his empty glass back on the footman's tray. 'How have you been this evening? Enjoying the show?'

'Yes, I'd forgotten how music can lift one's spirits.' Her eyes crinkled at the corners as they focused on something behind Sebastian. 'Is that the friend you said you'd invited? The Marquess? Ashton, is it?'

'Ashbrooke. And, yes I—'

'Begging your pardon, Your Grace,' Eames interrupted smoothly as he came up behind the Dowager.

'What is it, Eames?' she asked.

'It's Mr Alton, I'm afraid.'

'Alton?'

The gardener? What the devil did he want at this time of night? Sebastian wondered.

'What's wrong? Is he ill?' his mother asked.

'No, Your Grace. But he's asked me to relay an important message to you. He says there's a problem with the orangery. It seems the…' His white eyebrows drew together. 'The heating mechanism has failed. He's sent word to London to get someone to repair it.'

'Oh, dear…' Worry marred his mother's face. 'I should go and see to it.'

Sebastian placed a hand on her shoulder. 'Mother, there's no need for you to go now.'

'But I—'

'You shan't be able to do anything about it, and Alton has already done what needs to be done.'

'But the flowers. And the trees—'

'Will be fine for now.'

If he remembered correctly, when the system had been installed a few years ago the company that had provided it had said that if it should malfunction the heat would be retained for a day or two, provided they didn't open the doors too often.

'Mr Alton will take care of them. And someone will come in the morning to fix it.'

The line between her brows smoothed. 'You're right, darling. I should stay here with our guests. We are still to have supper after the musicale.'

Sebastian groaned inwardly. The only thing worse than having to sit two rows behind Miss Mason and Seagrave would be to once again watch them from across the table, flirting and carrying on during supper. 'Why don't I go and see Alton?'

'But the musicale…supper…'

'Don't worry, Mother.' He kissed her on the forehead. 'Enjoy your evening and I'll take care of everything.'

'Thank you, darling. Well, I should go. The next part is about to begin.'

'I'll let you know the situation in the morning.'

The Dowager Duchess nodded and strode off towards the ballroom.

'Eames, is Mr Alton at the orangery?' he asked.

'Yes, Your Grace.'

'Good. I shall go and see him now.'

There really was no need for him to see Alton, since neither of them could do anything with the broken heating system, but it was a good excuse to disappear from the party. Leaving the terrace had been difficult enough. Now he needed to put as much distance between himself and Kate Mason as possible, to erase the memory of that kiss that was still so fresh in his mind.

No, he needed to forget everything. Forget the moonlight. Forget the scent of lemons. Forget the feel of peach-soft skin and the taste of warm, sweet lips underneath his and the press of her supple curves.

He couldn't afford to play such dangerous games with her. Kate Mason was here for one reason: marriage. That alone was enough for him to stay as far away as possible. He reminded himself of that day when he had decided that he would do everything in his power never to turn into his father. Reminded himself of his vow to his mother, never to subject another person to what she had endured. The image of her pale, still body as she lay in bed would never be erased from his mind…

* * *

Kate hadn't thought it was possible to turn from hot to cold so quickly. Indeed, even when the Andersen had to be cooled down for maintenance, it took the better part of a day to lower its temperature after smothering the fire and emptying the boiler. But in a span of mere seconds Mabury had gone from fire-hot to glacier-cold.

Forgive me... I forget myself.

Kate braced her hands on the railing behind her as her knees were still weak and her body limp.

Damn him.

Why did he kiss me?

Why did I kiss him back?

She bit the back of her gloved hand to stop herself from groaning aloud. It wasn't as if it was her first kiss. She'd been kissed once before, by the son of one of her father's friends during a ball. The brazen young man had pulled her into a darkened alcove and she'd welcomed the kiss as they had been flirting most of the evening.

That, however, had been nothing like her kiss with the Duke.

'Argh!' She curled her hands into fists at her sides. This madness had to stop. She couldn't let her plans be derailed.

Focus, Kate.

That was what Pap would have told her. The solution to her Marriage Problem was right in front of her. She only had to reach out and grab it.

The shrill sound of a violin coming from inside told her the musicians had come back and were now warming up. She smoothed her hands down her dress and marched towards the door, carefully sneaking in. Thankfully the musicians didn't seem to pay her any attention, and she was able to slip into the adjoining room unnoticed. She spotted Seagrave by the refreshment table, chatting with the Marquess of Ashbrooke.

'Miss Mason, here you are,' the Duke greeted her as she reached them.

'Yes.' Kate forced a smile on her face. 'Here I am.' *And where were you?*

'I do hope you were able to soak in a breath or two of fresh air.' He lifted the glass of chilled champagne in his hand. 'Since you were feeling so warm, I took it upon myself to save you something cool to drink upon your return.'

She took it from him, tamping down the urge to swallow it and instead taking a small sip. 'You are so kind, Your Grace.'

Oh, Lord, he really is thick.

Kate wondered what she could have done to tell him more clearly that she'd wanted him to follow her out onto the terrace. Perhaps next time she should draw him a diagram.

'My, my...you do look refreshed, Miss Mason,' Ashbrooke remarked. 'The evening air does wonders for the constitution.'

The Marquess flashed her a hint of a smile that made Kate wonder if he suspected something—which made her take another sip of champagne. 'Yes, it does. Oh, it looks like the performance is starting again. Shall we head back in, Your Grace?'

'Of course.' Seagrave offered his arm.

With a quick nod to Ashbrooke, he led her towards the ballroom. As they walked in she couldn't help but scan the room for Mabury. *So I can avoid him*, she reasoned. Though the Duke had promised not to tell anyone about their episode on the terrace, she still couldn't risk running into him.

When they reached their seats, she sat down next to Seagrave, and Miss Merton appeared not long after.

'My dear, I've been looking all over for you,' the chaperone said. 'You weren't in the retiring room when I went to fetch you.'

'We must have missed each other. I was with His Grace and Lord Ashbrooke by the refreshment table.'

Miss Merton seemed to accept her excuse, and she settled into her seat as the orchestra once again began to play.

Though the second half of the programme was even better than the first, Kate couldn't bring herself to enjoy it. The moment she let the music carry her mind away, it drifted towards the kiss. Mabury's hands on her. The way he'd suckled on her bottom lip. The heat of him pressed against her.

'Bravo!' Seagrave called as he clapped vigorously when the orchestra concluded their final piece. 'Did you enjoy the music, Miss Mason?'

'Yes,' she said automatically, bringing her hands together to clap. Though she could not recall any of the music, the musicians at least deserved applause.

As the guests stood, Kate glanced around. Frowning, she realised Mabury was nowhere in sight. Maybe he had gone ahead to supper.

But he did not appear at the table. His usual seat was empty, and if anyone remarked upon his absence, Kate did not hear it because she was at the other end of the table, on the Dowager Duchess's side.

A stab of an unnamed emotion pierced her chest. Had he found their kiss so unpalatable that he had decided to leave for the rest of the evening? Maybe that was the true reason he'd promised to keep silent about their kiss: because she was so reprehensible he couldn't stand anyone knowing about it.

'Miss Mason? Are you enjoying the food?' Seagrave glanced down at the plate in front of her.

'Yes, I am.' She put a spoonful of the salmon mousse into her mouth and swallowed, not really tasting anything. 'Delicious.'

He dabbed at the corner of his mouth with his napkin. 'I was wondering…hoping, maybe…that perhaps tomorrow I might call upon you? Just you, I mean.' His cheeks went red before he added, 'And your chaperone, of course. During which time I would like to ask Miss Merton for permission to take you on a carriage ride later in the week.'

'That would be…wonderful,' she replied, mustering up as much enthusiasm as she could.

He seemed pleased with that and continued eating his salmon mousse.

Kate knew she should be thrilled. Finally things were progressing in the right direction. The solution to her problem was on the horizon. Jacob would be thwarted, Pap's memory and his contributions to the world would live on, and her sacrifice would be worth it.

Full steam ahead.

Chapter Eleven

Seagrave called on her in the morning and, as promised, asked Miss Merton for permission to take them out on a carriage ride sometime in the next few days. Miss Merton accepted, and when Seagrave left, the chaperone was positively giddy.

'A duke, Miss Mason!' Her cheeks flushed with excitement. 'I knew you would be able to find a man of quality.'

'He is indeed.' Kate bit her tongue so she wouldn't blurt out the qualities that made Seagrave appealing—which were that he was titled and eager to marry into wealth. 'I have grown quite fond of him.'

'And I'm sure in time his feelings for you will grow.'

Maybe he'll even like me as much as his horses.

But, then again, she couldn't fault those poor creatures. Thoroughbreds were expensive to maintain, after all, and Seagrave would do anything to keep his prized horses. That desperation not only made him an excellent candidate for her husband, but would mean he'd keep himself busy after they married and she could pursue other things.

The other day, the jaunt into the orangery and the

smell and the roar of the engine had reminded her of her beloved factory and Pap. Hope sparked inside her. Once she was married to Seagrave, she'd get away from Jacob's clutches. Then Pap's legacy would be saved. But first she had to secure the Duke.

Later that afternoon, as they waited for the Dowager Duchess at luncheon, Miss Merton told the other women about the Duke's visit.

'You really have done well for yourself, Kate.' Caroline tossed her blonde locks over her shoulder. 'He's a duke, yes. But his estate is so small, compared to the Duke of Mabury's.'

Kate trained her gaze on Caroline. An unknown emotion threatened to leap out of her throat, but she quickly quashed it. Caroline hadn't bothered to hide her aspiration to marry Mabury, at least not amongst their party, so why did Kate feel such hostility towards her?

'Oh, and what about the Marquess of Ashbrooke?' Eliza tittered. 'So utterly charming and handsome.'

'Ah, yes...' Caroline let out a long-winded sigh. 'We spoke at length during supper. I suppose a marquess would be a good second choice. I didn't see him at breakfast, but I believe he stayed the night.'

'And how would you know such a thing?' Maddie enquired.

'My maid shared that bit of gossip with me this morning.' Caroline's eyes positively gleamed. 'And he hasn't left yet. He's out riding with the Duke now.' A devious smile spread across her lips. 'I think I shall wear my other blue gown tonight, Mother.'

Before Eliza could reply, the Dowager Duchess strolled in, prompting all of them to rise and curtsey.

'Apologies for my lateness, ladies.' She nodded at Eames to signal that the servants should start the luncheon.

As they sat down together Kate couldn't help but notice the distress on the Dowager Duchess's face. Though she tried to hide it, Kate observed that she looked dispirited, and there was a furrow between her eyebrows throughout the meal. Despite the lively conversation the older woman seemed distracted and quiet, and not her usual lively self.

After they'd finished luncheon, and everyone had headed out of the dining room, the Dowager Duchess stayed behind to speak with Eames. With her curiosity getting the better of her Kate slowed her steps, allowing everyone else to walk ahead of her. Then she returned to the dining room, stopping just on the threshold. She focused her hearing, straining to hear the conversation between the Dowager and the butler.

'And they're certain no one else can come to repair it?'

'Yes, Your Grace, I'm afraid so. Not for a fortnight.'

'This is terrible news. Whatever are we to do with the heating system broken?'

'Mr Alton says he will do what he can for the plants and trees…but he doesn't know if they will last for more than a few days.'

'This is my fault. I shouldn't have… I mean, if I had been here…'

The butler cleared his throat. 'Your Grace, if I may speak freely? It's not your fault. Nor anyone's fault. These newfangled machines do break every now and then.'

'Thank you, Eames, you are too kind. Do give Mr Alton my thanks and tell him that whatever he needs to keep the plants alive he may have.'

'I shall, Your Grace.'

Kate backed away, lest the butler catch her eaves-dropping.

So, that's what's bothering the Dowager Duchess, she thought to herself as she hurried away from the dining room. However, instead of turning at the main corridor, so she could go back to her room, she headed left, towards the exit to the gardens.

Straightening her shoulders, Kate made her way to the orangery. Surely the steam-powered system used to heat the building wouldn't be that much different from a locomotive engine? Indeed, as Pap had taught her, all steam engines were similar. He himself had first learned from working on the engines that had pumped water out of the coal mines, and the basic principles were the same: heat combined with water equalled steam. She was confident she'd at least be able to diagnose the problem, if not fix it.

As she approached the orangery she walked past the front door—she already knew the heating system would not be inside. It would be too noisy, for one thing, and when she had been inside she had only heard a faint hiss of the boiler as steam rose through the grates. So she walked around to the back of the building. Sure enough, at the far end, where the walls were thicker, was a door that had been left ajar. She slipped inside and took a spiral staircase to the lower level. A familiar smell hit her nostrils. Oil and ash and iron. This had to be the right place.

Reaching for the lone gas lamp burning there, she turned it up, the flame growing brighter. She found the rest of the lights and lit them one by one, as well as a handheld lamp which, thankfully, was working. Swinging the lamp around, she surveyed the room.

'Hello,' she said to the long brick countertop along

one wall. Only it wasn't a countertop. From the grates along the side, and the small tubes rising up the wall to the ceiling, she knew that it had to be the main boiler.

She put the lamp down and pressed her hand to the iron grates of the firebox. Practically cold. The fire must have died out a while ago. Residual heat should keep the orangery warm for the rest of the day, assuming the door stayed closed, but the clock was definitely ticking.

'What went wrong?' she said to no one in particular. It was a habit she'd picked up from Pap, who, when faced with a problem, had always liked to talk aloud.

'Helps me think,' he'd said.

Straightening her shoulders, she unbuttoned her spencer and placed it aside. She frowned down at her white muslin dress. It would get dirty, for sure; the hem would already be covered in soot by now.

Oh, well.

Shrugging, she grabbed the ends of the sleeves and tugged at them, hearing the seams ripping as she pulled them up to her elbows. Taking the hand lamp, she raised it and began to investigate.

'Are you really not going to tell me what happened on the terrace last night with Miss Mason?' Ashbrooke asked as they slowed their horses to a walk.

Sebastian scrubbed a hand down his face. 'Christ Almighty, you're persistent, Ash. Has anyone ever said no to you?'

The Marquess flashed him a good amount of pearly white teeth. 'Not yet. Well…?'

Sebastian ignored him and nudged Thunder to walk faster. Ash, of course, kept stride. 'How do you even know I was on the terrace with her?'

'For one thing, when you realised she had disappeared you tore out of the room like a madman,' he explained cheerfully. 'And then I ran into Seagrave at the refreshments table, all by himself. Although I have to say when Miss Mason did reappear she did not look thoroughly debauched at all. Not even a little bit.' He tsked. 'I'm ashamed to call you my friend.'

'I'm not your friend,' he replied flatly.

That didn't seem to slow Ash down. 'You had her alone in the dark for ten minutes and—' He sucked in a breath. 'Oh, God.'

Sebastian slowed again, then turned to him. 'What's wrong?'

'Dear God, no.' Ash groaned. 'Say it isn't so.'

His patience was starting to dwindle. 'Just tell me what the hell is the matter.'

'You're infatuated with her,' Ash declared.

'What?' His shout startled Thunder, so he grabbed the reins tighter. 'You're jesting.'

The Marquess looked completely serious. 'The only time a man refuses to speak about his romps with a woman is when he truly has feelings for her.'

'I am not infatuated with Miss Mason,' he said.

'Ah, denial is another sign.' Ash shivered visibly. 'Please don't tell me you're going to be shackled soon. I told you...you're my only friend left.'

'We are not—' Sebastian rubbed the bridge of his nose with his thumb and forefinger. 'I am not—nor will I ever be—infatuated with Miss Mason.'

Or with any woman, for that matter. That vow he'd made would never be broken. His very soul depended on it.

'So you care nothing for her? Have absolutely no feelings for her?'

'No. Absolutely none.'

'Then you won't mind if I have a go at her, then?'

A growl escaped Sebastian's throat and the Marquess barked out a laugh.

'I thought so.'

Blowing out an impatient breath, Sebastian turned towards the manor. 'I should check on the orangery and see if Alton has any more news about the repairs.'

The boiler company should have sent someone out this morning, but according to Eames he hadn't even received a message from them yet. His mother was probably fraught with worry over the whole thing—especially since it had been years since she'd seen the orangery in full bloom. Indeed, before she'd left it had been one of her favourite places in Highfield Park.

'Tell me, Mabury, do you do anything else except work on your estate?' Ash asked in an exasperated voice. 'There are more things to life, you know. Live a little. You used to not be like this,' he continued. 'I remember back in our university days you'd be the one asking me to play truant, and you'd be the first one at the public house, buying ale for everyone.'

A spark of nostalgia hit Sebastian, and for a moment he longed for those carefree days when he hadn't had the burden of responsibility on his shoulders. But it was quickly extinguished as a coldness gripped within him. His very being now rebelled at the thought of idleness. After all, he'd seen the consequences of it first-hand.

'By the way,' Ashbrooke began, 'I do have a bit of gossip I'm sure you'll be interested in.'

'I'm sure I won't.'

'Even if it pertains to Miss Mason?'

Thunder let out a protesting whinny when Sebastian reflexively dug his heels into the horse's sides. He muttered an apology to the animal. 'What is it?'

'In the last few weeks there's been this boorish American fellow trying to get into all the clubs in London. Jacob Something-or-other is his name. Anyway, he doesn't know how memberships work and he thinks he can just barge in and pay to join.'

'And what does this have to do with Miss Mason?'

'Well, whenever the club managers politely decline him, he tries to make his case by telling them he's the cousin of Arthur Mason, locomotive magnate of New York, and saying that they'll be begging him to join once he owns half the railways in England.' Ashbrooke's expression darkened. 'I didn't think anything of it until I met your Miss Mason and made the connection. Arthur Mason must be her father and that odious man her second cousin.'

'She's not my Miss Mason.'

And such matters shouldn't concern him. Not after last night, when he'd vowed to stay clear of her.

'You're not curious? At all?'

Ignoring Ash's question, Sebastian brought Thunder into a canter until they'd reached the gardens, then tied him to a nearby tree before dismounting. Ashbrooke followed suit and they made their way to the rear of the orangery building.

'Alton's probably down in the furnace.' Sebastian nodded at the open door that would lead to the lower level. 'You don't have to come. There's nothing interesting down there.'

'I might as well—nothing interesting out here either.'

Sebastian went inside first, holding on to the handrail as he descended the stairs. The lamps were ablaze, which meant Alton or perhaps the repairman himself must be puttering around.

'Alton?' He walked inside and peered into the dim

room, finding a dark shape on the other side. As his eyes adjusted, he realised that it was not Alton, and nor was it a repairman.

'My, my...and you said there was nothing interesting here,' Ashbrooke mused.

Miss Mason turned around. 'Who in the—? Your Grace!' There was a tremble in her voice that set his instincts flaring. 'What are you doing here?'

'Shouldn't I be asking you that?' He crossed the room towards her with ground-eating steps. 'Are you—?' He stopped as she raised a handheld lamp, illuminating herself further.

A sheen of perspiration covered her brow and tendrils of dark hair hung loose around her face, a few of them stuck to her neck. She had taken off her jacket, leaving her in a light muslin dress, and the cuffs had been torn to expose her from wrist to elbow. A layer of sweat had the cloth sticking to her shoulders, but the bright yellow glow from the lamps behind her outlined the curves of her body through the thin folds of fabric.

His mouth went dry at the sight of her looking so naturally dishevelled.

'Good afternoon, Miss Mason,' Ash greeted her. 'Lovely to see you again.'

'My lord.' Her eyes darted from him back to Sebastian.

'Ash,' he said in a warning voice as he heard the Marquess's steps coming closer.

'Yes?'

'Get out,' he growled, and he turned his head to send the other man a menacing stare. Some irrational part of him didn't want Ash to see her like this.

'Ah, right... Of course.' Ash grinned. 'I'll stand watch outside.'

Stand watch? 'Wait, that's not what I—'

Ash saluted him. 'Say no more, old chap.'

And with that he retreated, his footsteps fading as he ascended the metal steps. A loud slam a few moments later indicated that he was gone and Sebastian and Miss Mason were alone.

Damned Ash.

Turning back, he saw that Miss Mason hadn't moved an inch, and those cornflower-blue eyes were widening as she stared at him. Thankfully, he managed to speak. 'Miss Mason, what are you doing here?'

Quickly, she spun on her heel to face away from him. 'What does it look like I'm doing?'

Placing the lamp on the counter, she stuck a foot into one of the iron grates and attempted to hoist herself up—with no success. Her skirts prevented her from lifting her legs high enough to reach the counter.

'Are you insane?' He was next to her in an instant. 'You're going to get hurt.'

She harrumphed. 'I'll be fine. I only need to take a closer look at that pipe over there.' Bracing her palms on the counter, she tried to climb up once again. 'Blast it. Help me, will you?'

'I beg your pardon?'

'Help me up,' she said. 'Just hold my skirts, Your Grace.'

'Only if you let me know why you need to get up there.'

She let out an exasperated sound and turned to face him. 'I think I know why the boiler has stopped working. If I'm right, I should be able to fix it. But to do that I have to check on that pipe up there.'

'You have to check it? Where the bloody hell is the repairman?'

'He's not coming.' She bit at her lip. 'Eames said the company won't be able to send anyone for at least a fortnight. By then it will be too late, and all the plants will have died. Now, are you going to help me or—? Oh!'

Sebastian didn't know why, but he'd grabbed her by the waist and placed her so she sat on the counter. 'There. Now...' He knelt and reached for the bottom of her skirts.

'Your Grace!' she exclaimed.

'You're the one who wanted help,' he reminded her.

Her lips pursed together. 'Fine. Go ahead.'

Gathering the hem of her dress, he compressed the layers of fabric with his arms, then helped her up to stand so she could plant her slippered feet on the counter. 'There.'

She moved closer to the pipe and got on her knees. 'Hand me the lamp, if you please. Thank you.' She raised it towards the wall lined with pipes. 'Hmmm...'

'What is it?'

'I'm not sure. One moment... Ah, just as I thought.' She leaned forward. 'Bulged surface...thick-lipped fissure...'

'In English, please, Miss Mason.'

'The pipe has burst. Scale deposits, most likely,' she explained. 'The good news is that's the reason why the heat couldn't make its way up to the orangery.'

He swore to himself. 'That's the good news?'

'Yes, it means that the boiler itself isn't broken and only the pipe requires changing.'

'I'm afraid I don't employ a full-time plumber.'

She turned to face him and smiled. The first real smile she'd flashed at him that day. 'Well, now, it's a good thing you have me, then.'

His heart rioted in his chest at her words.

'Here, help me down.'

He found himself reaching out to her, gripping her

waist to lower her down, and reluctantly releasing her as soon as her feet hit the ground.

'Now…' she began, dusting her hands together. 'I recognise this heating system. Made by an American, correct?'

'I believe so. My fath— The old Duke had it installed a few years ago. He said this was made by the same fellow who first built a similar system in the hothouses of the Governor of the Bank of England. How did you know?'

'I recognise the pipe socket design.' She grabbed the handheld lamp, then marched to the other end of the room. 'Ingenious, really. Threading on both the left and right side, so that two pipes can be joined together. And that makes them easily replaceable.' Raising the lamp, she swung it around. 'Now, there should be a… Oh, here you are.'

She pulled at something on the wall. He came up behind her and saw she had found a cabinet filled with tools and pipes. She rooted around in it for a few seconds, inspecting each pipe before shaking her head and putting it back. Finally, she picked one up, checked the ends and exclaimed with glee.

'Perfect.' Checking the rest of the cabinet, she grabbed a few tools. 'Now to put it in the right place.'

They walked back to where the broken pipe awaited and he helped her up onto the counter once again. Sweat had begun to build on his brow, so he discarded his jacket and cravat.

After she'd finished arranging her skirts, she manoeuvred herself into a kneeling position. 'If you wouldn't mind, Your Grace, could you hold the lamp up so I may see better?'

'Of course. But, please, I think we should dispense with the formalities.'

She tilted her head to the side. 'I beg your pardon, Your Grace?'

'Considering the circumstances—' he nodded at her, propped on top of the counter, and at the lamp in his hand '—could we call each other by our given names? At least for now, Kate?'

Even in the darkness he could tell that the prettiest blush tinted her cheeks. But she nodded anyway. 'As you wish… Sebastian.'

He did as she'd asked, rounding the edge of the counter so he could lift the lamp up, and then watched her work, eyebrows furrowed with determination, as she sized up the broken pipe, then took a wrench, and began to disassemble the array of tubes.

Sebastian didn't know what she was doing, exactly— in truth, he probably shouldn't just let her start ripping up a very expensive piece of machinery—but there was something about Kate Mason at this moment that made it difficult to say no to her. The Kate Mason before him seemed an unstoppable force, so self-assured in her capabilities that if she'd told him that jumping off a cliff would fix the boiler, he would have done it.

And damned if he didn't find it irresistible.

'Are you sure you know what you're doing?' he asked.

'I've been around steam engines since before I even learned to read, Your Gra— Sebastian. My grandfather started as a coal miner back in West Virginia, but he worked his way up to become an engineer. Eventually, when my father had established his company in New York, he sent for us and then financed Mason Railroad & Locomotives so he could manufacture an engine of his own design.'

Ah, her grandfather… She had spoken fondly of him

to John Lawrence. 'And you've always worked with machines?'

She frowned at something and peered closer. 'Could you lean in a little closer, please? With the lamp, I mean. Yes, that's it… And yes, I've always worked with machines. Pap taught me.'

'Why would he teach you?'

'What do you mean, "why"?'

'You're…well…you're a woman.'

Her plump lips pursed as she picked up a tool from the pile by her knees. 'So?'

No one had ever replied to Sebastian in such an impertinent manner—he was a duke, after all. Yet he had never quite met anyone like Kate Mason, either. But why all her pretence whenever they weren't alone? She was capable enough to build a wall and fix a boiler pipe. So he continued to prod her.

'Shouldn't you have been at home, learning how to run a household?'

She smiled wryly. 'We were poor before my father left and made his fortune in New York. I'm afraid there wasn't much of a house to run except for a shack with dirt floors. Since my mother died in childbirth and there was no one to care for me, Pap didn't have a choice but bring me to work. And since then, I never left his side. Until his death, that is.'

'I'm sorry.'

'Don't be sorry. Ah!' The broken pipe came off in her hand. 'Hand me the new pipe,' she ordered.

He grabbed the piece and handed it to her. 'Why shouldn't I be sorry about your grandfather's death?'

Taking the pipe, she pushed it into position, trying to find the right fit. 'Because for most of my life I got to spend every moment of every day with Pap. I watched him do something he loved, and I was able to share that with him. Every day until he died.'

She paused as she turned away from him to grab a wrench, though Sebastian did not miss the hitch in her voice.

'And every time I work on a steam engine or a boiler or an engineering problem I think of him. It's as if I can hear his voice in my head—as if he were right here, telling me what to do. It's like just for a moment I have him back.'

And there it was again—the same smile on her face as that day when she'd worked on the wall and spoken of her grandfather. He could hear both the sadness and the joy in her voice. Had he ever felt something like that for anyone? Perhaps he would have for his own father, had he been the person Sebastian thought he was.

'And...' She gave the wrench one more turn. 'There you go. That should do it.' The corner of her mouth lifted. 'It wasn't so difficult. Didn't even need joining material for the pipes, thanks to their ingenious design.' More of her hair had come undone, and a smudge of dirt or perhaps oil marred her perfect ivory skin. 'Now we just have to get someone to light the firebox and prevent it from happening again...'

Sebastian stood there, watching her as she rambled on about hard water and ash pans, and his mind tried to reconcile what was happening before his very eyes.

Mechanical genius. Fairy. Sprite. Innocent temptress. Who *was* this woman?

Whoever she was, she sure as hell wasn't the same person he'd been observing for the last few days. And certainly not the woman putting on that farce for Seagrave.

'Sebastian?' She waved a hand in front of him. 'Are you quite all right?'

He nodded.

She glanced down at her skirts. 'Would you mind assisting me once again?'

'Of course.'

Moving from her kneeling position, she twisted her body to face him. This time as he placed his hands on her waist he moved closer and took his time, letting her body slide down between the counter and his. He heard her sharp intake of breath and leaned forward, his nose lightly touching her hair. The smell of her, mixed in with her sweat, was a heady perfume.

'Sebastian,' she whispered, lifting her head to his as she placed her hands on his chest. 'Please…'

Sebastian wasn't sure if she arched up to meet his lips or if he bent down to hers. Maybe they met halfway, because before he knew it their mouths had met in a soft, sensuous kiss.

Much as it had last night, his body raged with longing and desire. Unable to hold himself back, he slid his tongue across the seam of her mouth, coaxing her lips open. His hands cupped her face as he parted her petal-soft lips and she gasped as their tongues touched. When she pulled back he slid his fingers around her nape, seeking the downy soft hair there.

A moan of pleasure escaped her, and he captured her mouth again. This time she opened to him, tilting her head back instinctively to let him explore her. He deepened the kiss, tasting her erotic sweetness. Her hands moved up to his shoulders, clinging to him as she pressed against him. The touch of their bodies sent his blood sizzling and his shaft hardened. He pushed her back against the counter, rubbing his hips against hers, the friction making them both groan aloud.

He slid one hand down to the back of her neck, and when he found the top buttons of her dress he undid them deftly and slipped his fingers under the fabric. Her skin was perfect and smooth and warm and everything he dreamed of. And he wanted—needed—more. He opened the rest of the buttons and then loosened the ties of her stays.

She gasped again and he devoured her lips, thrusting his tongue between those soft petals as he pulled down her garments. She cried out into his mouth as his hand cupped a soft breast through her thin chemise and rubbed a nipple to hardness.

'Kate…' he groaned, as he pulled his mouth away.

She shivered as he made his way lower, nibbling and kissing the soft skin of her neck and collarbone. His tongue teased at the delicate lace edge of her chemise, licking down to where the hard point of her other nipple poked through fabric. When she let out a frustrated whimper he wet the silk with his tongue, then drew her nipple into his mouth, making her mewl.

His hand released her other breast and reached under the layers of her skirts until he touched a slim stockinged leg. He looked up, watching her face twist with pleasure as he continued to suckle on her nipple, then moved his hand up, feeling for the slit between her drawers. When he found it, he parted her thighs, and his fingers inched towards the apex of her womanhood.

'No!' she cried, and then pushed him away. 'You can't…'

The heat of passion fizzled out and Sebastian leapt away from her, cursing to himself. How the hell had this happened? And why had he done it again?

She crossed her arms over her chest. 'I'm… We can't…'

'We shouldn't be together.' He raked his fingers through his hair. 'This isn't right.'

She stiffened, but nodded in agreement. 'Yes. I can't. Not with you.'

Those last three words hit him as if he'd been struck with an axe to the chest. *'Not with you.'* But she would with someone else.

'Of course. Your duke.'

Seagrave didn't bloody deserve her.

Despite her attempts to hide it, she was smart and witty. Capable, too. And she wasn't ashamed of her humble beginnings. Seagrave was so far beneath her in many ways. The thought of them together sent his blood boiling.

Then again, he knew all about men who didn't deserve the women they married. And what happened to those women when they stayed in such unions. He'd seen it with his own eyes.

And then it struck him—a memory from long ago that he'd tried so hard to repress rose to the surface of his consciousness. His mother had loved her husband so much that his betrayal had driven her to do the unthinkable.

He'd been wrong about Kate all this time. She wasn't chasing after a title, but something else.

'That's not real love,' he recalled her saying that first night in the gardens at the Houghton Ball.

'So you do believe in love.'

Her mouth parted as a breath escaped it, her chest heaving.

'And you seek a love match,' he concluded.

She didn't say anything. She didn't have to. He already knew the answer. His bubbling rage froze into ice in his veins. Had she merely wanted a title to elevate her social status, he could have given her that easily. But anything more was out of the question.

'Whatever this is between us, we must ignore it from now on.'

Her head bobbed up and down vigorously as she hauled her stays and her dress over her torso. 'Yes.'

'We must stay apart and avoid each other as much as possible.'

'Of course.'

She reached behind her, her arms bending unnaturally as she attempted to button her dress. When he approached her, she shrank back.

'I only wish to assist you. Please.'

She eyed him with suspicion, but nodded and turned around. Though he had more experience in undoing women's clothing, he somehow managed to quickly lace her stays and button her up.

'Th-thank you,' she stuttered, and then turned to face him. 'And for not—'

He raised a hand. 'No need. And forgive me for—'

'Let's not speak of this ever.'

'Agreed.'

They stared at each for a few more moments, then broke away at the same time.

Sebastian gestured to the staircase. 'After you.'

She gave him a nod and marched towards the stairs, smoothing her hair into place. He grabbed his jacket and cravat, then followed behind her until they reached the top.

The bright sun temporarily blinded him as he staggered out, and he squinted against the light. Much to his dismay, once his vision cleared, he saw that the Marquess stood outside, hands on hips. His lips twitched, as if he was trying to suppress a laugh.

'Well, now…' Ashbrooke began. 'That didn't take too long.'

Kate's face flushed. 'We were… I mean, I just… We fixed the boiler. That's all.'

'Of course, Miss Mason. I believe you.' The Marquess winked at her mischievously. 'And please do not fret. Sebastian is my dearest friend. He—and you—can count on my discretion.'

'It's not… We didn't… You don't…' she blustered, her face turning even redder.

'What Ash means is that you needn't worry about anything because nothing happened,' Sebastian said smoothly. 'You should get back before anyone sees you.'

Her lips pulled into a tight line. 'Thank you, Your Grace…my lord. And please do tell Mr Alton to start the firebox at once. It will take a few hours to get it up to the proper temperature to heat the orangery.'

'I shall inform him personally.'

'Thank you.'

He kept his gaze on her as she turned towards the house and marched off, unable to look away. But he had to. And not just look away, but also to remember his vow never to be like his father, to break the cycle. Now that he knew what she was really after it was more apparent than ever that he could never be with her lest she suffer the same fate as his mother.

Ash chuckled. 'Now, *this*, my friend, is what thoroughly debauched looks like.'

'I did *not* debauch Miss Mason,' he said through gritted teeth.

The Marquess grinned at him maniacally. 'I wasn't talking about her.'

Chapter Twelve

Somehow Kate managed to sneak into the house without anyone seeing her. She quickly made her way up to her room, her heart threatening to escape her chest, and slammed her door behind her.

She rushed to the washstand and poured some fresh water from the jug into the porcelain bowl, then wet a clean washcloth and scrubbed at her face. Streaks of soot came away on the white cloth. The dirt was easily washed away from her skin, but when she recalled what had happened with Mabury she felt marked all over again. Not with grime, but with his mouth and hands.

Another rush of heat went straight between her legs and she staggered away from the washstand. While she was a virgin, she wasn't totally ignorant in the ways of men and women. Once she'd begun her monthly courses, in the summer she'd turned fourteen, their old housekeeper, Mrs Hargrave, had taken her aside and explained how children were conceived. Indeed, it had been quite pragmatic of the woman to take the task upon herself, as Kate had had no mother or other female figure in her life to explain such things.

So, yes, she knew what might have happened. She'd

just never thought it would be so…exquisite, or that she would feel like that. Now she had experienced a taste of it, she longed for something she'd never had before.

You shouldn't have kissed him.

It was a good thing she'd come to her senses before they'd gone too far. Well, they already had gone quite far, but at least she wasn't ruined, and things could go on as planned.

Dear Lord, how could she have forgotten about the solution to her Marriage Problem? And Seagrave? If she and Mabury had been caught, even a nitwit like Seagrave would have been smart enough to avoid a scandal.

Nothing is lost, she thought with grim determination. She and Sebastian were at least in agreement that they needed to ignore each other. He was a duke who didn't need the dowry of an American heiress with no name and no breeding. It was a bitter truth that she quickly swallowed.

'*So you do believe in love.*'

In that moment he'd caught her off guard with his conclusion that she wanted a love match. Kate wasn't sure, but seeing as nothing could ever happen between them it was better if she let him think that she wanted to find love with Seagrave so he would leave her alone.

She couldn't risk her match with Seagrave—not when she was so close. Besides, had she forgotten that Sebastian had vowed never to marry? Those were some of the first words he'd uttered to her at the Houghton Ball. A dalliance with him would not help her with her problem. And she was not unscrupulous enough to force him into marriage—especially when he was so vehemently against it.

At least Seagrave wanted to be married. There would be no force involved. And she wanted marriage too—if only to protect Pap's memory—though the deception made an uneasy emotion settle in her stomach like a lead stone. But perhaps she could slowly show Seagrave that she knew quite a lot about engineering. Though she knew there was very little chance of it, she had hope that he might even allow her to work on the building of the factory or run it.

Or maybe not, she thought glumly. *Duchesses don't work, after all.*

But it would be worth it. Future generations would remember Henry Mason's work and how his engine had changed the world. Never running her own factory or designing an engine would be a small price to pay.

Reaching behind her, she managed to undo the top buttons of her dress and ripped off the rest, tossing the garment aside before crawling into the massive four-poster bed. Her naked skin against the silk sheets made her think back to Sebastian and their encounter. How his hands had felt on her…his lips…that tongue.

She rolled onto her back and blew out a breath.

Kate, you fool! How could you lose sight of your goal with just a few kisses?

Well, they hadn't been just kisses.

Kate sat up quickly and crossed her arms over her chest. She couldn't let a few moments of passion over-rule her mind. Indeed, if losing herself and her control was the result of a few of Sebastian's kisses and an embrace, it was better that she forget about him and focus on Seagrave. While she didn't feel the same blazing and intense emotions with Seagrave, there was every chance that once they were married he'd show a different side of himself to her.

In a few days she would go on a carriage ride with Seagrave. She would have to make certain to ignite his interest enough for him to propose, and then Mason R&L would be away from Jacob's clutches. Once she was married to the Duke of Seagrave, Pap's legacy would be safe.

For the next few days Kate focused all her attention on securing Seagrave. As promised, they had gone on their carriage ride through the beautiful Surrey countryside, and since then he'd been invited to almost every event at Highfield Park.

Seagrave had been the perfect gentleman every time. And they were never alone, as they were always accompanied by Miss Merton or surrounded by the Dowager Duchess and the other ladies.

Kate was thankful for them—especially Maddie—because the truth was, being around Seagrave was monotonous. In the time they had known each other Seagrave had only ever spoken of his horses, and whenever anyone introduced a new topic he just showcased how obtuse he was. Only yesterday the Dowager Duchess had been talking about Napoleon, and he'd revealed that he thought Waterloo was in France.

But he would be the perfect husband for her. She had come so far, and there was nothing that could stop her. Nor distract her, for that matter. Not even Sebastian.

So far no one had found out about their encounter, or that she'd even been in the orangery. The Dowager Duchess had been told that a plumber had come and repaired the boiler, and she hadn't seemed too worried about the details, simply happy to know that her dear plants and trees would be saved.

Sebastian had also kept his promise about staying away from her, and Kate hadn't seen him at all. It was unreasonable of her to feel slighted, but his rejection still stung. To think that he'd found his attraction to her so disagreeable that he had to slink around his own home… Still, it saved her from the awkwardness and embarrassment of having to see him again.

Yet whenever she had her thoughts to herself, she found her mind would wander to that day in the furnace. But just as quickly as the passion between them had dissipated she'd dismissed those thoughts. Although that didn't stop them from creeping in…especially at night as she lay alone in her bed. And sometimes… sometimes she allowed herself to think of what might have happened if she hadn't stopped him.

'My dear, there's a letter for you.'

The Dowager Duchess's voice jolted Kate out of her scandalous thoughts. *Blast it.* Now she was thinking about him during breakfast, too.

'Another one?'

Her stomach was tied into knots; she knew who it was from. Her fingers trembled as she opened the cream-coloured envelope.

Kathryn,

Since I have not heard from you, and Miss Merton has not relayed any offers of marriage, I can only assume that this venture is on the brink of failure. Thus, I have accepted Her Grace's open invitation and will be arriving at Highfield Park in one week with Jacob, so we may discuss your future prospects.

Signed,
Father

The only reason Kate didn't crush the letter in her hand was because the people around the breakfast table were looking at her expectantly. 'My father wishes to accept your invitation to visit,' she told the Dowager Duchess. 'He will be here in one week's time.'

'Of course,' the Dowager said graciously. 'He is welcome.'

Kate lowered the letter to her lap. Her father coming here with her second cousin to discuss her 'future prospects' only meant one thing: he was going to force her to marry Jacob.

Desperation clutched at her chest. *Oh, why hasn't Seagrave proposed, or even asked for permission to court me?* Time was truly running out now. At this point Seagrave was her only chance, since she hadn't entertained any of the other gentlemen the Dowager Duchess had invited to the house.

'Kate?' Maddie whispered, a look of concern marring her face. 'What's the matter?'

Sweet, sensitive Maddie. Of course she knew something was wrong. 'Nothing. It's fine.'

She didn't look convinced, and continued, 'You know you can tell me anything.'

Not quite everything. 'Yes, I know, Maddie.'

Maddie lowered her voice even further. 'If you're not occupied after tea, you should join me in the library.'

'The library?'

'Yes. We can speak in private there. I've been spending some time there by myself, to get away from Caroline and Mother. I had meant to invite you…but you've been busy.'

With Seagrave, Kate added silently, as Maddie would never say it aloud. She'd been such a dear friend all this time, never complaining or expressing envy at Kate's success while she remained a wallflower at every event.

It had never even occurred to Kate that she'd ignored her until now.

'Of course I'll be there.'

It would be nice to spend time with Maddie without anyone else around—especially Caroline and Eliza.

As she'd promised, Kate sneaked off to the library after tea. Maddie was coming down the corridor at the other end and they met outside the door.

'Kate, you made it.' Maddie grabbed her hands and led her inside, directing her to sit beside her on a settee by the fireplace. 'I'm so glad you came.'

'I'm glad you invited me, Maddie.' Smoothing her hands over her lap, Kate decided to get straight to the point. 'Maddie, I'm sorry if I've been too occupied to spend time with you. I have left you at your mother and Caroline's mercy.'

'I am quite used to them,' Maddie replied, 'so think nothing of it. And as for your being occupied, I certainly understand—especially since you have caught a duke's eye.'

Kate's heart jumped, but then she realised Maddie was talking about Seagrave.

'May I speak frankly, Kate?' Maddie continued, when Kate didn't respond. 'Since we are friends?'

'Of course.'

'Seagrave is a wonderful catch, of course. Caroline is boiling with rage that you are so much closer to a match than her. But perhaps…you should not be in a rush?'

'I shouldn't?'

'Er…yes. I mean…' Maddie paused. 'Seagrave is handsome and titled. But he seems quite…er… He's…' Her cheeks turned bright pink.

Kate knew what her friend was trying to say, so she spared her the trouble. 'He's as thick as porridge.'

'Yes.' Maddie giggled, which made Kate burst out laughing. They continued to roar and howl in the most unladylike manner, until tears were streaming down their cheeks.

'Oh… I…' Maddie inhaled a deep breath and sat up straight. 'I thought you would be offended, but I just wanted to make sure—'

'I know.' Oh, dear, sweet Maddie. 'It's just…' It was time to tell her friend the truth. 'It's my father…' Taking a deep breath, she confessed her father's ultimatum, and her own plan to thwart him. 'And so you see… I have no choice. I must get Seagrave to propose, or my father shall force me to marry Jacob. And once he has control of Mason R&L I won't be able to stop him.'

'No. Oh, no.' Maddie shook her head. 'We can't let that happen.'

'We?'

'Yes. We.' There was a determined steely look in Maddie's eyes—something Kate had never seen before in her sweet, mild-mannered friend. 'Your Pap worked so hard. Kate, *you* worked so hard. I won't allow anyone to take that away from you.'

'Oh, Maddie…' A tiny flare of hope sparked inside her. 'But Seagrave hasn't even hinted at a proposal, and my father and Jacob are arriving next week.'

'Then the Duke must make haste in proposing. Or we can help him hurry.' Maddie's teeth sank into her bottom lip. 'I think you should get him alone tomorrow…during the picnic.'

The Dowager Duchess had arranged for a picnic in the grounds and Seagrave had agreed to come.

'Get him alone?' she repeated.

'Yes—and you should k-kiss him,' Maddie stammered, the colour returning to her cheeks once more. 'I mean, you h-haven't kissed yet, have you?'

The memory of Sebastian's kisses flashed in Kate's mind. 'No,' she replied hesitantly.

If Maddie noticed her hesitation she didn't mention it. 'We'll find a way to get you alone. I'll distract the others if I have to. Then you can get him to kiss you. That should make it very clear that you want a proposal.'

'What if I'm wrong? And he really doesn't want to propose?'

'Kate, please—you're much smarter than that. You know he wouldn't be spending this much time with you if he didn't have intentions.'

'But a kiss…'

'Is just a kiss—or that's what Caroline says,' Maddie said. 'If we are wrong, and no one else finds out, then there's nothing to worry about. You can still move on to the next suitor and ensure you don't have to marry Jacob.'

Maddie's words reminded her of why she was doing this in the first place. 'All right. I'll do it.'

Still, her insides twisted at the thought of kissing Seagrave. And she couldn't stop thinking about kissing Sebastian. Would Seagrave kiss her with the same passion? Would he make her feel the way Sebastian had? Ignite something in her—something scary, but at the same time something that made her feel alive?

But then she remembered that Sebastian didn't want her.

And I don't want him.

His kisses might have awoken something in her, but at the same time she'd felt like a spinning top, losing all her senses and her mind. And like that top she would eventually run out of momentum. She could not afford to lose control like that. All her life she'd been under her father's command. This time, at least, she would have a say as to who she was going to marry.

It's just nerves, she convinced herself.

Once she had Seagrave alone she would find a way to kiss him. Then he would have no doubt that she would accept a proposal from him.

It'll be all right, she told herself. *Everything will go according to plan.*

Chapter Thirteen

The following morning started out well enough, with the Dowager Duchess gathering everyone at the manor and explaining that the picnic would take place in a lovely meadow on the estate. The servants had gone on ahead to set up tables, food, and some amusements like archery and nine pins. The guests would have a lovely stroll to the picnic spot.

The food was scrumptious, as usual, with plenty of cold sandwiches, salads, teacakes, and lemonade and ginger beer to go around. When they'd finished the meal, the Dowager Duchess invited everyone to go for a walk in the wooded area nearby.

'I have an idea,' Maddie whispered to Kate. 'You, Seagrave and I will stay in the rear of the group. When we get deep into the woods, pretend that you've lost something. A piece of jewellery, perhaps. Tell Seagrave that it has much sentimental value to you. He'll offer to help you find it, and you can retrace your steps to lead him back. Once you're alone, then you must kiss him.'

'All right…' It was worth a try.

The party gathered and marched towards the dense woodland. One of the guests, Sir Elliot Mimsby, was somewhat of a nature-lover, and pointed out various flora and fauna along the way. While everyone was engrossed by Sir Elliot's lecture about the difference between a chaffinch and a bullfinch, Kate brought a hand to her ear, unclipped her earring, then dropped it into her pocket. Then she gasped and covered her mouth with her hand.

'Oh, dear, where is it?'

'What's wrong, Miss Mason?' Seagrave asked.

'It seems my earring has fallen off.' She tried to sound distressed. 'It was my dear grandmother's, too.'

'A priceless heirloom,' Maddie added for effect. 'Whatever will you do?'

'I must find it,' Kate replied. 'It's the only thing I have left of her.'

'You must help her, Your Grace,' Maddie urged Seagrave. 'Please.'

'But what about the others?' He gestured at the rest of the group, who had gone on ahead as Sir Elliot dragged them to a tree to point out a nest of baby birds.

'I'm sure the earring must have fallen somewhere behind us on the trail.' Maddie smiled sweetly at him. 'You can catch up with us.'

'Oh, please, Your Grace?' Kate batted her eyelashes at him. 'It would mean so much to me.'

He seemed to hesitate, but then nodded. 'Of course, Miss Mason.'

When Seagrave had turned and retreated down the path Kate straightened her shoulders and followed as he craned his head left and right, looking for the lost earring. When the path turned a corner, she retrieved the earring from her pocket, then tossed it halfway between them.

'Your Grace!' She strode closer to him. 'There!'

He swung round and looked down. Spying the earring, he bent to pick it up. She did the same thing, hoping he would accidentally bump into her, even angling her body sidewards. He moved much faster than she'd anticipated, however, and when she leaned down he raised his head, knocking their foreheads together.

Seagrave let out a curse and slapped a hand over his right eye. 'Ouch!'

Pain shot through her temple and she staggered backwards. While she didn't fall over, she also didn't realise what was behind her—until her left foot sank into a shallow pool of water. The sensation of her boot sinking into wet mud made her cry out in surprise and completely lose her balance. Before she knew it she had landed on her back with a loud, wet *splash*.

'Heavens!' Seagrave exclaimed as he stumbled forward, catching himself before he also took a dive into the water. 'Dear me…is that a pond?'

No, it's the Atlantic Ocean, you nitwit, Kate fumed as she sat up.

'Why, yes, Your Grace. I believe it is.'

Her hair was soaked and the water had reached her hips, and was now quickly seeping in through her garments, making them stick to her skin. She braced her hands beneath the surface, feeling the mud squishing through her fingers as she somehow managed to hoist herself up.

'Oh, dear…' The Duke continued to stare at her. 'You're wet.'

'Yes, that tends to happen when one falls into water.'

Seeing that Seagrave was making no move to assist her, she grabbed at her skirts and hiked them up as she trudged out of the pond. When she heard the sound of voices approaching, she let out a loud groan.

'Kate? Where are—?' Maddie's blue eyes widened.

'What is going on?' Miss Merton rushed forward, huffing and puffing, then stopped when she saw Kate. 'Miss Mason, what in heaven's name has happened to you?'

'I… I fell.' There was no other way to explain it, really. Just her luck that she hadn't seen the pond a few feet away from the trail when they'd walked by it.

Glancing behind the chaperone, she saw the Dowager Duchess, Caroline, Eliza, and the rest of their party approaching.

Oh, blast it all.

'My dear, why are you so muddy and wet?' The Dowager Duchess's mouth formed a perfect *O*.

Behind her, Caroline sniggered, and Eliza clucked her tongue in disapproval.

'I slipped and fell.' Kate grabbed a handful of her skirts, peeled most of them off her legs, and wrung out the excess water, not giving a whit that there were other people around.

'We should head back,' the Dowager Duchess said. 'Before you catch a cold.'

'I'm fine.' She waved a hand away.

And I am done.

Obviously, today was not the day when everything would go according to plan. And, considering her bad luck, she wasn't about to tempt fate further.

'Please don't cancel the rest of the day's activities because of me.'

'But you'll get ill,' the Dowager Duchess countered as she came closer, and offered Kate her shawl.

Kate waved the shawl away. 'I'll walk back to the manor and get changed. It's a warm day. I'll probably be quite dry by the time I arrive. Please, Your Grace,' she added in a whisper, 'I've embarrassed myself enough for today.' She glanced surreptitiously at the Duke. 'My ego can only endure so much.'

'Ah, I understand.' The Dowager Duchess patted her hand. 'Let me get a footman to accompany you.'

'It's not that far, Your Grace. I'll be faster on my own. Thank you very much for your concern, though.'

After sending a sheepish smile to Maddie, Kate trudged away, her wet walking boots squelching as she made the journey back. When she saw the manor ahead, she sighed with relief and picked up her pace. When she reached the front door she didn't dare enter with her muddy boots, so she took them and her stockings off and went inside on her bare feet.

Kate stopped and glanced at her reflection in the hall mirror. *Oh, heavens, I look a fright.*

Her coiffure had come undone, and her wet tresses trailed down her shoulders and back. The entire bodice of her yellow gown remained wet and now stuck to her torso. Her corset could clearly be seen underneath the almost transparent fabric.

I need to get to my room before anyone sees me!

Grabbing her sodden skirts, she hurried as best she could up the long staircase, thanking her lucky stars that only some of the servants were at home, since most were still at the picnic. She cheered herself on as she neared the top without having been caught.

'Almost there,' she muttered. 'Just a few more—'

Her breath stuttered when she looked up and found herself staring at a pair of familiar dark eyes.

When he'd arrived at the manor, after another long day helping John Lawrence, the last person Sebastian had expected to see was Kate Mason. And certainly not a bedraggled, wet, yet still lovely Kate Mason, with her dress moulding indecently to the luscious curves of her body. A body that had been torturing his every waking and sometimes sleeping thought for the last few days.

Cornflower-blue eyes grew wide as saucers. 'Y-Your Grace.' Somehow she managed a curtsey on the step.

Stunned, he said the first thing that came to mind. 'What the devil happened to you?'

'I—I fell.' Her cheeks heightened with colour.

He peered closer to her face and noticed some discolouration above her eye. 'Is that a bruise on your forehead?'

'A small…mishap. If you would excuse me…?' Straightening her shoulders, she continued to trudge up the stairs. When she reached the top she attempted to brush past him, but he blocked her way.

'Kate, you will tell me exactly what has happened to you this instant.' Lord, he was exhausted from physical activity, and all he wanted was a bath and a nap. But seeing her like this had his emotions swinging from lust to rage.

She attempted to sidestep him, but with his great bulk it was impossible. 'Please, Sebastian, I need to—'

'Kate, I won't repeat myself.'

Anger flashed in her eyes. 'Why in heaven's name would I say anything to you? I do not owe you an explanation.'

His jaw hardened. 'I want to know.'

'I am tired and wet and I have no patience to argue any more.'

'Then stop arguing and *tell me*.' He searched her face. 'Was it Seagrave?'

Her expression faltered. 'It's not what you think.'

Bloody hell, he didn't *want* to think about it, because

in the time he'd been away thoughts of what might be happening between her and the Duke were the only things plaguing him.

'Did he force himself on you? Try to kiss you?'

'Did he what?' she spluttered. 'I told you—it's not what you think!'

'Enlighten me, then.'

She hesitated, then said, 'If you must know, *I* was the one trying to kiss him.'

Rage tore through Sebastian and his fingers curled into his palms. 'And did you succeed?'

'That's none of your business.'

He had almost convinced himself that he would find a way to overcome this foolish attraction to her and keep her at a distance. But now here he was, in exactly the position that he had wanted to avoid all this time. It was too risky. There was too much at stake. And he wouldn't be able to give her what she wanted. A love match was out of the question, because after the events of five years ago he didn't even know if that was an emotion he could ever feel.

'I can't stand it,' he said.

'Can't stand what?'

Her breathing came in deep pants, and it was difficult to ignore the rise and fall of her chest as it thrust up towards him, her cleavage clearly outlined through the wet fabric.

'Seeing you. Being around you—'

'Then allow me to leave your sight immediately.' She sidestepped him and began to walk away.

'I can't stand being around you but not being able to have you.'

And that was the truth he hadn't been able to admit these past weeks. The truth he had been running away from. But maybe it was time to stop running away from the inevitable.

His words seemed enough to stop her in her tracks, as her frame went rigid. Slowly, she turned on her heel to face him again.

He continued. 'When you're around, I can't concentrate on anything else.'

She took a step closer.

'The only thing I want to do is take you in my arms and kiss you until every bit of breath has left your body.'

And closer.

He couldn't hear anything except for his heart pounding madly in his chest, but he couldn't stop all the words spilling out of his mouth. 'It's driving me mad—you're driving me mad.'

She was so near now, their bodies nearly touching.

'It's as if I might burst from the inside if I wait one second more to have you.'

They stood there, just staring at each other, for what seemed like the longest time.

'Why, Kate?'

'Why, what?'

There were so many 'whys' he wanted—no, needed—to be answered, so he asked the first one that came to mind. 'Why him? No matter how much you may...care for him, he's not the right one for you.'

'You don't understand.' Her voice hitched. 'Never could understand.'

'Why not?'

'You never want to marry,' she began. 'And you'll never have to if you don't want to.'

'So, this is about what society expects you to do?'

'I'm a woman.' A wry smile touched her lips. 'From the moment I was born I've always been under a man's

control, and I will continue to be so until the day I die.
At the very least I can have some choice in *this* matter,
limited as it may be.'

Something in him wanted to shout *You have another
choice aside from Seagrave.* Unfortunately, the bigger
demons he'd been keeping inside managed to wrestle
him down. Even if he could marry her, he wouldn't. Not
when the memory of his father's deeds haunted him.

'You men have it so easy. Everything just drops in
your lap. You can do whatever you want. You can choose
to be anything you want to be. You are free.'

Sebastian ground his teeth together. 'If only that were
the case. Men aren't as free as you think. Sometimes
we're bound by society too. We must play by its rules
and be what other people expect us to be or suffer the
consequences. Or have our loved ones pay the price.'

She tilted her head to the side. 'What do you mean?'

'Nothing,' he replied quickly. 'Nothing at all.' This
entire conversation was turning futile, so he decided to
end it. With a quick nod, he tore his gaze from her and
stepped back. 'I should leave—'

'Wait.'

His head snapped back to meet her eyes. 'Why? What
do you want from me, Kate?'

The question seemed to stun her for a moment. But
then to his surprise she reached out and once again
crossed the distance between them.

Lord, he couldn't stand it any longer. She didn't fight
him when he leaned down. No, she pushed herself up
and fully opened to him, lips parting to welcome his
kiss. Lord, he'd missed this. Missed her. The entire time
he'd stayed away from her his body had been akin to
a wound spring, ready to snap if he did not see, smell,
and taste her again.

Tearing his mouth away from her, he trailed kisses down her jaw to her neck. She sighed and leaned her head back, exposing more of her soft skin to his mouth. Tentatively, he touched his tongue to the spot behind her ear. She mewled when he grazed his teeth over her skin, so he pressed his lips there and sucked. That sent her body buckling forward, so he caught her and then slipped a hand to the back of her dress, undoing just enough buttons to pull the garment down and peel the fabric from her chest. Moving his lips to her front, he reached the tops of her breasts and nibbled on the soft, white flesh, inhaled her distinct, sweet scent.

She cried out when he popped one breast from her corset and wrapped his lips around the nipple, licking it until it puckered in his mouth. He drew it in deeper, enjoying the sounds of her whimpers and moans as her body writhed deliciously against his. Her fingers dug into his hair, and the sensation of her nails raking on his scalp sent tingles down his spine.

'Please,' she moaned. 'I…'

He released her nipple. 'Please, what?'

'Please…we can't be seen out here.'

He slipped his hand under her knees, lifting her up into his arms.

'You're right,' he murmured against that spot again. Her pulse jumped, sending a surge of excitement straight to his manhood. 'I'm taking you to my rooms.'

She didn't protest. Instead she wrapped her arms around him, then nuzzled at his neck, and his shaft hardened painfully against his constricting clothing.

Sebastian wasn't sure how he managed it, but somehow they made it to his rooms undetected. Setting her down on the floor, he clicked the door shut and locked it, then turned to face her.

The sunlight streamed in through the windows, bathing her in an ethereal light that made her skin glow. However, it was the haze of desire in her eyes that had his own simmering lust boiling over. Seizing her once again, he backed her up towards his bed, stopping just at the edge.

His hand trembled as he reached up to tip her chin with his finger. 'Do you know what's about to happen?'

Her lashes lowered, but she nodded, her skin flushing prettily.

'And you still want it?'

Lord, if she said no he would turn back right now. If she told him she loved Seagrave and he loved her in return he would send her packing before they did something that they couldn't undo. The thought strung him tight, but all she had to do was say she didn't want this.

Slowly, she raised her gaze to meet his. 'I want…you.'

And with those words Sebastian knew there would be no turning back.

Chapter Fourteen

Kate's world had turned upside-down at her admission. When Sebastian had confessed his desire for her on the staircase she hadn't quite been able to believe it—not because she didn't think it was true, but because he had described her own emotions so perfectly.

'It's as if I might burst from the inside if I wait one second more to have you.'

How could he possibly have put it so succinctly? Every feeling, every ache, every longing had been encapsulated in his words, as if he'd reached into the depths of her soul and plucked them out. This raging attraction between was like a runaway locomotive, a powerful force neither one of them could stop.

And, Lord help her, she didn't want it to stop.

But, more than that, it was as if something had changed between them. In that moment she'd seen a side of him that had made her want to know more about him. Made her want to be closer to him.

'What do you want from me, Kate?'

She wanted him. She wanted this moment. To grab this intense passion by both hands, like a hunk of burning coal, and hold on to it for as long as she could. And damn the consequences.

His head swooped down, his mouth devouring hers, while his hands made quick work of the rest of the buttons at her back. Fabric pooled around her ankles as he shoved her dress down, then undid her corset until it too met the floor. Somehow her petticoats and hoops had also joined the rest of her clothing, but she didn't notice as he once again found that delicious spot under her ear with his talented mouth.

'Lovely,' he whispered, as he stepped back to look at her.

Despite still being dressed in her damp chemise and drawers, she felt exposed under the gaze of his dark eyes. A hand cupped her chin, tilting her head back as he pressed his lips to hers again. This time his kiss was surprisingly gentle, though his hands roamed lower, over her breasts and down her hips, before grabbing handfuls of her chemise.

'Oh!' she gasped, when their mouths broke contact so he could lift the undergarment over her head.

'Kate…' he began as his hand spanned her abdomen. 'Have you ever…touched yourself?' He moved lower, his fingers leaving a trail of heat in their wake. 'Down here?'

She sucked in a breath when his callused palm covered the downy triangle between her legs. 'I… A few times.' The sensation had been pleasant, she recalled, but it had felt entirely too wicked, so she'd refrained from exploring further.

'And did you…?'

'Did I what?'

A finger slid up to the top of her mound and brushed

against the swollen bud there. A cry tore from her mouth as the most delicious sensation rippled through her body.

'From the look on your face I can guess you did not.'

'Did not…what?'

He murmured non-committally and continued to stroke her, his pace increasing, and at the same time those pleasurable shocks came faster. Kate's knees buckled, so she clung to him, her fingers digging into his forearms for support and her face pressed against his chest as he switched to a circling motion.

Her body tightened and tensed and felt hot all over. Unsure what to do, she rolled her hips against his hand, wanting more… She didn't know what, exactly, but she just knew she had to have it *now*.

'Sebastian…' She whimpered against the linen of his shirt as her body climbed a peak. Higher and higher. Until she was sent reeling over the edge. Falling. Drifting. Sapped. Back to earth. Her legs shook when she tried to straighten herself out, so he pushed her down on the bed.

'That.'

Obsidian eyes filled with promise bored into hers, and the heat she'd thought had drained from her body came rushing back, making her feel dizzy.

Mrs Hargrave never said anything about this feeling so good.

'Is there more?' she asked breathlessly.

'Oh, yes. There's so much more.' He stared boldly down at her naked form, spread on top of the covers, leaving nothing unseen.

A sense of shame and mortification washed over Kate, and she reflexively crossed her arms over her breasts and cupped a hand over her mound. 'Please, you— Sebastian…' She shut her eyes tight. 'Could you…draw the curtains?'

'No.'

A rough hand held her ankle, then planted it on top of the mattress, then did the same with the other. Kate could imagine how she looked—what he was looking at, at this moment—and her entire face, all the way to the tips of her ears, heated with embarrassment.

'I want to see all of you, Kate.' He brushed her hand aside. 'And taste you.'

Oh, Lord, he couldn't possibly…

'Oh!' His tongue slid up the crease of her sex. Teasing and licking at her. Sending shocks of pure pleasure up and down her body. It coiled in her, winding tight like a spring, and just when she thought it couldn't possibly get any better she felt something—his finger—slip inside her. The sensation made her claw at the sheets with her fingers.

The maddening rhythm of his tongue and the deep carnal thrusts of his finger were too much. Too incredible. Too pleasurable. They sent her to dizzying heights once more, and this time her entire body convulsed and shook with ecstasy, making it hard to breathe. She let out a hoarse cry, trying to get as much air as she could, until her body collapsed back on the mattress and her lungs learned to function once more.

'You are exquisite.' He nuzzled at her thighs, sending a few aftershocks over her skin. 'Look at me, Kate. Please.'

Somehow, she found the strength to open her eyes and glance down at him. The blurriness of her vision faded until his face appeared before her. He looked entirely too wicked, kneeling between her thighs, dark eyes burning as their gazes crashed into one another.

Slowly, he stood and discarded his jacket, then began to unbutton his shirt, exposing all that golden skin. Mortification coloured her cheeks as she remembered that day when she'd spied him similarly undressed. The view from the telescope, however, had not done him any justice. His shoulders were broader than she'd imagined, the muscles bulging and flexing as he continued to discard his clothes. A thick mat of dark hair covered his wide chest, trailing downwards towards...

She couldn't stop the gasp from escaping her mouth as he pulled his loosened trousers and his drawers down in one motion, freeing his manhood. Heat rushed up her cheeks as she watched the heavy, jutting member rising from the nest of dark curls between his legs.

He came forward, the mattress dipping under his weight. Slowly, he moved over her, slipping his arms under her and then hauling her body higher on the mattress. When he nudged her knees apart instinct made her clamp them together and turn her head away.

'Shh... Kate...' He leaned down and pressed his lips to her cheek. 'Relax.'

A hand slid up her thighs, coaxing them to open. Once again, his fingers did the most delicious things to her most secret part. Kate allowed herself to calm down and unclench. He breathed a sigh, too, as if he'd been just as anxious as her.

'This will hurt,' he warned her as his body covered hers, his heavy sex jutting against her belly. 'But only for a short while. And then it will feel so good.'

She wanted to trust him. No, she *did* trust him. At least in this, she did.

Nodding, she spread her legs even more to accommodate him. He gathered her against him, then planted soft kisses on her neck, moving up to capture her lips again.

She welcomed his mouth on hers, his ardent kisses making her shiver with pleasure. She hardly noticed the blunt tip of his sex as it nudged against her cleft and pushed inside her.

Oh.

The sensation was like nothing she'd ever felt before. It wasn't terrible, but she couldn't describe it. His hips moved further, and she gasped. There was more…so much more of him. Her passage clenched at the intrusion, and she let out a soft cry and squeezed her eyes shut.

'I'm sorry.' He kissed her again. 'I need to…'

'Please…not so fast.' It was overwhelming. The sensations. The invasion. The building pain.

'Shh…' A hand moved between them, searching for the bundle of nerves right above the place where they were joined. He teased her there again, his fingers playing her expertly, until she felt a rush of wetness. 'It will be over sooner if I just…'

'If you—? Oh!' She hadn't expected the immediate thrust.

He continued to brush the crest of her sex with his rough fingertips. The burning hurt terribly, but as he promised it was over quickly. She found herself relaxing, and then rolling her hips at him.

'You feel…incredible…' He groaned when she pushed up, and seated more of himself inside her. Shifting his weight, he drove his hips back and then pushed inside her once more.

The sensation jolted her eyes open. He did it again, the pressure from his pelvis rubbing her just right, eliciting from her a hoarse cry.

'Kate?'

'It's…good.'

Hands slid under her buttocks, lifting her up to meet him. 'Better?'

'Much.'

He buried his face in her neck, whispering soft words that she didn't quite understand. He drew back, then thrust inside her again, each time driving deeper. His mouth found that spot under her neck once more and the pleasurable sensations intensified. Still, she wanted more. A greedy craving grew exponentially inside her with every stroke.

His mouth caught hers again in a savage kiss. Their tongues danced, teeth clashed, his hips all the while continuing that maddening rhythm that provoked sensations she'd never felt before. She wrapped her arms around his torso, fingers digging into his back as she arched up into him, urging him to give her more. He stroked parts of her that no one else had, parts she'd never even known existed inside her.

With each thrust she sobbed and cried out in joyful surrender. A wave of pleasure pushed her once more to the edge, sending her soaring. His arms tightened around her, his thrusts turning erratic as she continued to plummet to the blissful depths. He let out a guttural groan and she felt the oddest sensation of him spasming inside her, then warmth flooding her, before he slumped forward with a deep shudder.

They lay still for what seemed like eternity. She should have been bothered by his body on top of hers but, truth be told, the weight of him was rather pleasant. She felt…enfolded and cherished at the same time.

He breathed deep, then rolled away. Disappointment flooded her as he left her body, but before she could protest he tucked her against him and brushed the hair at her nape to the side.

'Rest,' he whispered lazily, to the column of her neck.

She was about to protest, but only a yawn escaped her mouth. Her body, drained from the physical and mental exertion of the day, relaxed in his arms and she let blissful sleep take over.

When Kate woke up, the first thing that registered in her mind was the strange sensation of sheets on her body. *How odd.* It was as if she was naked.

Bolting upright, she glanced around her. She was *definitely* naked, and that was *definitely* Sebastian behind her.

Dear Lord, it hadn't been a dream.

Her head snapped towards the window. While the last time she'd been awake the sun had been high in the sky, it was now slowly sinking beneath the horizon, casting the room in the glow of twilight.

Oh, heavens.

She slid to the edge of the bed, wincing as pain throbbed between her legs.

Another realisation smashed into her brain.

They had—

'Kate?'

His low baritone was enough to make her knees weak—especially when she remembered the wicked things he'd whispered in her ear.

'It—it's getting late,' she stammered. 'Everyone must have come back from the picnic by now. They're all probably getting ready for dinner.' She scampered off the mattress and grabbed at the clothes on the floor. 'If I can sneak off—'

'What the devil are you going on about?'

He sat up in bed, eyes fixed on her. There was no

time to feel shame or mortification at her current state of undress—or his—so she tore through the pile and picked up her chemise and drawers. 'If I'm found here—'

He was beside her in an instant. 'Kate, what's done is done. Do you regret what happened between us?'

The question made her pause. *Did she?* Perhaps if she considered only the pleasure they had given each other she could say she didn't regret any of it. But now, as the light grew even fainter, the consequences of her actions came crashing into her. Her plan to save her grandfather's legacy was in peril.

But not everything was lost.

Shrugging, she tugged and tied her drawers on and threw her chemise over her head.

'We cannot undo what we did.' He was behind her now, his presence looming over her.

'Yes, that's generally how time works.' She smoothed the chemise down over her body. 'But as long as we are discreet no one will find out.'

'No one will—?' He blew out a breath. 'I've ruined you.'

'No one needs to know. We haven't been caught.' But she had to get out of there before anyone did see them.

A dark look crossed his face. 'You are—*were*—a virgin. I think your future husband will be able to tell if you come to his bed in this state.'

She gritted her teeth. 'I'm sure Seagrave won't mind.' *Blasted nitwit probably wouldn't be able to tell, anyway.*

'Seagrave?' he thundered. 'You still think to marry him?'

'Of course.' She spied her corset in the clothing pile and bent down to pick it up. He was supposed to believe she loved Seagrave, right? 'Who else am I supposed to marry?'

'Me. Marry me.'

The words had flown out of his mouth without thought.

She stopped moving, her limbs frozen in place. 'You're jesting.'

'I am not. I have ruined you and now I must pay.'

Yes, that was it. That was the only reason that didn't sound insane right now. Because, despite his vow never to marry, Miss Kate Mason was the one person in the world who had managed to make him say those two words.

'You must *pay*? Like…like having to recompense a shopkeeper for breaking a trinket on a shelf?' She snorted. 'My, what a romantic proposal, Your Grace. It's what every girl dreams of.'

'That's not what I meant! You simply must marry me now.'

'Oh!' She threw her hands up. 'So now you are ordering me to marry you?'

'For God's sake!' He scrubbed his hands down his face. 'Kate, I know I can't give you what you want—'

'At least we are in agreement on that!'

Pain plucked at his chest, but he ignored it. 'But we have no choice in the matter now.'

'Only if anyone else finds out.'

'If you are with child, then they will definitely find out.'

She opened her mouth, but nothing came out. She clamped her lips shut. Silence hung between them until she finally spoke. 'Well, we will find out soon, I suppose. My courses will come...or they will not...and once we are certain we can deal with it.'

Deal with it? Was she insane?

'Listen, Kate—'

'No, *you* listen!' She waved her corset at him as if she were brandishing a fencing foil. 'This should be a boon to you. A tumble with no consequences. Why must you insist on doing the right thing when it's quite apparent that you want to marry me about as much as I want to marry you?'

That pain in his chest spread, making it difficult to breathe. He could only watch as she slipped the corset over her chemise and tugged on the ties at the back. He couldn't move, couldn't speak.

By the time she had finished knotting her corset, the throbbing in his temple had stopped. 'You will tell me if you are with child.'

She didn't answer. Instead shook out her gown on the floor, then stepped into it.

'There will be no child,' she stated.

'You don't know that.'

Kate pulled the dress over her torso, reached behind her to close the top buttons, then arranged her hair to cover the rest. 'We can't know for sure either way, so let's assume for now there is no child.'

Damn her logical mind.

'This discussion is not over,' he said.

'Oh, I think it is.'

Finally she was somewhat fully dressed, and she strode over to the door. She opened it and stuck her head out, glanced around to check if anyone was outside, then slipped out and tiptoed away down the corridor.

Why he'd slept with her, he didn't know. Actually, he damned well *did* know. He'd wanted her. And it was quite obvious she'd felt the same way. Kate had been a virgin—she was not the kind of woman who took a tumble in anyone's bed for no reason.

So why had she said no?

Why had he proposed in the first place?

Because I did ruin her.

Despite Kate's protests about being a trinket, that was the truth—at least, that was how the ton would see it.

In the past it had been easy to avoid virgins. Hell, even when he'd been a thoughtless rake he hadn't dared seduce virgins so he could avoid being forced to marry too early. But now his actions had consequences.

Just as with his father's actions, someone else would be paying for them.

He'd done exactly what he'd been trying to avoid all these years. Which meant he had to put right this mess he'd created. Unlike his father, he wasn't going to bury his head in the sand. No, he would face the consequences and take responsibility for his actions.

Kate had to marry him. There was no other way.

Chapter Fifteen

Kate's heart hammered so loudly she feared it might burst out of her chest. But by some miracle she managed to make it all the way to her room without being seen by anyone. When the door clicked shut behind her, her limbs weakened, as if all her energy had been drained from her very bones.

She leaned against the door and closed her eyes.

What had she been thinking? She had been swept up by passion and his kisses. By pleasure she'd never imagined she could feel. Even now her sex clenched at the thought of him inside her.

I'm no longer a virgin.

She didn't feel different at all—except for the stinging between her legs. Speaking of which…she needed a hot bath, and then she'd have to get dressed for dinner. While she considered begging off tonight, and pretending she had caught a cold, she knew it would be a waste of an opportunity for her to spend time with Seagrave—especially now that her father would be arriving in six days, with the odious Jacob in tow.

A thought made her heart crash into her ribcage.

Mabury had wanted to marry her.

And, God help her, for a brief moment she had wanted to say yes.

But she hadn't.

Some might think it a stupid decision to reject him, but his impulsive proposal had done nothing to sway her. In fact, it had felt like an insult—as if she now had even less value as a person because she'd lost her virginity, and only he could bring her back from perdition.

'I have ruined you,' he'd said. *'Now I must pay.'*

Her chest had tightened at those words. Words that had made what she had thought a beautiful, passionate experience into a sordid affair.

And then he'd made it even worse, ordering her to marry him! Why, he was no better than her father, forcing her to marry.

She couldn't afford to lose this one choice—this one bit of control she had over her life. Seagrave was the right husband. She had thrown caution to wind with Sebastian, and now look where she was. With Seagrave she might never experience that intense passion, but she wouldn't get burned either.

Nothing would stop her from getting him to propose. Not her father, not Sebastian, nor—

Her hand went to her abdomen. Surely she couldn't be... If she were...

Kate straightened her spine and curled her hands into fists at her sides. She would deal with that later. If Seagrave asked her father for permission to court her, then that would at least ward off any notion of her marrying Jacob. Should she be with child, her second cousin would surely never agree to marry her anyway.

Feeling resolved, she rang for her maid so she could dress for dinner.

* * *

Somehow, Kate kept her composure for the duration of the meal. However, she couldn't help but feel that anyone who looked at her would know what she and Sebastian had done—as if a visible mark had appeared upon her person to indicate that she was no longer a virgin. Still, she kept her mind on her goal and focused her attention on Seagrave.

For his part, Seagrave seemed genuinely apologetic for what had happened and not helping her sooner. She, of course, forgave him.

'It was an accident, Your Grace. No harm done.'

No harm except that she had lost her innocence to another man.

And, speaking of Sebastian, he seemed to have no trouble at all in keeping his countenance aloof. Indeed, he acted as if Kate didn't exist at all. When he entered the room, after being announced, he greeted everyone with a nod, his gaze passing over her as it always did. And when he sat down to dinner he spoke only with his mother and the guests around him, but only if they asked him a question first.

This is what he's really like, she supposed.

Maybe, like her, he'd been caught up in the blazing passion between them. It was hard to believe this cold, imposing figure was the same man who had kissed her so wickedly on the neck and the shoulders and well… everywhere.

Everything had changed between them. She was a fool to think otherwise. But it wasn't just their making love. She had glimpsed a side of him she'd never seen before—something he usually hid behind that cold and aristocratic façade.

'Men aren't as free as you think… We must play by

*its rules... Suffer the consequences... Or have our loved
ones pay the price.'*

What did he mean, exactly? She'd been too caught up
in their passion to think about it then. Now she couldn't
stop thinking about it, and another instance afterwards.
It had been the one moment when she'd thought that
there was something more driving his proposal. When
she'd told him that she didn't want to marry him there
had been a subtle change in his expression, but Kate
hadn't been able to ignore it. He'd looked almost…hurt.

But he was the one who didn't want to marry at all.
Why would her rejection affect him?

'Are you all right, Miss Mason?' asked Miss Merton. 'You seem listless all of a sudden. Are you coming
down with a cold?'

'Oh, dear.' Seagrave clicked his tongue. 'Perhaps you
should have stayed in bed.'

At the word 'bed' the Duke of Mabury's head snapped
towards her and a jolt of excitement shot straight to her
abdomen. 'I—I'm perfectly all right. It's just rather…
warm in here tonight.'

'Indeed, the weather is changing,' the Dowager
Duchess remarked.

'Your Grace,' Caroline began, 'don't you think we
should celebrate? Celebrate that spring is here, I mean,'
she added quickly. 'Maybe you could host a bigger gathering?'

'Oh, yes!' Eliza clapped her hands together. 'That
would be lovely. A large soirée. Perhaps you could invite more people to attend?'

The Dowager Duchess seemed to contemplate the
idea. 'Well, I suppose that could be arranged…a ball,
perhaps?'

Caroline squeaked. 'Oh, yes.'

'A ball sounds wonderful, Your Grace,' Miss Merton said. 'If you are amenable to such a thing.'

'A small, intimate ball…a party with dancing, really,' the Dowager Duchess qualified. 'We could invite everyone who's already come to Highfield Park.'

'Hopefully we can all dance?' Caroline sent a hopeful look at the Duke.

'It's settled, then,' the Dowager Duchess declared. 'Five days from today—that will be enough time to prepare. Eames, what say you? Are you up to the task? There is no one else I would trust to help me put together an event like this.'

The butler stepped forward and gave the Dowager Duchess a nod of his head. 'It would be my deepest honour, Your Grace.'

'Thank you, Eames.' She turned to the rest of the table. 'And of course everyone here is invited.'

Excitement buzzed amongst the guests.

Beside Kate, Seagrave cleared his throat. 'Miss Mason?'

'Yes, Your Grace?'

'I…uh… I hope I am not overstepping my bounds, but I overheard Miss Merton tell Mrs DeVries that your father is expected to arrive.'

'Oh. I mean…oh, yes.'

'I was wondering…if you think it would be wise… if I might speak to him…perhaps…' He looked around and motioned for a footman to refill his glass.

Just say it! she wanted to scream at him as he took a big gulp of his wine.

'Yes?'

'Um…' He breathed in. 'What I mean to say is… I would like to approach your father about the possibility of courting you.'

Kate paused, waiting for…she didn't know what. It felt as if she'd been anticipating this moment for eternity, and now that it was here she had imagined it would feel more…well, just *more*.

'Miss Mason?'

'Yes…?' she choked. 'I mean, yes, of course.'

When his face lit up, Kate breathed a sigh of relief.

'Miss Mason, I am so glad to hear that.' He wiped his lips with his napkin. 'All these weeks I have been trying to gauge your interest, and I'm glad my feelings are returned.'

She forced a smile on her face. 'Of course, Your Grace.'

The doors opened once again and the footmen came in with the third course. A hush fell over the table as the trays were set down and the silver domes lifted to reveal a scrumptious pheasant dish.

Kate cut into her roasted fowl and put a morsel in her mouth, but it turned to ash on her tongue. Yes, her plan was coming along nicely, but there was an uncomfortable sensation in her stomach—an uneasiness that told her something was not quite right.

Unwillingly, she glanced towards the head of the table. Her chest tightened as she looked at Sebastian, so devilishly handsome under the glow of the candlelight.

'Marry me.'

If he'd said those words under different circumstances would she have said yes? If he had used softer tones, or if he hadn't said that he'd ruined her and therefore had to pay?

She didn't dare let her fantasy play out. It only made her chest constrict. Besides, what was the point of mulling it over now that it was done?

Seagrave was her best choice, she reminded herself.

And now that marriage to him was finally within her reach she couldn't afford any missteps. Pap's legacy was at stake.

Kate didn't know how long she'd been staring at him, but when those dark eyes met hers a slow heat began to build low in her belly. Unable to keep looking at him without losing herself, she quickly turned away.

She had to remind herself of the plan. All she had to do was wait until her father arrived. She couldn't re-call ever in her life looking forward to seeing Arthur Mason or Jacob the way she did now.

Sebastian fumed silently, wishing for a cloud or a thunderstorm or a cyclone to spoil the beautiful clear weather outside. *Or perhaps a lightning strike would be better*, he thought. But only if it could be directed to the current object of his ire—the Duke of Seagrave, who as of this moment was helping Miss Kate Mason into his carriage.

It was as if God or the Devil himself had cursed him, so that he'd happened to look out of the window of his study just in time to watch her flirting with Seagrave. The only thing that stopped him from storming outside was the fact that Miss Merton was accompanying them, even though it was perfectly acceptable for Kate and Seagrave to drive together in an open carriage.

At least someone around here has some sense.

'Your Grace?'

Clearing his throat, he turned and faced his solicitor, Mr James Hall. 'Yes, James?'

'The machinery, Your Grace?'

'What machinery?'

James nodded to the papers on his large oak desk. 'The new machinery you ordered. I just wanted to make sure the amounts were accurate so I may release payment to the company.'

'Ah, yes.' Sebastian glanced outside one last time, grinding his teeth as he watched the carriage drive away, before striding back to his desk. After a quick check of the numbers and a few calculations in his head, he knew something was off. 'There's an error in the addition… I think your accountant must have mistaken that seven on the third invoice for a one.'

James took the papers. 'I shall have him redo this.'

'Now, is there anything else we need to discuss?'

'No, Your Grace.' The solicitor stood up. 'Thank you again for your time.'

'Thank you for coming all the way here, James; I do appreciate it. Allow me to walk you outside.'

'I'm sure you have more business to attend to. There's no need—'

'It's no trouble at all.' Sebastian rounded his desk. 'Come.'

He would not be able to concentrate on his work in any case. For the last five days his thoughts had been plagued with only one thing—or rather, one person. His damned emotions were scattered all over the place, swinging from lust to anger to frustration, and it was all because of one slip of a girl.

His burning desire for Kate he would eventually be able to conquer. Even the anger would eventually subside. But Sebastian's frustration stemmed from the one thing he just couldn't understand: why she was insisting on marrying that buffoon.

Granted, Seagrave was young and handsome, but his estate was in near ruins. The match would obviously be advantageous to the Duke, but for the life of him Sebastian didn't know how Kate would benefit—especially when she could find better prospects. Anyone who had even a modicum more sense and intelligence than Seagrave would suit her.

Like you? a voice inside him mocked.

He quickly quashed that thought. Besides, she had made it perfectly clear from her rejection of his proposal that she wouldn't even consider him for a husband, despite what had happened between them. Really, he should be rejoicing. He'd already tried to do the right thing by offering for her, and if she hadn't accepted that was not his fault.

I can't give her what she wants.

Love.

She wanted love. She hadn't denied it when he'd asked her outright in the furnace room.

She believed in love. Sought it out. And, despite her obvious attraction to Sebastian, somewhere deep inside she must know that he had no capacity for such an emotion.

In fact, no emotion could move him, and he was convinced that all sentiment had been removed from his person five years ago.

His throat went dry as the vision in his head became clear. As if he were reliving the nightmare again.

The candles burning.

The empty bottle on the bedside table.

His mother, lying motionless in her bed.

He was no better than that cad who had sired him... who had seduced and whored his way through London. Sebastian had sworn an oath never to marry and sire a child so that he would stop the cycle. So that he would never turn out like his father. Yet he had done exactly that, and that was why he had to make it right.

He'd ruined Kate. That he'd taken her virginity without even thinking of the consequences for her left a terrible dread in his stomach. But even though Sebastian should regret taking Kate into his bed, for the life of him he couldn't. They had both wanted what had happened between them.

'You don't understand. Never could understand.'

What had she meant when she'd said that, exactly? He understood that, as a woman, she didn't have a lot of choices. Lord, he understood that most of all, after what had happened with his own mother. But there was something else. Something she wasn't telling him.

'Thank you once again, Your Grace.'

James's voice yanked him from the grip of the past. Sebastian had been so deep in thought that he hadn't realised they'd made it all the way outside. 'Of course. I shall see you in a fortnight, James.'

'Have a good day, Your Grace.'

Sebastian turned back to the manor and walked inside, nearly bumping into Eames.

'Apologies, Your Grace.' The butler stepped back and bowed his head low.

'It's quite all right, Eames.' Looking behind the butler, he saw two maids carrying large white bundles, their faces turning pale and eyes widening as soon as they realised he was there. They both nearly fell over, trying to curtsey. 'What the devil is going on, Eames?'

Eames gave the two maids a stern look. 'Mrs Grover forgot to inform the maids that they need to prepare two bedrooms in the east wing. They are pressed for time, so I'm escorting them through the front of the house instead of via the servants' entrance. Apologies. It won't happen again, Your Grace.'

'Why are they preparing two bedrooms in the east wing? Who are we hosting now?'

'Mr Arthur Mason and his cousin are arriving in the morning, Your Grace,' Eames answered smoothly.

'Arthur *Mason*?' Even the sound of Kate's surname had him responding like a dog hearing its master call.

'Yes. Miss Kathryn's father is coming for a visit, along with his cousin.'

'Her fath—?' A throb pulsed behind his eyes.

Kate's father was arriving tomorrow. And Seagrave had visited every day since the night of the picnic, sometimes staying for dinner. This only meant one thing: Seagrave was going to ask Mr Mason's permission to court Kate. He must have made his intentions known, which was why Kate's father was coming to Highfield Park.

'Bloody hell!' In his own home, too!

Eames's face drained of colour. 'I'm sorry, Your Grace! I shall tend my resignation and—'

'For heaven's sake, Eames! I wasn't cursing at you!' The throb was now a painful hammering, growing by the second. 'Send word to John Lawrence and all the other tenants that I'll be indisposed for the rest of the day.'

'Of course, Your Grace.'

Whirling on his heel, he stormed down the corridor and made his way back to his study. He went straight to the table by the fireplace, where he kept a bottle of brandy. After filling the snifter halfway, he swallowed the entire contents and then poured himself another before sinking down on the nearest chair.

So, Seagrave has found the bollocks to make his intentions known. Bloody fantastic.

Why in God's name should he give a damn, anyway, when she didn't want to marry him?

There could still be a child.

Yes, that was the reason he should give a damn. From the way Kate had spoken, Sebastian thought it would be some time before she was certain whether or not she was with child. Or perhaps she did already know and had accelerated her courtship with Seagrave as a result. Maybe she'd already slept with him so he could take responsibility for any child she bore.

That she would be bound for ever to someone else had him gasping for breath—as if his body couldn't bear the thought that he would never see her again. Or, worse, see her beside another man.

But why should she bring such emotions within him?

He took another sip. The smooth liquor slid down his throat, straight to his belly. While the alcohol should have dulled his mind, it only brought more questions to the surface. Questions he should have asked himself in the first place.

Kate wanted a love match, and yet she had slept with him. If she was in love with Seagrave, why had she willingly come to his bed?

Something about this whole thing did not make sense. There was something that he had missed. And, dammit, the nagging urge to find out what wouldn't go away.

One way or another, Kate would tell him the truth before the day was over.

Chapter Sixteen

Despite his earlier state of intoxication, Sebastian was clear-headed and sober by the time the ball began—thanks to Robeson. His valet had tutted disapprovingly at his master's inebriated condition, but worked hard to make Sebastian presentable for the ball. To do that, however, the valet had forced some vile concoction down his throat that had him swearing off liquor for the rest of his life.

Miraculously, the foul potion seemed to have worked and he was now sober as stone.

Frankly, Sebastian didn't know if he should fire Robeson or give him a rise.

'It's been a while since I've seen you in your finery, darling,' his mother remarked as he escorted her towards the ballroom. 'You do look so handsome in black and white.'

'And you're ravishing, as always.'

'Thank you. And, darling…?'

'Yes?'

'Thank you for everything.' Her smile seemed to light up the room. 'I know my guests have disturbed your peace.'

Sebastian bit his tongue so he wouldn't ask if she

knew anything about one particular guest and her possible engagement to a certain duke. Thankfully, Eames
announced their arrival before he could speak, and they
headed to the middle of the dance floor to open the ball.

When they were in position, Eames nodded to the
orchestra's conductor and they began their dance.

'Are you looking for someone, darling?' his mother
asked, lifting a brow quizzically.

'Looking for someone?'

'Yes. Your eyes are roving the room, I thought perhaps there was someone you were hoping to find?'

'I was simply wondering who you had invited. Apologies. I have been too busy and didn't look over the guest
list.' He focused his attention on the dance steps, hoping
his mother would accept his explanation.

When the dance finally ended, he bowed to his
mother, then escorted her to the side of the room, where
a group of their neighbours had congregated.

For the next hour, Sebastian did his duty and stayed
by his mother's side, engaging in conversation and dancing with a few matrons. This 'small' ball was much
larger than he'd anticipated, and while he used his time
whirling around the dance floor to search amongst the
guests, he hadn't spied Kate nor Seagrave yet.

It was as he led his latest dance partner back to her
husband that he saw the Duke escorting Kate to the
dance floor for a quadrille. He couldn't take his eyes off
her. Kate looked even lovelier tonight, in a green satin
ballgown, her mahogany hair pinned in curls around
her head, her creamy skin glowing under the light of
the chandelier.

His jaw hardened as the couple took their positions.
Unable to stop himself, he watched them like a hawk,
each smile and whisper making his ire grow.

Finally, the dance finished, and Kate and Seagrave walked to the corner where the DeVries ladies were waiting. He excused himself from his current companions and strode over to the group.

'Good evening, Seagrave…ladies.'

'Mabury,' the Duke greeted him. 'Splendid ball tonight. It seems half the county is here.'

'It was all my mother's work.'

His gaze fixed on Kate. The low neckline of her dress displayed her creamy skin and a generous amount of décolletage. He couldn't help but remember how she'd tasted, and her soft mewls as he'd suckled on her nipples.

'Your Grace, are you ready for your next dance?' Caroline batted her eyelashes at him. 'Because I am.'

'Indeed, I am ready.' Sebastian cleared his throat. 'Miss Mason, may I have the honour of the next dance?'

'I'm afraid I'm otherwise occupied, Your Grace,' she answered in a sweet tone.

'With whom?' Seagrave asked. 'You said your dance card was completely empty until I asked you.'

A flash of exasperation crossed her face, but she held out her hand anyway. 'Thank you, I would love to, Your Grace.'

Taking her hand, Sebastian led her to the dance floor. When a waltz was announced, she flinched. Sebastian, on the other hand, relished the closeness the dance required.

He slid his hand around her waist and pulled her to him. 'Put your hand on my shoulder.'

She did as he asked, but turned her head away as the dance began.

Undeterred, he continued. 'How lovely you look tonight, Kate.'

'Just because we are dancing, it does not mean we must talk.' She craned her head further away from him.

He leaned down, dangerously close to her ear. 'That's quite all right, because all I need is for you to listen.' She stiffened in his arms. 'Once our waltz is over I will escort you back to Seagrave and your friends. When the next dance finishes you will make up some excuse and meet me in the library.'

Her eyes snapped up to meet his gaze. 'I will do no such thing.'

'Yes, you will.' He lowered his voice. 'If you do not, I shall tell Seagrave that there is a possibility you are carrying my child.'

'You wouldn't dare!' she breathed.

'Would you like to put me to the test, Kate?'

Her plump lips pressed tight as she seemed to contemplate her choices. 'All right.'

'Good.'

The rest of the dance went by in silence, but he couldn't help the satisfaction he felt, holding her close in his arms. It seemed like a lifetime ago that she had been in his embrace.

When the music ended, she curtseyed to him and he led her back to the side of the room. 'Remember what we talked about.'

'Yes, Your Grace,' she mumbled.

'Thank you for the dance,' he announced loudly to her group. 'If you would excuse me, Seagrave, ladies? I think I see my mother waving at me. I must fulfil my duty as host.'

With a final nod, he turned on his heel and disappeared into the throng of guests. He greeted a few people, chatted with some long-time neighbours, and once the current dance was halfway done slipped out of the ballroom and made his way to the library.

Inside, he lit a few of the gas lamps, then settled on one of the chairs by the large oak table in the middle. Anticipation thrummed in his veins, and when the audible click of the door echoed through the empty room he got to his feet.

Kate emerged from out of the shadows, her arms stiff at her sides as she marched towards him with a determined stride. 'Tell me what this foolishness is about this instant.'

While the thought of riling her further tempted him, he decided he'd waited long enough. 'Your father is arriving in the morning.'

'So?'

'What convenient timing—considering he has not come for a visit these past weeks. Tell me, has Seagrave finally found the courage to ask his permission to court you? Or perhaps something has happened in the last five days to give him reason to speak to your father?'

'I beg your pardon!' she spluttered. 'What are you implying?'

'What do you think I'm implying?'

Her eyes narrowed into razor-sharp slits. 'How dare you imply that I would…? Seagrave is a complete gentleman and would never try anything untoward.'

That knot that had seemed permanently lodged in his throat since that afternoon loosened. *She hadn't slept with Seagrave.* Not yet, anyway.

'Then what are his intentions? Did you summon your father here? Did he?'

'Ha!' Her hands flung in the air. 'As if Arthur Mason could be *summoned* by anyone. For your information, my father wrote to *tell* me that he would be coming to Highfield Park.'

Ah, so it was a mere coincidence.

'But if you must know,' she said snidely, 'His Grace does intend to ask permission to court me.'

'He will do no such thing. What if you are carrying my child?'

'If His Grace wishes to speak with my father then that is out of my control. Besides, we agreed to wait until we are certain that I am… I am…in that way.'

'I don't recall agreeing to anything.'

'Before I left, I said the discussion was over.'

'I recall saying it was not,' he countered. 'Tell me, Kate, is your plan to string Seagrave along until he is so in love with you that he would marry you even with another man's child in your belly? Or perhaps you are going to sleep with him during your courtship so he has no choice?'

'You rotten scoundrel of a—'

'Tell me what your grand scheme is, then! What is the purpose of all this deception?' His fists slammed on the tabletop behind her, making her start. 'Make me understand why you would lower yourself to marry a man who's not worthy of you. Why are you hiding your intelligence, Kate? No—' He held up a hand when she opened her mouth. 'I'm not a feather brain like Seagrave. I know you are clever and skilled, despite your obvious attempts to conceal your knowledge. You helped rebuild that wall and you repaired that boiler by yourself. Do you love Seagrave so much that you would pretend to be stupid just so you can marry him?'

Her eyes grew wide, and her lower lip trembled. 'N-no.'

'Then tell me why!' His frustration made his entire body tense like a wound coil. Because the truth he didn't want to say aloud was ready to burst out: he would move heaven and earth and give his very soul to the Devil to stop her from marrying Seagrave.

The muscles in her throat bobbed as she swallowed hard. 'It's not what you think.'

Tension seeped away from his muscles as he recognised the look of defeat in her eyes. Now was the time to push further. 'Then tell me, Kate.'

'I'm not in love with Seagrave.'

'Why lie to me, then?'

'I didn't lie to you. You came to that conclusion on your own.'

His thoughts went back to that day in the orangery furnace. *'So you do believe in love.'* She hadn't confirmed or denied it. 'Why let me keep on believing you wanted a love match, then?'

'It just seemed simpler.' She bit her lip. 'I need to get married to a titled lord or...'

'Or what?'

'Or my father will force me to marry my second cousin Jacob, and I can't let that happen!' She drew herself up to her full height. 'I told you about my grandfather and Mason R&L. After he passed away, I took over the management of the company. So when my father brought me here I thought he meant for me to start our England factory, like we've been discussing for the past year.' She let out a rueful snort. 'But I was made a fool; he never intended me to run a factory here—or any factory. He brought me here so I could find a lord to marry. See, he hasn't had any luck starting Mason R&L in England because he can't even get his foot in the door. My marriage to a lord would help smooth things over in Parliament and allow him to acquire the land he needs to build lines for the railway. Should that plan fail, then he'll marry me off to my cousin.' A fire blazed in her eyes. 'And if that happens that vile man will destroy everything my grandfather built. All Jacob wants is to take the credit and reap the rewards without doing any of the hard work.'

He searched her eyes and face for any signs of deception and found none.

'So, you see, that's why I have to marry Seagrave,' she stated fervently. 'To protect my grandfather's legacy. I want to see his name live on for ever, even if it means having the Duke spend my dowry on his estate and horses. I would rather fulfil my role as his wife and never work on an engine again than have Pap's hard work destroyed. I owe Pap that much.'

So, that's what it is.

She wasn't looking for a love match. No, she needed a powerful name and a title to enable her father to gain a foothold in the English railway business and dissuade him from marrying her off to her cousin. All to protect the name and legacy of the man who'd raised her.

Now, those things he could give her.

'Marry me, Kate.'

'Wh-what?' Her jaw dropped.

'Marry me.' He moved closer. 'Marry me and you'll have everything you want. I'll use my influence in Parliament to make sure your father's railway lines are approved. Your dowry will be put in trust for you to use however you please. You can pour it back into the factory. I don't care. I have no need of it. Nor will I do anything to destroy your grandfather's legacy or name. We'll call the factory whatever you wish.' A thought occurred to him, as he remembered how brilliant she was at engineering. 'And once it's built, you can even design your own locomotive.'

Her expression shifted. 'My own engine... I've always wanted to... How did you know...?'

There it was. The spark of interest in her eyes. He had no doubt she could create an engine of her own. 'Spend all day working at the factory if you wish.'

As long as you spend your nights with me.

'But what about your vow to never marry?' she asked. 'I will not force a man to do something he doesn't want to do.'

'Forget I said it.' Desperation clawed at him. 'Forget every damned word I said about not marrying. Besides, there could already be a child on the way.'

'We're not sure yet. I could still get Seagrave—'

'Damn bloody Seagrave to hell!' he roared. When Kate shrank bank, he immediately regretted it. 'Kate, please...'

This time, she pursed her lips and crossed her arms over her chest. 'You brought me here and forced me to reveal my plan, and now you're telling me to forget you ever said you didn't want to marry? Are you a liar, Your Grace? Did you lie to me about not wanting to marry? Or are you lying to me now, with your proposal?'

'No,' he said through gritted teeth. 'I wasn't lying then and I'm not lying now.'

'But the two concepts conflict with each other. You shouldn't have to marry me—'

'That's not the point.' He raked his fingers through his hair. 'Kate, when I said those things to you I didn't know... I hadn't thought...'

'Hadn't thought what?'

Sweat beaded on Sebastian's forehead as he tried

not to let the memories come back. But perhaps telling her the truth was the only way she would understand.

A heartbeat passed before he began. 'When I was a child, I absolutely adored my father. He doted on me, and I thought him to be the most wonderful man on earth. Then, when I grew up, I realised who he really was...' Swallowing hard, he fought the tightness in his throat to continue. 'I realised that when he died five years ago.'

She reached out and placed a gloved hand on his cheek. 'I'm so sorry.'

The touch soothed him, so he covered her hand with his, closed his eyes, and focused on the warmth of her palm through the silk. 'I'm not. It turns out he wasn't the most wonderful man on earth. He was a wastrel who let the estate decline. It was barely surviving when I inherited the Dukedom. But worst of all was what he did to my mother.'

Kate gasped. 'Did he...hurt her?'

His grip on her hand tightened. 'He did not strike her, but he might as well have. You see, he died during a fight in a brothel. Turns out that after my mother gave birth to me he decided he was done with her. Made his way through every brothel in London and perhaps most of England, too. She never said a word about it, and I was too blinded by my adoration for him to know any better. I think she hid it from me because she saw how much I loved him.'

'You were a child,' she whispered. 'You didn't need to know that.'

'Maybe I should have,' he said bitterly. 'Then I would have seen the truth. That she loved him so much and so deeply that it drove her to drink a whole bottle of laudanum in an attempt to take her own life.'

'Oh, no.' Kate's face turned completely ashen. 'You were the one who found her, weren't you?'

It hurt to breathe, but he continued. 'Mrs Grover, the housekeeper, had fallen while reaching for some linens on a top shelf, so a doctor was already at Highfield Park. Had Dr Hanson arrived a minute later she would have died that day. She survived, but barely, and she hasn't been the same since. The scandal and the gossip drove her away from society, and she's kept herself locked up for the last five years.'

Taking her hand away from his face, he placed her arm back down at her side.

'She survived death, but that didn't mean she came back to life. She withdrew from public life, then eventually moved to Hertfordshire. And I know it was because she couldn't stand being here, in the home she had shared with her husband, and being with the son who reminded her so much of him. From that moment on, I promised myself I would never be like my father. I did everything in my power to undo everything he'd done by working on the estate and restoring it. But that didn't seem enough. I knew I couldn't let the cycle perpetuate, so I also vowed never to marry or have offspring, so that no woman would have to suffer the same fate as my mother.'

'I see.' She stepped back and leaned against the oak table. 'Then why ask me to marry you? What would you get out of it if you don't even want an heir? Our match wouldn't be advantageous for you.'

Why did it feel as if she were slipping through his fingers? No, he would not let that happen.

'When this…situation between us arose, I came to a conclusion. You have an honourable reason for getting married and, like me, you don't believe in love, which

means you won't become like my mother,' he reasoned.
'Also, I've heard about your father. Anything Arthur
Mason touches turns to gold, and I would profit hand-
somely if I went into business with him. Should we
produce an heir, then that will be an additional benefit,
but not a requirement. I already have an heir—a distant cousin, who would inherit the title. But don't you
see, Kate? Our marriage will be a mutually beneficial
arrangement, which is much better than one built on
something as unsteady as sand, like love.'

For a moment, he thought he saw hesitation in her
eyes, but then she said, 'Yes, Sebastian. I will marry
you.'

Thank God.

Feeling emboldened, he leaned down to her ear. This
close, he could smell her wonderful scent.

She moaned when his lips clamped over that spot
under her ear. She braced her palms on his chest, then
moved them up to his shoulders.

Dear God, he'd missed this. Missed her touch, her
taste, her scent. He nibbled at that spot until she was
melting against him. Sliding his hands into her hair, he
pulled her back so he could kiss those luscious lips. Immediately, she opened to him and he dipped his tongue
to savour her sweetness. He could take her here, right
now. Make love to her on top of the table and say to hell
with the ball. To hell with the entire world.

However, she pulled away. 'We can't…not here.'

'Of course.' Reluctantly, he released her.

'What do we do now?' She took a step away from
him. 'We need to get back to the ball before someone
discovers we're missing.' Her hand went to her chest.
'Think of the scandal…'

Frankly, he didn't care what anyone thought, but she

was right. 'Will you wait here a moment?' He knew what he had to do. 'I'll take care of this.'

She nodded. 'Of course.'

Walking past her, Sebastian strode out of the library and made his way back to the ballroom. He stopped the first footman who passed by and whispered instructions. The footman bowed and scurried away. A mere moment later, the footman came back, his mother trailing behind.

'Sebastian?' Lines of worry wrinkled her brow. 'Dalton says you require my assistance. What's the matter? Has something happened?'

'Thank you, Dalton,' he said, dismissing the footman. 'I do require your assistance, Mother.'

Before she could ask anything else, he guided her back to the library by the elbow.

'Sebastian, why are we in the—?' She gasped when she saw Kate inside. She looked back to Sebastian. 'Are you trying to ruin Miss Mason's reputation? Taking her in here with no chaperone?'

'I'm sorry, Your Grace.' Kate covered her face with her hands. 'I didn't—'

'I wasn't trying to ruin Miss Mason, Mother,' he stated. 'I was trying to convince her to marry me.'

'You were trying to—what?' For the first time in his life—and probably hers—his mother looked completely flabbergasted. 'Oh. *Oh.*' She took in a sharp inhalation of breath. 'And did you say yes?' she asked Kate.

'Of course she did.'

Kate shot him a rueful look, but answered, 'Yes, I did, Your Grace.'

'That is…wonderful news!' The Dowager Duchess clasped her hands together.

Sebastian hadn't even thought of what his mother

might say about his relationship with Kate, but her wholehearted approval was nonetheless a welcome reaction. 'Thank you.'

'My dear…' Coming closer, she took Kate's hands in hers. 'I never thought…' Her eyes shone with tears. 'I was hoping he would…and you… Oh, no.' Her face fell. 'Seagrave… I thought— I mean, Miss Merton said that he was on the cusp of asking your father for permission to court you. Was she wrong?'

'Ah, yes.' Kate's shoulders sank. 'Right… This was… unexpected.'

Sensing her embarrassment, Sebastian draped an arm around her shoulders. 'But not completely out of the blue. I saw Miss Mason from across the room at the Houghton Ball. It was there that I became acquainted with her.' That part was true. 'I couldn't stop thinking about her afterwards.' Also true. 'And then, to my surprise, she turned out to be your guest. You could say that I've been keeping my feelings hidden because… because of my initial request to you about not involving me with your matchmaking schemes.'

Yes, that was it. He congratulated himself on coming up with such a brilliant explanation on the spot.

'I am a duchess, Sebastian. I do not *scheme,*' she said haughtily. 'And so all this time…?'

'Yes, all this time.'

He sent her a warm smile and pulled Kate closer, hoping it would be enough to convince his mother that this was not merely a case of unwarranted lust.

'And Seagrave's attentions spurred you to take action?'

'It wasn't my intention to use the Duke to make Sebastian jealous,' Kate said quickly.

'Of course not,' Sebastian assured her.

'My feelings for Seagrave were genuine.'

'Yes, I'm sure they were.'

'He is an honourable man, and I would be lucky to—'

'That's enough, darling.' He gave her shoulders a squeeze. 'I believe what Kate is trying to say is that she was unsure of my intentions as I had given her no indication of my feelings for her.'

She bit her lower lip. 'I must tell the Duke… He was to speak with my father tomorrow.'

'There, there, dear.' The Dowager Duchess patted her hand. 'It will be all right. The poor man was besotted with you, but I'm sure he'll take the news with grace.'

'I shall speak with him as soon as possible,' Kate said.

'A capital idea.' Sebastian tightened his grip on her shoulders. 'Mother, would you be so kind as to find Seagrave and escort him here?'

'Here?' Kate exclaimed, shrugging his arm off. 'Have you lost your mind?'

'You think I would allow my future wife to speak to another man alone?' he thundered. 'If so, then you are the one who has lost your mind.'

'Why, I—'

The Dowager Duchess tsked. 'Now, now, lovebirds. Calm yourselves. I shall bring the Duke post-haste.'

'Thank you, Mother.'

'But he and Kate will speak out in the corridor and, Sebastian, you will stay in here.'

'Here? I think not. What if—?'

She held a hand up. 'I shall ensure they are properly chaperoned. No more arguments.'

'But—'

'I said, no more arguments,' the Dowager Duchess

declared. 'Now, darling, try not to maul Miss Mason before I get back?'

However, Sebastian could have sworn he saw the corners of her lips lift before she turned and left the room.

'What in heaven's name were you thinking?' Kate whacked him on the shoulder with her palm. 'Coming up with that…that lie about the Houghton Ball?'

'Lie?' he asked. 'Tell me, what falsehoods did I tell my mother? I did see you across the room at the Houghton Ball and we did make each other's acquaintance that night.'

'And what about…about…?' The loveliest blush stained her cheeks. 'The part about not being able to stop thinking about me?'

He answered her by planting his hands on her waist and drawing her closer. 'Who said that was untrue?'

She shivered visibly, but then pushed away from him. 'Sebastian, why are you making it appear as if this is a love match? I thought that was the last thing you wanted?'

A strange twinge plucked at his chest at her words. 'Because…because I am trying to preserve your reputation. And my mother's,' he added quickly. 'Your father sent you here under her protection. What would he say if he found out I'd swooped in like some predator to seduce you?'

She let out a rather unladylike snort. 'He doesn't give a whit about my reputation or whom I marry, as long as my future husband is able to advance his business interests.'

For some reason he found himself getting unreasonably angry with this man he'd never met. 'In any case, I was also doing it to protect you from the wagging tongues of the ton. They're already going to gossip because I want us to marry as soon as possible. In one month.'

'One month? But that won't leave us time for courting, and then a proposal, plus all the preparations...'

'One month,' he said firmly. 'The sooner we marry, the sooner we can come back from our honeymoon and begin the construction of your factory. If we delay any longer, we might have to wait until Parliament reconvenes after the summer. Besides, you might already be with child. Think of the scandal if the child is born too soon after our wedding.'

She seemed to contemplate that. 'All right, then.'

Thank goodness she was American, and not familiar with the prevalence of 'premature' babies amongst the newlyweds of the ton, most born eight, seven, or even six months from the wedding night while still being suspiciously healthy. Since the couples were already safely shackled anyway, even the most notorious of gossips didn't think that kind of news juicy enough to spread.

'Come, Kate.' He planted a soft, innocent kiss on her lips and let his hand drift to her waist. 'Tomorrow I shall speak to your father, and all will be well.' He led her towards the door. 'Now you must let your erstwhile beau—' Lord, his mouth turned sour even as he said that word '—know about this turn of events.'

Snatching Kate away from Seagrave should have left him feeling completely triumphant. And his plan to have a marriage based on business interests and mutual needs should allay his fears that Kate might end up like his mother. He would at least ensure that she would never worry for money for the rest of her life and that she would have her factory. And as long as they felt nothing except lust for each other he needn't worry, even if he did become like the man he hated.

* * *

Kate was still in a state of shock as Sebastian led her out into the corridor. This was not where she'd expected the events of tonight would lead.

He planted a kiss on her temple. 'I'll be just inside the library, so do not fret.'

'I'm not fretting,' she retorted.

'Then why the frown on your pretty face?'

She pursed her lips together. 'It's just… I worked so hard to even get Seagrave to approach my father, and—'

'How hard, exactly?' he asked, an edge to his voice.

'Oh, please, there is no need to feign jealousy—your mother isn't around. But I do owe him an explanation. Maybe—'

The sound of approaching footsteps made her halt. Her chest tightened and dizziness came over her, as if she were standing on the edge of a cliff. She looked ahead, and as the forms of Seagrave and the Dowager Duchess came closer she thought, *He would be the safe choice.*

It was not too late yet. With Seagrave, she'd know exactly what to expect and how to plan her future. With Sebastian, on the other hand, it would be like starting a project without a blueprint. Or leaping into the unknown and hoping she would not end up broken and battered when she plummeted back to earth.

But everything Sebastian had promised her was too tempting. She could run the factory. Heavens, she'd be able to build her own engine! But, more importantly, Pap's legacy would be safe.

'I think Her Grace has returned.'

He bowed his head and turned on his heel. 'I will give you your privacy.'

She stared after him as he disappeared into the library, but before she could further process what had happened she heard voices coming from the opposite end of the corridor.

'Are you sure she's all right, Your Grace?'

'Yes, Miss Mason is unharmed.'

They're here!

Kate quickly ran a hand over her coiffure and down her bodice, making sure everything was in place. 'Your Grace,' she greeted Seagrave, and then the Dowager Duchess. 'Your Grace. Thank you for your assistance.'

'Of course, Miss Mason. Now, I shall stand over here...to admire these paintings...while you have your little chat.'

The Dowager Duchess turned away from them, then strode a few feet away to stop and look at the picture hanging on the wall.

'Miss Mason?' Seagrave searched her face. 'The Dowager Duchess said you had to speak with me. Are you hurt or ill?'

'I'm quite fine, Your Grace. I just wanted to see you as soon as possible.' Taking a deep breath, Kate considered her words carefully. 'Your Grace, I want you to know that I have truly enjoyed our time together these past weeks.'

'As have I.'

'I am grateful for your attentions, but I must ask that you not speak to my father tomorrow.'

'Not speak to your father?' He gave her a flummoxed look. 'Why not?'

'Because...because I'm afraid I have accepted an offer from another.'

He paused, then blinked twice. 'Oh. I didn't realise you had other suitors.' His shoulders looked deflated. 'Who is he?'

There was no use concealing it from him as he would find out anyway. 'His Grace the Duke of Mabury.' She waited for a violent protest, but none came.

He let out a resigned sigh. 'I should have realised a prize such as you would not be ignored. Perhaps it is my fault that I waited too long. If only I had acted sooner.'

Kate did not know if she should be relieved or vexed that he seemed to accept the news so easily. 'Let's not talk about ifs and buts, Your Grace. It is not your fault. He and I were acquainted before I came to Highfield Park and I found myself...' She scrambled for the appropriate words to say. 'Infatuated with him. But, as you know, the Duke can be quite reserved, and he did not confess his...er...feelings for me until today.'

'I understand.' He patted her hand. 'Your heart had simply been fixed before we met.'

'How...er...perceptive and wise you are, Your Grace.' She was glad he had said it, because she didn't want to lie to him any more than she had to.

He swallowed hard. 'If you would excuse me, Miss Mason? I shall bid goodnight to our hostess and be on my way home.'

'Of course. Goodnight, Your Grace.'

'Goodbye, Miss Mason. I wish you well.' He walked over to the Duchess. 'Your Grace, I thank you for your invitation, but I must cut my evening short. I'm sure you understand.'

'Of course, Your Grace.'

He gave her a deep bow and then walked away, disappearing down the darkened corridor, along with the safe, reliable future Kate had striven for.

'Are you all right, my dear?' asked the Dowager Duchess as she hurried over to Kate. 'I hope you aren't too distressed.'

Kate wasn't sure how to describe how she was feeling at this moment. Relieved? Not quite, as the gravity of her new situation weighed heavily on her. In the morning, her father would arrive, and Sebastian would be speaking to him.

'Is he gone?' Sebastian asked, seemingly manifesting from nowhere.

'Yes, he's gone.'

He frowned. 'Did he cause you worry? Did you argue?'

'No, it's fine. I am just…glad it's over.'

'Well, now…' The Dowager Duchess's smile practically lit up the room. 'It seems we must plan a wedding.'

'Please, Mother.' Sebastian groaned. 'Do control yourself for now. I still have to speak to her father.'

'Pish-posh, let me have this moment,' she teased. 'Don't look at me like that. I know how to keep a secret.'

'Of course you do, Mother.'

'Now, let's go back to the ball before anyone notices our absence.'

'Must we?'

'Yes, we must—for appearances' sake.' The Dowager Duchess shook a finger at him. 'And don't even think about having a midnight rendezvous with Miss Mason.'

'Mother—'

'I am deadly serious. I will not have anyone gossiping about your future duchess.' She cast an apologetic look at Kate. 'Forgive me, my dear, we are being awfully rude…speaking as if you are not here.'

'Not at all, Your Grace.' Her stomach had flipped at the words *future duchess*.

'Now, Sebastian, promise me you won't give anyone cause to speak ill of Kate.'

'Mother, may I remind you that this is my house, and

I will do as I please?' Coming from him, it wasn't a reminder so much as a statement.

'You have said it yourself: you still have to speak to her father.' The Dowager was equally determined. 'Sebastian…?'

'Oh, all right.' His teeth gnashed together. 'I promise.'

'Good.' The Dowager Duchess seemed satisfied. 'Come, now, let us rejoin the guests.'

Looping her arm through Kate's, she pulled her along and they made their way back to the ballroom.

This was it. Her fate was sealed. She was going to be his wife.

This was what she'd wanted, wasn't it? Sebastian wanted to marry her, instead of being forced to marry her. They would be on an equal footing. She would save Pap's legacy, and he would never have to worry about repeating history. This was her choice. Finally.

But there was still something else—something that felt unresolved. And because her logical mind was tuned to solve problems, she just couldn't stop thinking about it.

Her stomach knotted and her nerves felt frayed, as if she stood on the edge of a precipice, facing an unknown future.

Chapter Seventeen

Just as Kate had predicted, convincing her father to accept Sebastian's suit was not difficult. However, being the businessman that he was, Arthur Mason could not resist bargaining, even if the terms already suited him from the onset.

'Never accept the first offer,' he always said.

'So, you want to marry my daughter?'

Arthur Mason's countenance had been cool and collected from the beginning, and he spoke as if he were asking about the price of a hat at the milliner's.

The moment he and Jacob had arrived, early that morning, Eames had immediately ushered her father to Sebastian's private study, where she and the Duke had been waiting.

'If so, should she be here while we discuss this?'

'Yes, I believe that is what I said,' Sebastian replied, equally composed. 'And, seeing as she happens to be the subject of our talk, her presence is required.'

'Shouldn't you be asking my permission to court her first?'

'I should. But why waste my time or yours when we know the outcome will be the same anyway?'

That seemed to mollify her father enough to continue their conversation. Or negotiation.

While Arthur complained about the date of the wedding, and Kate's dowry, Sebastian was just as tough. In the end, Arthur relented on having the wedding in a month, as Sebastian planned, in exchange for a percentage reduction on her dowry, plus an extra seat on the board for someone of Arthur's choosing once the London company was established.

It seemed that at some point the two men had decided to pursue the railway business together, along with their marriage discussion.

'I feel as if I'm a side of beef at the market,' Kate muttered to her new fiancé. 'Did you really have to bargain so hard?'

His mouth turned into a grim line. 'It was he who began the bargaining, Kate. And I would have given him his every demand, except that he acted as if you were an inanimate object. He doesn't know it yet, but you're a great loss to him and the factory back in New York. With you staying here in England, I'll be gaining a brilliant engineer and manager.'

A nagging thought materialised in her mind. 'How can you be sure of that? You've never even seen me on a factory floor.'

What if he decided that her style of management didn't suit him? What if they clashed on the way things would be run?

'I meant what I said when I proposed. While I know how to run an estate and deal with tenants, I won't be able to absorb everything about factories and engines before the ground-breaking. It's obvious to me that you will have to be in charge of everything from the beginning.'

The sincerity in his voice and eyes told Kate that he was telling the truth. Still…

'But you fought my father so hard about retaining your majority ownership of the company. You could have allowed him to invest more of his money, like he offered, and reduced your own personal risk. He would have given you something of value for more control.'

'But that would mean you wouldn't be able to do what you want.' Dark eyes met hers, pinning her to the spot and boring straight into her. 'And he did give me something of value—even if he didn't know it.'

The words made Kate's heart stutter in her chest.

She couldn't quite remember what had happened for the rest of the day, as she'd felt as if she were floating on air. And now here they all were, having refreshments in the parlour during the usual pre-dinner gathering. Sebastian and the Dowager Duchess had yet to arrive, so after introducing her father and Jacob to the other guests Kate stood with Arthur by the window.

'I must admit, Kathryn,' Arthur began, 'you've done much better than I expected.'

And from Arthur Mason that was the best compliment Kate could ever hope for.

'His Grace the Duke of Mabury,' Eames announced. 'And Her Grace the Dowager Duchess of Mabury.'

As everyone bowed and curtseyed, Kate sneaked a glance at Sebastian, who looked devilishly handsome in his evening clothes. When she caught the Dowager Duchess's eye, she sent Kate a knowing smile.

'Good evening, everyone,' Sebastian began. Tonight, only the house guests were dining. 'Allow me to welcome our newest guests to Highfield Park, Mr Arthur Mason and his cousin Mr Jacob Malvery.' He gave them a brief nod of acknowledgment, which they returned. 'Now, before we begin our dinner, I have some news to share with you. Mr Mason, Miss Mason, if you please...?' He held out his hand to them.

Every single pair of eyes was riveted on Kate, leaving her unsettled. But she kept her head held high as her father led her towards Sebastian and the Dowager Duchess.

'After speaking with Mr Mason today, it is with pleasure that I announce my engagement to Miss Kate Mason.'

A stunned silence hung in the air, and the guests' faces held varying degrees of surprise, shock, and befuddlement—except for Jacob, whose face showed no emotion. She guessed her father had already told him about her engagement to Sebastian.

Perhaps he didn't wish to marry me after all.

'That's such wonderful news,' Miss Merton exclaimed, and clapped her hands.

Thankfully, everyone else followed, and surrounded them to offer their congratulations before Eames announced that dinner was served. This time Sebastian led Kate to the head of the table, where she took the highest position after her father. She was glad—not because of the honour it brought, but because she would have time to collect her thoughts before being bombarded by questions from everyone.

When the scrumptious dinner had concluded, the men and women separated as usual. As soon as they arrived in the parlour for tea Eliza dashed towards Kate, dragging Caroline and Maddie behind her.

'Miss Mason, my deepest felicitations on your engagement to His Grace.' She curtseyed low. 'I always knew you would make a great match. And because you are the best and closest friend of my dear daughters, we hope you will welcome us to the many social gatherings you will have once you take residence in London.'

'She's not a duchess yet, Mother.' Caroline's mouth was pressed into a straight line. 'My, my, you've done well for yourself, Kate,' she said, her tone laced with snideness. 'And I thought you had Seagrave wrapped around your little finger, too. What has happened to the poor Duke?'

'We simply decided we weren't suited,' Kate stated.

Caroline lifted an elegant blonde brow. 'And you and Mabury are?' She let out a mocking huff. 'I didn't realise he even knew you existed. After all, why would the bumblebee hover over a daisy when there are so many roses around?'

Before Kate could retort, Eliza interrupted. 'But now the other bumblebee…er…the Duke of Seagrave is unoccupied, perhaps we can ask Her Grace to invite him back to Highfield Park. Or maybe Miss Merton could arrange for us to visit him.'

'Assuming he would even want to associate with more Americans,' Maddie said under her breath.

Caroline's pretty face twisted. 'As if I would take Kate's leavings! I would be a laughing stock back home.'

'Caroline…' Eliza warned. 'Come, I must sit down. My knees are bothering me. Then you can fetch me some tea. Excuse us, Miss Mason.' She sent Kate an apologetic look before dragging her younger daughter away.

Maddie actually chuckled. 'That was absolutely delicious.'

'Hopefully you won't bear the brunt of her anger,' Kate said sympathetically.

Maddie smiled wryly. 'In private, maybe, but Mother won't let her disrespect you—not if she wants to be in your good graces. Caroline may actually have to be nice to me now, seeing as you and I are good friends,' she added with glee.

The rest of the evening continued as they usually did—although Caroline's mood only grew more sour, and she continued to send subtle jabs towards Kate— and not so subtle when Eliza was not within hearing distance. She ignored her as best she could. Especially since, at least for one evening, Maddie wasn't her sister's target.

When the hour grew late, the Dowager Duchess declared she was weary, which was the signal that the evening was over. The ladies retired and went to their separate rooms, and after her maid had helped her out of her dress and into her night rail Kate slid under the covers. She had barely closed her eyes for five minutes when a soft knock came at the door. Had her maid forgotten something?

Climbing out of bed, she trod towards the door. 'Anna? Do you need something?'

No answer.

'Anna…?'

'It's me,' came Sebastian's voice from behind the door. 'Don't make a sound.'

Sebastian? She opened the door a crack and sure enough there he was, standing just outside. 'What are you doing here?'

'What else? A midnight rendezvous.'

'I thought you promised your mother you wouldn't come to my room?'

'I promised to wait to speak to your father,' he countered. 'And now I have.'

She didn't know what to say. On the one hand, her body had started vibrating with need the moment he'd

declared his intentions. After all, they had already
made love before, and another few weeks wouldn't
make a difference. On the other hand, her instinct told
her to be on her guard. While she was seemingly about
to get everything she wished for, and continue Pap's
legacy, there was still something not quite right. Again,
there was a feeling that there were things left unsaid
and unresolved.

'Well? I can go—'

'No!' Reaching for the lapels of his robe, she dragged
him inside. 'I mean…don't go.' She slid her fingers over
the silk material, feeling his hard muscles underneath.
'Stay.'

Perhaps just for tonight she could lose herself in his
embrace and that feeling would go away.

Chapter Eighteen

The room was still dark when Sebastian opened his eyes, but the familiar feeling of dread slid into his stomach like a heavy stone.

'Sebastian?' Kate murmured, her voice rough from sleep. 'Is it time?'

He shut his eyes tight. It was, unfortunately, time. Time to go. However, the press of her warm body against his had him protesting. So he held her tighter and brushed away the hair at the nape of her neck to press a kiss on her soft skin.

'Oh…' She half-moaned, half-yawned. 'Please…'

'Please what?' His hand slid down over her abdomen to the triangle of curls between her thighs.

'Anna will come soon to light the fire.' And yet her legs opened to give him better access. 'You must— Oh!'

His finger slipped into her tight passage, now growing slick with her desire. 'I must what?'

She let out an annoyed grunt, then pushed his hand away. 'Sebastian…' she warned, twisting around to face him.

Though he could only make out the outline of her head, he could picture the admonishing expression on her face. Those cornflower-blue eyes would be narrowed, plump lips pursed together. He let his gaze wander lower, imagining her naked breasts on display.

'Are you ogling me in the dark?' she asked, miffed.

'What do you think?'

That was a rhetorical question, but before she could answer he rolled her onto her back and covered her, rubbing his hardening shaft against her belly.

'Sebastian…' she warned again.

'What? It's been two weeks and we haven't been caught.'

Two glorious weeks of sneaking into her bed each night, exploring every inch of her body. Sebastian had thought that surely, by now, the edge of desire would be dulled. But if anything he wanted more of her. All the time. What Kate lacked in experience she made up for in enthusiasm, and he was eager to keep pushing her limits.

'Haven't been caught *yet*, Sebastian…'

'Oh, all right,' he grumbled.

Despite the fact that he'd had her twice last night, he still wanted her. *Two more weeks*, he told himself. In two weeks they would be man and wife, and he would have access to her any time he wished. They would spend all their nights together. And he'd be able to wake up next to her and watch the morning light…

The idea made him pause. *Wake up next to her?* For the life of him, he couldn't remember ever having done that with a woman. Nor had he ever wanted to. He'd made it a rule always to leave the bed before dawn. He couldn't even recall having breakfast with any previous mistress.

'Sebastian?'

His chest tightened, but he rolled off the bed and reached for his discarded trousers.

'Are you cross about something?' she asked.

'I'm not cross with you, Kate. I am just...' He searched for the right words as he finished buttoning his trousers but could not find them.

'Grumpy?' she offered.

He reached for the candle by the bedside table and lit it. Turning to face her, he let his eyes greedily soak in the sight of her—head propped up on one hand, naked torso aglow in the candlelight, like a half-clothed reclining Venus in one of those scandalous Italian paintings.

'I don't mean to be grumpy.' He leaned down and allowed himself one kiss. Anything more and he would say damn her maid, and damn any potential scandal, and climb back into bed with her. 'It's the lack of sleep, that's all.'

'And whose fault is that?' She chuckled. 'By the way—your mother asked me to remind you that you are to be dressed no later than half past six tonight.'

'Half past six?'

'You've forgotten, haven't you?'

'Er...'

She rolled onto her back, making her breasts jiggle deliciously. 'Tonight is our engagement ball.'

'Ah, right.' *Damn.* 'Why do we need to make an announcement to the ton about our upcoming marriage? Can't we just go straight to the ceremony without all this pomp?'

'I would agree with you,' she said wryly. 'But apparently news of our nuptials has set the ton ablaze. After the wedding, tonight's ball is the most sought-after invitation of the Season, despite being miles away from town. Besides, aren't you looking forward to seeing your friends?'

'I have no friends.'

'What about the Marquess of Ashbrooke?'

'Unfortunately, he is the only one who has declined the invitation.'

Ash had begged off, saying that he was occupied that night. *God knows with what.* But the Marquess had promised to be his best man for the wedding, despite the fact that Sebastian hadn't actually asked him to fulfil such a role.

'What do you mean, you don't have friends?' She frowned at him.

'I don't have any real friends. Not the kind who would be happy for me.' As sad as that sounded, it was the truth. He didn't know anyone who truly cared about him who would come to celebrate his triumphs.

'Who are all these people coming to the wedding, then?'

Sebastian scoffed. 'The same people who spread all the nasty gossip about the old Duke five years ago. If I had my way, none of them would be invited at all, but then it would be a very small party.'

'Sebastian,' she began, placing a hand over his, 'we don't have to invite any of those people to the wedding.'

'Unfortunately, we do, as we will need many of those peers on our side once Mason R&L begins the process of applying for permits for its railway lines.'

'Are you sure?'

'Absolutely. In any case, it doesn't matter. There are other things to worry about. And I promise I will be dressed on time. My mother has surely conspired with Robeson anyway. Now, try to get some sleep.'

'Mmm-hmm,' she murmured drowsily, then hugged a pillow to her torso and closed her eyes.

After he'd finished dressing, he allowed himself one last glance at her beautiful form and committed it to memory, hoping the image would be enough to sate him until tonight.

As he made his way back to his rooms, his mind clicked onto the business of the day. He had a meeting with Arthur Mason after breakfast about plans for building the factory, which might possibly run on until early afternoon.

One might think that after spending two weeks with him Sebastian would have got to know his future father-in-law better. But he still didn't have a clue who the real Arthur Mason truly was—the person, not the industrial magnate. When he'd mentioned this to Kate she had merely scoffed and told him that the hard-nosed business-man *was* the real Arthur Mason. And after a fortnight of discussions and meetings Arthur had yet to even enquire about the wedding plans or his daughter's future as Se-bastian's duchess, prompting him to think Kate was right.

While he found Arthur's treatment of Kate appall-ing, he could see why her father was the successful businessman he was today. Whip-smart and completely ruthless, Arthur Mason did not stop until he'd got what he wanted. He rather reminded him of Kate and her determination to save her grandfather's legacy, though without the bloodthirsty edge. Sebastian guessed that had Kate been born a man she would have taken her fa-ther's place in his empire. Unfortunately, Arthur's clos-est male relation was Jacob Malvery.

Sebastian's mood darkened, as it always did when his thoughts turned to Malvery. While it was unjustifiable to abhor a man on sight, Jacob Malvery had nonethe-less elicited from him only feelings of intense loathing. Malvery was a spineless sycophant, whose one skill in life was to obey his rich cousin's orders like a trained dog. He now understood why Kate would have preferred someone like Seagrave over being married to Malvery.

When Sebastian reached his suite and entered Robeson was already there, choosing his clothes for the morning. The valet didn't bat an eye at his dishevelled state.

'Good morning, Your Grace,' he greeted him in his usual serious tone. 'Shall I fetch your paper and your coffee, or would you like to nap for half an hour first?'

The man didn't even have the decency to pretend not to have seen Sebastian sneaking into the room, or that he didn't know his master had been out all night.

'Coffee would be fine. Thank you, Robeson,' he said, dismissing the valet.

As soon as he was alone he began to strip, but stopped halfway as he lifted his shirt over his head. A lingering trace of Kate's scent tickled his senses and brought back memories from last night. He'd been so eager for Kate that he hadn't even bothered to remove all his clothes. He'd pushed her up against the door and unbuttoned his trousers, lifted her nightgown out of the way and made love to her.

He dropped his hands to his sides. *Made love to her?* he scoffed. He'd never called it that before. Not with anyone. Yet he couldn't bring himself to use the typical words for the sexual act with Kate. *Screwing. Tupping. Diddling.* Somehow the thought of those words made him irrationally angry.

Idiot, he told himself. They were just words. Many words had different meanings. And what had transpired between them had no meaning at all. It was just an act between two people—a release for their pent-up energies.

Surely after the wedding the newness of their sexual congress would wear away...like the polish on a pair of new shoes. He reminded himself that their marriage was a mutually beneficial business arrangement. His estate would be enriched further with the profits from the railway company. And once the factory was running she would be preoccupied with its day-to-day business and designing her own engine.

The thought that she wouldn't share her days with him made him regret the bargain they'd struck. While before he hadn't been able to fathom being with the same person day in and day out, now the thought of being away from Kate made him feel lost and lonely.

But if he tried to stop her from running the factory that would surely make her unhappy, and he couldn't have that. Kate couldn't end up like his mother. She was brilliant and beautiful. And he didn't deserve to have her all to himself.

Chapter Nineteen

Though Kate knew that today was the day of her engagement ball, the reality of it didn't quite solidify in
her mind until she saw herself in the mirror dressed in
her new gown—a gorgeous blue-grey concoction made
of silk and taffeta. The low neckline and bodice were
trimmed in delicate French lace, while the full skirt fea-
tured flounces on the bottom half that revealed a darker
layer of silk underneath.

'A perfect fit, Miss Mason,' exclaimed the dressmaker,
Mrs Ellesmore, as she turned Kate around to face the
mirror. 'We don't even need to make any adjustments.'

'Oh, Kate, how marvellous you look.' The Dowager
Duchess's smile was reflected in the mirror. 'You're a
genius with fabrics and sewing, Mrs Ellesmore,' the
Dowager said. 'Thank you again for entertaining us
at such short notice. I know this is the busiest time of
year for you.'

'Anything for you, Your Grace,' she fawned. 'It is my
honour to create Miss Mason's engagement dress and
her wedding gown.'

'I am also very grateful that you've agreed to come

to Surrey to make all the arrangements instead of having us travel to your shop on Bond Street.'

'My pleasure, Your Grace.'

With what Sebastian was paying her she could probably afford to set up shop in Highfield Park for the rest of the month, Kate thought wryly. And, of course, the dressmaker would become even more sought-after now that she was making the future Duchess of Mabury's trousseau.

But Sebastian had wanted the best dressmaker in London, and Mrs Helena Ellesmore was the best of the best.

Mrs Ellesmore offered Kate a hand and helped her off the dais. 'My assistant will press and hang the dress for you. She will also remain here to assist you before tonight's ball, as I must be off back to London. Is there anything else you'd like to discuss before I leave?'

Kate shook her head. 'I don't have any changes since the last time we spoke. Your Grace, do you have anything to add?'

'No, no...' The Dowager Duchess strode over to her, the sunny smile still on her face. 'It is your wedding. Please do not let me interfere.'

'Not at all.' Kate chuckled. 'I'm afraid out of everyone here I'm the least experienced in this particular field. Your Grace, surely you have some advice to give? Did you have nerves on your wedding day?'

The Dowager's smile faltered for just a second, but Kate noticed it. 'I'm sure you'll do just fine, dear.'

A feeling of dread formed in Kate's stomach. *Why did I bring up her wedding day?* The Dowager Duchess didn't need any reminder of her failed marriage or her bastard of a husband.

'Well, then, let's get you undressed, Miss Mason.'

Mrs Ellesmore helped her out of the dress and into her lavender morning gown. When she emerged from behind the screen Kate could still feel the strain in the air. She hated that feeling—couldn't stand it.

I must make things right and apologise.

'Your Grace, if you're not busy, may I have a private word?'

The older woman paused. 'Of course. Why don't we go to the orangery? It's quite lovely there in the mornings.'

They bade goodbye to Mrs Ellesmore and made their way outside into the gardens and to the orangery.

'This is my favourite time of year in here.' The Dowager inhaled the humid, loamy scent in the air then turned to her. 'Now, Kate— Oh! Do you mind if I call you that?'

'Not at all, Your Grace.'

'Thank you, Kate. And you know you may call me Mama after the wedding. If you would like to.'

Mama. The word sounded strange, even in Kate's mind.

'Or not,' the Dowager Duchess added quickly.

'Oh, no––please don't think I don't want to,' she assured the Duchess. 'It's just that I've never called anyone that in my entire life. My mother died in childbirth.'

The Dowager Duchess took her hand and squeezed it. 'I am so sorry.'

'It was a long time ago; I don't remember her.' And that was the truth. It was difficult to mourn a woman she hadn't even known. 'I was raised by my grandfather.'

'And what a lucky man he was, having such a granddaughter as you.' A few beats of silence went by before the Dowager Duchess spoke again. 'Kate, dear, what is it that you want to speak with me about?'

Oh, right. Maybe she could still salvage the situation if she chose her words carefully.

'I couldn't help but notice that when I asked you about your wedding day, you seemed…sad.' Kate took a deep breath. 'If I said or did anything to offend you, I apologise.'

The Dowager Duchess's expression turned inscrutable. 'What has my son told you about his father?'

'He…mentioned he had passed away five years ago.'

'And?'

Oh, Lord, what else was she supposed to say? Should she tell the Dowager what Sebastian had confessed to her? It was such a private matter. Perhaps she should lie. Pretend not to know anything else and save them from embarrassment.

The older woman's complexion turned pale as she read Kate's silence. 'He has told you everything. No need to deny it, my dear. I can see it on your face.'

Blast it, I've mucked it all up.

'Forgive me, Your Grace.' Embarrassment made her want to run away. 'We needn't speak of it.'

'So, you know what happened. With his father. And what I did afterwards.' Recovering quickly, the Dowager tucked Kate's hand into her arm. 'But not the entire story. At least, not my side.' The Dowager Duchess led her deeper into the orangery. 'When we met, Charles completely swept me off my feet. I fell so deeply in love with him I even threw away a chance at…' She shook her head. 'Let's just say that I gave up something very important to me. We were happy for a few years. But… Well, it turned out that I didn't know my husband as well as I thought.'

They stopped in front of the fountain located in the middle of the orangery, and the gurgling sound of the water filled in the long pause.

'I'd long suspected he was unfaithful to me, but I didn't say a word. I didn't even want to admit it to myself.'

The awkwardness grew heavier than the humidity in

the air. 'Forgive me, Your Grace,' said Kate. 'You don't have to continue.'

'But I must.' The Dowager's head snapped back to her. 'You need to hear this.' Those dark eyes, so familiar, captured her gaze. 'So you can understand.'

'Understand?' she echoed.

'After his father died, Sebastian changed. He had always been a precocious child, but growing up he was easy-going and carefree, with a devil-may-care attitude. Very much like his father.'

Kate couldn't imagine Sebastian as the Dowager had described him. That person seemed the exact opposite of the man she knew.

Her future mother-in-law continued. 'He had no idea what Charles was really like. I thought I was being a good mother, trying to hide his father's flaws. Sebastian loved him so much, you see... I should have told Sebastian, but... Anyway, Charles's death affected him deeply and I don't think Sebastian has fully recovered. I'm partly to blame, too, because these last five years...' A vacant expression took over her face. 'I was too swallowed up by my own grief to see that my son had turned into a hard, bitter man.' She paused. 'This match between the two of you... I know there's more to it than you are telling me. And I'm happy with that. I just hope...'

Kate held her breath. Was the Dowager Duchess going to tell her she didn't approve of her as Sebastian's wife? Perhaps she'd decided Kate's social standing was too low or her money too new. Or maybe she thought Kate would be unfaithful to Sebastian, like his father had been to her. Her stomach tied into knots at the thought of all of the things the Dowager Duchess might object to.

'I hope...you give him a chance.'

Now, *that* Kate hadn't expected. 'A chance?'

'Yes.' The Dowager Duchess smiled warmly at her. 'I think you are the best thing to have happened to him. The fact that he has confided in you fills me with much confidence. And while I'm proud of what he's accomplished—restoring everything his father lost and growing it tenfold—I would rather have my carefree son back.' The line between her eyebrows deepened. 'Now, I haven't told you all this so you will pity him—or me. But I think he believes that he is incapable of anything more with you than just an amicable partnership. Because he's afraid.'

'Afraid of what?'

'Of getting too close to someone. Of emotional intimacy. I suspect he doesn't want what…what happened to me to happen to him.' She took Kate's hands in hers and squeezed them. 'But now you've given me something to look forward to. Given me hope that maybe you can help bring back my old Sebastian.'

Kate wasn't sure how to respond to that. But, looking at the Dowager Duchess's face, she couldn't dash the other woman's hopes with the truth: that she and Sebastian had agreed their marriage would be one that was merely mutually beneficial.

The Dowager Duchess thought that Sebastian confiding in her meant his cold façade was melting. That he was ready to bring down the walls he'd erected after his father's death and his mother's attempted suicide. But Kate had a feeling that wasn't true.

If there had ever been a major problem at the factory she and Pap had always found a quick fix to prevent the production line from completely halting and putting them behind schedule. However, a patch here or a fastener there had only temporarily assuaged the situation. No, they'd had to find the cause of the problem and solve it—or else it might turn into a disaster.

Perhaps humans weren't very different.

But what did it matter to Kate, anyway? Theirs would be a marriage of convenience. It would be better that Sebastian didn't think he was capable of any emotional entanglement. And perhaps it was time that she started guarding her heart around him—because it would be so easy to fall in love with someone like him.

Fall in love? she chided herself. *Don't be ridiculous.* Love had no place in their arrangement.

The Dowager Duchess's face crumpled. 'Oh, dear, I haven't upset you, have I?'

'What—? Oh, no, not at all,' she said reassuringly.

'Excellent.' The Dowager Duchess straightened her shoulders. 'Come, let's see how the trees are doing, shall we?'

Swallowing the growing lump in her throat, Kate smiled and nodded.

'Oh, it's so beautiful!' Maddie exclaimed as she looked around the ballroom. 'The Dowager Duchess has really outdone herself.'

Kate would have replied with her agreement, except her breath had been taken away by the marvellous sight before her. The ballroom had already been an opulent space, with its polished wooden floors, glittering crystal chandeliers, and walls decorated with intricately carved twisting vines and leaves in bronze with a gold trim, but now it was a magnificent fairy-tale wonderland.

Potted trees and shrubs from the orangery were dispersed across the room. Cream and gold-coloured bunting intertwined with gauzy white fabric hung from the ceiling. A sixteen-piece orchestra played while the footmen, donned in their finest livery, roamed around as they offered guests titbits and refreshments.

'Kate, who are all these people?' Maddie asked.

Remembering what Sebastian had said that morning about his guests made Kate's blood boil. *Snakes. Scandalmongers. Sycophants.* Clearing her throat, she said, 'Mostly other peers from London.'

Everyone tonight was beautifully dressed and turned out. And every single one of them had their gazes fixed on Kate and her father as soon as they were announced.

On the surface, they were all polite, even enthusiastic about being introduced to them, but she could already guess what they were thinking: who was this American heiress who'd managed to bag one of the most coveted bachelors in England?

Kate didn't care much for these vile people, and didn't even bother to remember their names. Her father, of course, seemed to have committed their titles and faces to memory, and after he'd deposited her with her friends he'd promptly left to mingle with the Earl of What's-His-Face and Viscount No-Distinguishing-Features.

Still, these people were peers and, as Sebastian pointed out, they'd need their approval for the factory and the railway lines. But she didn't have to like them.

'Where is your fiancé, by the way?' Maddie asked, glancing around the room.

'He's not my fiancé yet,' Kate reminded her. 'Not until the announcement at midnight.'

That was why she and Sebastian had arrived separately and he'd opened the ball with his mother—they were not officially betrothed yet. However, the news of the Duke of Mabury's engagement had spread through the ton like wildfire, even before the ink on their contract had dried. Kate wondered if there was a way to harness that mode of communication and use it for the signals on train tracks…

'Cousin Kate, Miss DeVries…how are you this evening? I'm so glad to see you both.'

Kate expelled a breath as she turned to face Jacob, who had seemingly appeared from out of mid-air. 'Cousin Jacob, you are…here.' She couldn't quite bring herself to lie and say she was pleased to see him, because he was the last person she wanted to see right now.

'Such a beautiful party.' His greedy eyes lingered a little too long on Maddie's décolletage—which unfortunately, at her height, was nearly at eye level for him. 'Are you enjoying yourselves?'

'Yes, we are, Mr Malvery,' Maddie said politely, though she cast a wistful look at the sea of dancers.

'I don't think I have personally congratulated you on your engagement, Cousin,' Jacob began. 'I've heard nothing except how fortunate you are to have made the match of the Season. Indeed, we are blessed to have someone such as the Duke joining our family.'

'Thank you, Cousin.' Kate was taken aback by Jacob's words, and she didn't know how else to react.

'Cousin, would you do me the honour of joining me for the next dance?'

Kate cursed herself, because she knew she couldn't find an excuse to say no. Not when everyone in the ballroom had their attention on her. 'Of course.'

She let Jacob lead her to the floor with the other dancers. When the galop was announced, Kate sent out a prayer of thanks to the heavens. The lively, energetic rhythm of the dance usually left little time for conversation. Not that it stopped Jacob from trying.

'Cousin, I was wondering if we could speak in private?' Jacob asked as they slowed for a turn.

Kate paused long enough for the beat of the music to change, indicating a change of partners. She stepped away, reached for the woman on her left, and continued on with another gentleman until she returned to Jacob and they once again started the brisk steps of the main dance.

Thankfully he did not attempt any more conversation until the dance had ended.

'Such a…spirited dance,' Jacob huffed, his cheeks red from exertion. 'As I was saying—'

'May I have the next dance?'

Every fibre of Kate's being lit up at the sound of Sebastian's voice. Turning around, she looked up into those magnetic obsidian eyes. 'We are not supposed to dance until after the announcement,' she said under her breath.

His expression remained cool, but the energy vibrating from him felt barely contained. 'And who set this rule? This is my home, my ball. I think I'm entitled to dance with whomever I please.'

Kate could feel several pairs of eyes on them and so, not wanting to garner any negative attention, said, 'Of course, Your Grace.'

She nodded to Jacob, who stepped away. Sebastian took his place without even a glance at the other man, and placed a hand on her waist and pulled her close, as if they were starting the waltz.

'Your Grace, they haven't yet announced—' She stopped short as Eames called out the waltz, then lifted an eyebrow at him. He said nothing, but merely smirked at her as they began the dance.

'What were you and Malvery talking about?' His expression turned stormy. 'What did he say to you? Did he upset you?'

'Jacob? Nothing. We didn't have a chance to talk during the dance.'

Wait—was he jealous? Over Jacob? Her heart fluttered in her chest. *Don't be ridiculous,* she scolded herself. He could never be jealous over another man dancing with her.

As they danced, she glanced around the ballroom. Everyone was definitely watching them now, so she tried to focus her attention on something else. Her gaze continued to roam, and she paused when she saw Maddie standing off to one side, swaying to the music as she drank some lemonade, a forlorn look on her face as she watched the dancers whirling about on the ballroom floor. A group of girls behind her giggled and pointed, making gestures that obviously mocked her height and childish dress.

Irritation pricked at Kate. Maddie was perhaps the one person tonight who was genuinely happy for her. She understood, in a way, what Sebastian had been saying about real friends. And she would be grateful for ever for Maddie's friendship.

'Kate? What's the matter?' Those dark brows furrowed together. 'Tell me what's bothering you and how I can make it better.'

Her heart did a somersault at his words.

'Ah...'

'Ah?'

'You are concerned for your friend.'

'It's unfair, really.' She let out a huff. 'Maddie is worth ten times as much as these insipid, vapid debutantes. Just because she doesn't fit the mould of what a young lady should be, society thinks she should be shunned. These people really are horrible, and I can see why you despise them. Frankly, I don't care any more. They can all go...jump off a bridge.'

His dark brows drew together, but he remained silent for the rest of the dance. Kate wondered if she'd offended him with her defence of her friend and her denouncement of the ton. But that would be strange because, as Sebastian had said, he didn't care much about the guests here tonight.

Once the dance had ended, Sebastian bowed to her and then led her back to where Maddie was waiting.

'Everyone's talking about you,' Maddie said excitedly. 'Mostly in a good way.'

'"Mostly" good is a positive thing with these people,' Sebastian said drolly. 'Miss DeVries, may I have the honour of the next dance?'

Maddie's jaw dropped. 'M-me?' She looked around. 'If you mean my sister—?'

'No.' Sebastian shook his head. 'I mean you, Miss Madeline.'

Kate's breath caught at the look of pure joy on her friend's face. *Oh, Sebastian...*

'Th-thank you. I mean, yes… Yes, Your Grace.'

Sebastian offered his hand and the two of them made their way to the dance floor for a lively reel. Maddie was surprisingly light on her feet, and graceful, her steps keeping good time with the music. With Maddie being only one or two inches shorter than Sebastian, Kate thought that being tall wasn't bad at all if it meant not having to crane one's neck up at a dance partner.

Maddie's delight at the dance was obvious, and even when they came back her pretty face was still all aglow. Kate knew it was not just because of the dancing, but because now half the gentlemen in the room were looking at her.

'You were wonderful, Maddie,' Kate gushed. 'I had no idea you could dance so well.'

'Thank you,' she said. 'Your Grace, thank you.'

'Thank *you*, Miss DeVries,' Sebastian said. 'You were a delightful partner.' He cleared his throat. 'If you would excuse Kate and I…? I believe my mother is getting ready to make a certain announcement.'

Kate looked at the large grandfather clock nearby. It was nearly midnight. Nerves twisted in her gut.

'Of course, Your Grace,' Maddie said, then leaned towards Kate. 'Good luck!'

She grinned at her friend, then followed Sebastian as they walked to the centre of the ballroom, where the Dowager Duchess was giving instructions to Eames.

'Have I made it better?' Sebastian asked.

'Made what better?'

'I told you.' His hand drifted to her lower back. 'I was going to make what bothered you better.'

Her heartbeat stuttered as everything came crashing into her like a wave. He hadn't just danced with Maddie because he'd enjoyed it, or to be a good host.

He did it for me.

'Well?'

Her throat burned as she felt moisture gather in the corners of her eyes. 'Yes,' she managed to whisper. 'You made it better.'

'Good. Now, let's go to my mother so we can make this bloody announcement.'

Kate's unladylike laugh dislodged the blockage in her throat.

As she and Sebastian strode towards the Dowager Duchess a feeling of dizziness came over her—but not in an unpleasant way. It reminded her of when she was a child and she would hang upside-down from the railings on the porch of their tiny shack in West Virginia, then quickly pull herself upright. It was heady, and it sent a thrill down to her toes.

'Ladies and gentlemen,' the Dowager Duchess began, and the guests lowered their voices until silence blanketed the room. 'Thank you for joining us here on this momentous occasion.'

As the Dowager continued her speech, Kate looked up at Sebastian—truly looked at his face, from his freshly shaven jaw to the line of his nose to the crinkles at the corners of his eyes. Her stomach turned topsy-turvy as she came to a realisation.

'And now...' The Dowager Duchess clapped her hands together. 'It is with great delight that I announce the engagement of my son, Sebastian, Duke of Mabury, to Miss Kathryn Mason of New York.'

Applause and cheers rang in Kate's ears, and as Sebastian lifted her hand to his lips she tried to decipher who this man really was. This stubborn, frustrating man, who annoyed her with his high-handedness, yet also made her melt with his kisses. Who loved his mother so much he'd do anything for her—even disturb his quiet life. Whose stare could turn a grown man to ash, but who had shown nothing but kindness to a wallflower everyone else had written off.

Oh, drat. I have feelings for him.

Impossible. She couldn't be developing any emotions for him.

This is supposed to be a business arrangement.

A marriage based on a solid foundation of mutual benefits. They were both getting what they wanted. That should be enough to make them happy and solve their problems.

Her thoughts turned back to her conversation with the Dowager Duchess that afternoon.

'The solution to a problem isn't just a quick fix,' Pap had always said. But for once in her life she wished he'd been wrong.

Chapter Twenty

Sebastian could not recall the last time he had enjoyed a ball so much that he'd danced until dawn. He had never even made it to the end of a ball, as he'd either left to continue carousing with his compatriots or been too inebriated to remember.

'You know, you really didn't have to dance with Maddie twice tonight,' Kate said.

Though many of the guests had left, a few still lingered, so he had whispered in her ear, telling her to join him outside the ballroom after he'd slipped out first.

'I know,' he replied. 'But she seemed to like dancing.' And, more importantly, it had made Kate happy.

'She loved it.' Kate was positively glowing. 'Thank you so much.'

He would dance with the Devil himself if he could see her smile as she did now.

'Though maybe you are right and it was greedy of me to take her out for more than one dance. Many other gentlemen were clamouring to get on her dance card for the rest of the evening.'

'All thanks to your stamp of approval.'

The grin she flashed him sent a warm feeling to his

stomach, and it wasn't just from all the champagne he'd drunk. Glancing around, he realised they were truly alone now, so he gently guided her along the corridor.

'Sebastian, where are we going?'

'To your room, of course. Where else?'

'My room? But you said you were tired.'

'That's what I told Sir Elliot, so he would shut up about those damned goldfinches,' he groused. 'But I'm never too tired for you.'

How prettily she blushed, even after all this time.

'We must not let anyone see us.'

Quietly, they made their way through the darkened corridors and up to her rooms. Thankfully, the servants knew everyone would be having a late night, so they would not disturb any of the guests too early. But, frankly, Sebastian did not care if half the staff walked into Kate's room to see him in her bed, naked as the day he was born.

They were going to have to get used to it, anyway.

In two weeks she would be his wife.

He'd hated seeing her across the ballroom, unable to dance with her as he pleased and having all those men look at her covetously without him being able to stake his claim.

Especially that vile cousin of hers.

When he'd seen her dancing with Jacob Malvery, he had decided to hell with propriety and claimed his dance.

And he was glad he had. Initially, he'd abhorred the idea of having an engagement ball, or even a big wedding. If it had been up to him he would have said to hell with it and eloped with Kate to Gretna Green. Imagining all those people who had caused his mother pain being there, in the same room, had made the anger from five years ago flood back.

However, seeing Kate out there, focusing his attention on her and making sure she was truly happy, he'd found that he was actually enjoying himself. With Kate by his side, nothing else mattered.

After what seemed like an eternity, they made it to her room. He pounced on her the moment the door closed, making her giggle. After battling with the layers of petticoats and silk, he succeeded in removing all of her clothing, then his, and they tumbled onto the mattress.

He worshipped her body, trailing kisses all over her naked skin, giving her pleasure with his mouth and hands. First he turned his attention to her breasts, pressing them together so he could lave the pert little nipples with his tongue. He teased her, making her whimper and protest. That only fuelled him, so he suckled at her harder, drawing one nipple deep into his mouth until she thrust her fingers through his hair and tugged hard. But he refused to relent and continued his sweet torture.

When he was done with her breasts he moved lower, his tongue tracing a path straight down over her ribcage and smooth belly to the valley of her sex. He tasted her sweetness, licking at her nether lips, then teasing at her button. Lifting his gaze, he stared up at her while continuing to feast on her. How he loved watching her sigh and shiver, especially from his vantage point between her legs, looking up as her moans and cries escaped her plump lips, her thighs pressing against the sides of his head.

When she was spent, he moved over her, covering her body with his. 'Do you trust me, Kate?'

She nodded.

'Good.' His hands slipped under her, then he rolled onto his back, settling her on his hips.

'S-Sebastian?' Her mouth rounded. 'Can it be done this way?'

'Oh, yes.' His hand traced up her ribcage to cup a breast, and he rolled the hardened nipple between his thumb and forefinger. 'There are many ways it can be done.'

'What should I do?'

'You're a clever woman.' Using his other hand, he reached for her mound, brushing the soft curls aside to seek out her slickness. 'You know what to do.'

Kate arched into his hand, mewling as he brushed his thumb against the bundle of nerves above her entrance. Nodding, she wrapped a hand around his now hard shaft, giving it a tentative squeeze before pointing it at her wet entrance.

'It's... Ah...'

Her head rolled back as she sank down onto him. Slowly, maddeningly, he filled her to the hilt. Neither of them moved for what seemed like the longest time, until she squeezed him. The sensation nearly had him losing his control.

Sebastian held onto her hips as she moved, slow and tentative at first. But when she pushed her hips forward and found a position that gave her the friction she was seeking, her mouth parted in a gasp. Then she began to move in earnest.

Lord, she was stunning, with her dark hair spilling over her creamy shoulders, breasts bouncing, and those small pants escaping her lips as she sought her pleasure.

A realisation swept over him—an emotion building in his chest that he could not recognise. He thought that for a brief moment a voice in his mind had whispered what it was, but he was too deep in his own pleasure to understand it. He needed more of her. No, he needed all of her. Now.

Her body let out a shudder, but he pulled her off him before it could go further. She let out a whine of protest, but Sebastian quickly rolled on top of her and once again filled her, making her moan as he moved his hips rhythmically to push them both to the edge. That earlier thought rushed back into his head, stronger now, but before he could say it aloud he bit the inside of his cheek to stop himself.

He gathered her in his arms, surrendering to the rapture of being deep inside her, filling her with his seed as ecstasy made his body convulse. Afterwards, he crumpled on top of her, fully drained. As the taste of iron filled his mouth he realised how close he had been to saying things he might regret later.

Much too close.

His body had barely recovered from the mind-numbing pleasure before a different kind of emotion ran through him.

Panic.

Anger.

And a coldness that gripped his insides like a vice.

He could only attribute it to one thing.

Fear.

With an inward curse, he pushed himself off her and onto his back, then swung his legs over the side of the bed.

'Sebastian?' Kate said in a breathless voice. 'Are you all right?'

'I'm fine,' he grumbled, then bent down to pick up his discarded trousers.

'Are you leaving?'

'It's almost daylight. I should go before your maid comes in.'

With a determined grunt, he pushed himself off the bed and continued to dress.

'Yes, but if there's something the matter—'

'I told you. I'm fine.' Half the buttons on his shirt still had to be done up but he left her room anyway, as the tightness in his chest threatened to suffocate him if he didn't get away that instant.

Swiftly, he escaped back to his rooms, and air only began to fill his lungs when he collapsed in the leather chair by the window.

Dear Lord, what had he been thinking?

Reaching towards the table beside him, he picked up a crystal decanter filled with amber liquid. He unscrewed the top and took a swig, hoping the burning path the liquor took down his throat would also raze the memories from the past threatening to overwhelm him here in the present.

The candles burning bright in the darkened bedroom. His mother so still and pale and barely breathing.

And once again he was transported back to that moment five years ago. The moment that had changed his life.

'Your Grace?'

Robeson's voice flung him back to the present. Sebastian blinked, then quickly shut his eyes as sunlight burned them. When the devil had it become so bright outside?

'Robeson?' he rasped, his throat feeling dry. 'What time is it?'

'A quarter past nine, Your Grace.'

'Quarter past—?' He clamped his mouth shut. He'd

been sitting here, decanter in his hand, for nearly two hours.

'Do you need a few more minutes, Your Grace?'

'No.' He tucked the empty decanter into a corner of the chair and then got up. 'Please have a bath prepared, Robeson. As quickly as you can. Don't bother heating the water.'

The valet didn't even blink an eye. 'Of course, Your Grace.'

Once he was alone, Sebastian strode over to the washstand and splashed his face with clean water.

This has to stop.

He could not let what had happened this morning—what had almost happened—happen again. Could not lose control. After half a decade of keeping a tight rein on his emotions he'd been on the cusp of letting all that hard work go to waste. Only he had the power to stop it. He could not be alone with Kate—not until their wedding. No more midnight visits, no more intimate glances, no more worrying about if she were happy or not.

Surely by then he would have put enough distance between them that he could get a hold on his emotions before they ran away.

He shut his eyes tight, drawing up an image of his mother in his mind. An image of what might be his future if he did not stop this insanity now.

Despite his weariness from lack of sleep, Sebastian managed to go through his usual routine for the rest of the day. He met with a few tenants, conducted another long meeting with Arthur Mason and the solicitors, then finally changed into his dinner clothes.

'You're looking a little the worse for wear,' the Dowager Duchess commented as they walked to the parlour.

'Aren't we all?' he muttered in reply.

She laughed. 'Indeed. I don't remember staying up that late in a long time.'

A fleeting expression of sadness crossed her face. Sebastian knew she was remembering what it had been like before her husband had shattered their lives and left her to pick up all the pieces. His resolve to keep his distance from Kate grew stronger. But of course his chest tightened in anticipation as they stood outside the parlour, at knowing she was mere feet away. When they entered, he could not help searching the room for her, his gaze stopping once he did find her.

'Come, let's begin dinner,' the Dowager Duchess said, leading them towards Kate and Arthur.

'Your Grace.' Kate's greeting sounded unsure as she curtseyed, her body wavering slightly. Still, she looked stunning in a violet evening gown, its modest neckline showing only the minimum amount of skin. Skin that he wanted to—

'Good evening,' he said, getting hold of his lust.

Lord, this would be a long meal.

She looked as if she wanted to say something, so he offered his arm to her and spoke first. 'Let's go in for dinner, shall we?'

The meal seemed longer than it really was—perhaps because he kept his eye on the clock on the mantel for most of it. He thought no one had noticed, but the Dowager Duchess raised a delicate eyebrow at him, the corners of her lips tugging up.

When they'd finished dessert, and the men and women were parting, Sebastian breathed a sigh of relief. It had taken all his strength to treat Kate as he had before, when all he'd wanted was to be alone with her again.

As they were leaving the dining room, Kate leaned over to him and whispered, 'I shall see you tonight, Your Grace.' She disentangled her arm from his and followed the other ladies back to the parlour.

His resolve nearly crumbled as he watched her walk away, hips swaying gracefully. Thankfully, Arthur and the other men hadn't noticed, and ushered him towards his study for port and cigars.

'Your Grace,' Arthur began, 'now that we are making headway in our plans for the factory, have you thought what to do for iron?'

His head snapped towards the older man. 'What about iron?'

'As you know,' he went on, pulling Cornelius DeVries forward, 'Cornelius here owns one of the largest iron forges in America. He's the best in the business.'

DeVries let out a jovial laugh. 'You are too kind, Arthur.'

'Nonsense,' Arthur snorted. 'If you weren't, I wouldn't be working with you. Though he and his family are only here for the girls, I think we can convince him to partner up with us in our little venture.'

'Is that so?'

Sebastian normally hated talking business after dinner—and with Arthur's enthusiasm for anything that had to do with making money, this might take all night—but it would be a welcome distraction from his urge to be with Kate.

'Tell me more, Mr DeVries.'

Chapter Twenty-One

Kate glanced at the door as she sat up in bed, fully awake, her body thrumming with anticipation, waiting for Sebastian to enter her room. She had nearly gone mad during dinner, acting as if everything was as it had been before last night, making polite conversation and keeping a modest distance.

Yet she knew things were not the same and nothing could ever go back to the way it had been before.

Now that she had a clearer picture of Sebastian's past, and the baring of her own growing emotions, the reality of it crashed into Kate like the rolling waves on the shore, smashing into her mind and sending her into a tizzy. But then, once it receded, she got her bearings and was able to think clearly.

This was a mutually beneficial arrangement. She needn't be concerned for him this deeply. This foolishness had to stop now.

She metaphorically straightened her shoulders and dug her heels in.

Then the wave came crashing back again, knocking her into the sand.

Oh, Lord, what was she to do?

Sebastian had been adamant that emotions could not be part of their marriage. And after her talk with the Dowager Duchess she could guess why. He'd been hurt because of what had happened with his parents, and his mother in particular. She couldn't even begin to imagine what it must be like to be in love with someone and then have them betray you.

But I would never betray him.

Once again, she found herself smashing onto the shore.

The worst possible scenario she could imagine would be Sebastian discovering her feelings, as then he might break off their engagement. That would mean her having to marry Jacob and wiping away all traces of Pap's legacy.

No, Sebastian could never find out about her feelings.

A noise from outside made her jolt. Her fingers clutched at the sheets, as she waited for Sebastian to enter her room. But the doorknob didn't turn, and the door did not open. She guessed it had to be past midnight, which was later than he usually came. In the past two weeks he'd arrived not too long after Anna had left as, when the men and women separated after dinner, Sebastian usually cut his evening short so he could be with her.

While she wished she could be a part of those discussions—because, knowing her father, they would be all about business—she knew she only had to bide her time and then her father would be thousands of miles away and she would be free to do as she wanted with the new factory and her engines. Indeed, her mind was already filled with ideas on how she was going to improve the basic design of a locomotive so it could run more efficiently.

She reached over to her bedside table and pulled out

a leather-bound notebook with a pencil attached to the strings that held it closed. Untying the knot, she opened it to the first blank page and began to sketch. Graphite flew over the pages as Kate's ideas materialised into rough designs and initial calculations.

Yes, that would work!

Her teeth sank into her lower lip.

But only if the factory floor space were doubled…

Then she'd double it.

Her hand paused. Sebastian had said she would be in charge of everything. From start to finish. The possibilities would be endless.

Filled with excitement, she continued to draw and plan, flipping the pages so fast they were nearly ripped out.

Oh, Pap, this is really happening!

When Kate reached the last empty page, she halted and looked up. Morning light had begun to filter through the gauzy curtains.

Goodness, I stayed up all night.

But it had been worth it. She clutched the notebook to her chest, her head light and dizzy from excitement.

But then her heart plummeted when she realised Sebastian hadn't come to her bed.

Maybe he was tired last night.

Feeling her energy drain from her body, she relaxed and sank back into the pillows. Yes, perhaps that was it.

I'll show him my plans later, she thought before closing her eyes and allowing sleep to take over.

Kate could understand it if Sebastian had felt tired for a night or two—Lord knew, she could use some rest from all this excitement herself—but it had been nearly a week since Sebastian had visited her at night.

I should have trusted my instincts.

Something was very wrong. She had felt it the last two times they had made love, and then on the morning of the engagement ball and the day after.

Her gaze went to the stack of notebooks on the bedside table. Each night she had sketched and planned until she was exhausted. She'd told herself that it was a good thing he was busy, so she could finish her work, and she couldn't wait to show him all her plans. But after a week she'd already revised all her ideas. And now all she could do was wait.

Leaning over the bedside table, she blew out the candle. With the room blanketed in darkness, she sank deeper into the covers. Perhaps it was better if they didn't sleep together any more—at least not until their wedding night. With her feelings causing chaos within herself, who knew what would happen if they were intimate and she suddenly confessed?

No, she had to keep it to herself. They were not married yet, and if it should fall through Jacob would be waiting to swoop in.

She turned on her side and hugged her pillow. The maid must have changed the sheets that morning, because they no longer had that trace scent of Sebastian's cologne. She closed her eyes tight, trying to convince herself to go to sleep. Not that it helped.

Kate found herself wide awake until the early hours of the morning, and it was only pure exhaustion that had her finally drifting off. By the time Anna came in to bring her some tea and toast, her eyes felt dry and swollen, her head was throbbing, and her chest was ready to burst with... With what she didn't know. But if she didn't get to the bottom of it she would surely explode.

With a determined grunt, she swung her feet off

the bed and instructed Anna to get her favourite peach morning gown ready. Once dressed, she marched to Sebastian's private study and knocked on the door. When she heard a voice telling her to come in, she pushed it open and strode inside.

'Sebastian, I must— Father?'

Arthur Mason sat behind Sebastian's desk, white brows furrowed as he read through some papers. Jacob, as usual, was behind him, looking over his shoulder.

'Yes, Kathryn?' her father said, without looking up.

'Father, what are you doing in here? Where is Sebastian?'

'Working,' he said matter-of-factly. 'And as for the Duke—he said he was leaving for London after breakfast.'

'London?'

He had never said anything to her about going to town. Her heart plummeted. Without another word, she whirled around and marched out through the door. It was early still, so maybe he was having breakfast.

'Kate?'

Jacob had followed her.

What now?

'I don't have time for this, Jacob.'

'One moment, please, Cousin.'

She slowed her steps but didn't stop. 'What do you want?' After no sleep the night before, she was irritable and exhausted.

'What has you so vexed this morning, Kate?' Jacob enquired. 'Are you and the Duke having a tiff? You didn't seem to know he was heading to London...and only a week before your wedding.'

As if she'd confide in him about such things. 'Everything is fine,' she said, mustering up as much confidence as she could. 'Is there anything else?'

'Nothing at all.'

'Good.' She curled her hands into fists. 'Now, unless you have something truly important to tell me, I must be off.'

Despite her exhaustion, she managed to race down the corridor and into the dining room. It was completely empty, so she dashed out into the receiving area, where the door was still open. She spied Sebastian's coach, pulling up outside on the drive.

'Sebastian!' she called when she saw his tall form standing in front of the coach, one foot on the steps. Not caring that Eames and the footmen were around, she picked up her skirts and ran out. 'Sebastian!'

He froze, his body stiffening. 'Kate.'

'You're...leaving?' she huffed between breaths.

His back remained to her. 'I have business to attend to.'

'Business? In London?'

He let out a breath and lowered his foot. Turning around, he finally faced her. 'Yes, business.'

'You're going without telling me?'

'I didn't realise I needed your permission.'

His cool, impersonal gaze told her that something was definitely amiss.

'Could we speak before you leave? It won't take too long.'

His expression darkened, but he nodded towards the carriage. She took the hand he offered and climbed in. Sebastian gave instructions to the driver to wait, and then followed her inside.

'What is this about, Kate?'

'I just... I just wanted to ask...' She bit her lip, not

really sure what to say. 'If you have changed your mind about the wedding.'

About me.

He didn't even flinch. 'Changed my mind? What in heaven's name are you talking about?'

His irritated tone clawed at her, making her lash out. 'You haven't been to my bed in days. And now you skulk off to London without so much as a by-your-leave. Not a word to me, your fiancée.'

Those obsidian eyes hardened into black steel. 'You're being ridiculous. I have business interests in London, and sometimes that requires me to travel into town at a moment's notice. Besides, the air in the country makes me weary at times, and I find myself needing...variety.'

The meaning in his words was clear. She knew what kind of 'variety' he needed in London.

'You don't mean that.'

'I beg your pardon?'

Her heart twisted in her chest, but she couldn't help it. 'Tell me this marriage is not just about our business arrangement. Tell me it is more than that—that you have other reasons why you want to marry me. That I mean something to you. Because you mean something to me.'

Please tell me.

All those nights together. The things he'd done to make her happy.

He must feel something for me.

'Kate,' he said in a warning tone. 'Don't—'

'I love you, Sebastian.'

She hadn't meant to say it, but the words had spilled out of her. No, they'd burst out—after a week of trying to break free.

'I can't help it. I do.'

There. She'd said it. Bared it all for him. She could

be sitting in front of him without her clothes on and she still wouldn't feel half as naked as she did now.

Silence hung in the air. He sat there, still as a rock, not saying a word. Finally, he spoke, after what seemed like for ever. 'You're mistaken,' he began in a low tone. 'We have agreed this is a business arrangement,' he reminded her. 'That's all.'

Kate couldn't move. Couldn't breathe. Knew that if she did she would shatter into a million pieces.

Sebastian felt nothing for her.

She had imagined that Sebastian breaking off their engagement and the destruction of her grandfather's legacy would be the worst scenario in the world.

Now she knew it was not.

She wanted to slink out of the carriage and escape back to her room. Bury herself under the bedcovers and not come out for days.

'But what good would that do?'

The words came to her in the form of Pap's voice.

'You've never been one to run away from your problems, my girl,' he continued. *'That's not how I taught you.'*

And so she dug her heels in. 'You are a coward.'

'I beg your pardon?' Sebastian replied in an ominous tone.

Her throat threatened to close, but she pushed on. 'You heard what I said. You're a coward, Sebastian.'

'How dare you—?'

'I am not done speaking.' Her palms slammed down on the plush upholstery seat. 'You're a coward—hiding behind your father's death and your mother's attempted suicide because you're afraid to face what's really scaring you. The fact that perhaps there's another reason you're obsessed with not becoming like your father.'

'I can't let the cycle—'

'That's not it.' The tic in his jaw told her she was getting close to the mark. 'All these years you've wasted, trying not to be that man... Sebastian, you are your own person. You could never turn into someone else. It's not inevitable, but something you choose. And right now you're choosing to let something out of your control hold you back.'

Once she'd started speaking it was like a tidal wave, and she couldn't stop.

'When you're truly honest with yourself, and address what's really wrong, then you can open up to the possibility that someone could love you and you could love them in return. Now, tell me, what are you really afraid of?'

'You don't know what you're talking about.' The air in the carriage had turned chilly. 'As I said, you're mistaken.'

So that was it. He had made his choice to live in the past instead of moving forward with her.

'Of course, Your Grace,' she managed to mutter, even though her heart cracked within her chest. 'Forgive me. Please, allow me to delay you no further.'

Tears blurred the edges of her vision, but she dared not let him see them. She reached for the carriage door and pushed it open. Ignoring the startled footman, she leapt off the steps and dashed into the manor.

She was halfway to her room when she stopped.

I can't go in there. There—the place where she had shared so many achingly beautiful moments with him.

She bolted in the opposite direction and made her way outside again, through the entrance that led to the gardens.

A walk should clear my head

Yes, that was what she needed. Some fresh air and sun. Time in nature, to contemplate and determine what she should do.

She trudged through the gardens, but even out here all she could think about was Sebastian—especially when she glanced up at the orangery. So she ambled out to the meadows and fields surrounding the manor, wandering aimlessly until her feet ached. The pain felt good, and for now it was enough to make her forget the stinging soreness in her chest.

I'm a fool for telling him I love him.

Of course he did not love her back. He had made it clear from the beginning that love would have no place in their marriage. Their partnership was to be built on a solid foundation of mutual need, not something unsteady like love.

She knew that, and yet she'd done nothing to stop her heart from falling into danger. And now that runaway train had plunged straight down into the abyss.

It felt as if she'd been walking for days, but really it couldn't have been more than half an hour as the manor was still in her sights, although in the distance. With a deep sigh, she began the long trudge back. What was she going to do? Perhaps she would figure it out by the time she reached the manor.

'Kate! Kate!'

She turned around at the sound of the voice. A figure in the distance came running towards her, and as it drew closer she cursed silently.

'Cousin Jacob? What are you doing here?' Kate couldn't even pretend to be glad to see him.

Jacob's face was red with exertion. 'Kate…you must come with me. There's been an accident!'

'An accident?' She pressed a hand to her breast. 'Who? My father?'

He shook his head. 'No…it's the Duke.'

Sebastian! A different kind of emotion gripped her chest like a fist. 'What—? Where—? But he just left for London.'

'It was a carriage accident.' Jacob continued to gasp for air. 'He'd only travelled a few miles from the estate when the horses got spooked. A fox or something must have crossed the road.'

'And Sebastian? How is he?'

Oh, Lord, please let him be all right!

Jacob's face turned grave. 'He's alive…but trapped under the carriage. He's asking for you.'

'Of course. I'll head back to the manor—'

'No!' Jacob seized a fistful of her sleeve. 'They sent me here to fetch you. I've taken your father's carriage by the back road—it's just down there—and I'm to bring you to His Grace right away.'

'Let's go now.'

Kate followed Jacob across the field towards the carriage waiting on the side of the wide path. She climbed in first, and scooted towards the opposite end of the bench. The cab dipped as Jacob clambered in, then settled beside her.

As the carriage began to move her chest squeezed tight with fear as images of what state Sebastian might be in sprang into her mind.

Please don't die, Sebastian. She didn't care if he never loved her back. *Just let him be alive.*

She wrung her fingers together in her lap, keeping her focus outside. Worry loomed over her like a storm cloud, creating a contrast to the beautiful English countryside. Right now the sun filled the bare land with golden morning light, but soon this field would be filled with flowers. What a beautiful sight it would be, with the sun shining on them.

Her heart crashed into her ribcage when she realised where the sunlight was coming from.

The sun was behind them.

Which meant they were travelling west—not northeast towards London, where Sebastian had been headed. She glanced around, noticing how the carpeting on the floor of the carriage was threadbare and the seat cushions so worn she could feel the hard wooden bench underneath them. Arthur Mason would never have rented such a carriage.

'Have you figured it out, Cousin?'

Her head snapped to Jacob. 'There was no accident.'

The smug smirk he flashed her confirmed it. 'You always were too smart for your own good.'

Oh, Lord. Jacob was kidnapping her.

Instinctively, she lunged for the door, but he blocked her and pushed her back. Her head hit the side of the carriage with a loud thud and pain exploded in her temple.

'Don't even think about it.'

The sound of a revolver being cocked made her blood run cold. Raising her gaze, she spied the barrel of the gun pointing straight at her. 'What's…this about?' She moaned, kneading the growing lump on the side of her head. 'Where are you taking me?'

'Where else do secret lovers go to escape their families?' Jacob sneered. 'Scotland, of course.'

'Lovers?' What in the world was he talking about? 'Scotland?'

'Yes. Gretna Green, to be exact. The letter you've left on your bed explains it all. You and I have been lovers all this time. We want to marry, but your father is forcing you to marry the Duke, so we've decided to elope.'

Despite her throbbing head, she quickly grasped the gist of his scheme. 'You rotten scoundrel!' Jacob *did* want control of Mason R&L. 'Greedy...*bastard*!'

Jacob only laughed. 'Did you think I was going to let years and years of hard work, of licking your father's boots and deferring to him, go to waste? I was the one who did all his dirty work, kept his hands clean so that everyone would remember Arthur Mason as a benevolent industrialist instead of the ruthless businessman we both know him to be.'

Kate couldn't deny that. In fact, when Pap had been alive, he and Arthur had often clashed over things like wages and the cost of materials. Her father always looked at maximising profit, while Pap had refused to sacrifice quality and had fought for his men to get fair pay.

'England is where I was going to build *my* empire,' Jacob continued. 'And now he's just going to hand over the reins to that stupid duke.'

His eyes had widened so much that Kate could see the whites around them.

'I will never let that happen. I worked hard for this. I deserve this. Deserve you.'

'I'll never marry you!'

'You won't have a choice, dear Cousin.'

'Not even the blacksmiths at Gretna Green will officiate a marriage where one party is unwilling.'

The corner of his lips turned up into a smile. 'That's the beauty of this, Kate. We're not really going to Scotland and nor are we getting married—not right away. We're heading west, and not north, just in case your dear duke tries to chase after us. After spending tonight at a coaching inn we'll make our way back to London, then send for Arthur in the morning. By then everyone will know what we've done. Once the gossip has spread, do you think your precious duke will still marry you? Will anyone believe you're still a virgin by the time we come back?' He snorted. 'Of course not. And that's all I need. Once you're spoiled goods, you'll have no choice but to marry me.'

Lord, she hated those words. *Spoiled goods.* Once again she was being treated like an object, not a person.

Unfortunately, though, Jacob was right. Once it came out that she was ruined, her father would only care that she be married one way or another.

What would Sebastian think of her? Would he believe her? Even if he did, he would break off their engagement if even a whisper of scandal touched his family again. And, heavens—the Dowager Duchess! She wouldn't be able to weather another scandal.

Feeling drained and hopeless, Kate slumped back in her seat.

'That's right…be a good girl. Don't bother fighting it.' Jacob grinned. 'Now, get some rest. It'll be a few more hours until we reach the coaching inn. Don't worry, sweetheart. I won't touch you in such a filthy place. No, we'll have a grand wedding in New York, and we'll have our first night together as man and wife in the finest suite at the Astor Hotel.'

The very thought of being in bed with Jacob made her insides revolt. Damn Jacob and his greed!

I can't lose hope.

Surely she could find a way to flee.

Think, Kate!

Even if Sebastian didn't want her, she would do everything in her power to escape this fate.

Chapter Twenty-Two

Regret filled Sebastian the moment the carriage door slammed shut. No, it had begun the moment he'd spoken all those lies that had brought pain to those beautiful cornflower-blue eyes. He couldn't have hurt her more if he'd struck her.

He sat inside his coach for what seemed like for ever, unable to move an inch. His stomach churned with bile as his mind played the events in his mind over and over, torturing him with a vision of Kate's face crumpling and how her eyes had shone with tears as he'd uttered those brutal words.

He'd had no choice. She couldn't possibly mean what she said. Did she have any idea how powerful those words were? How he could use them against her?

No, he hadn't had a choice. It was for her own good.

Well, he had wanted to push her away and he'd succeeded. Spectacularly.

'I love you, Sebastian.'

But those words weren't the only thing that bothered him. It was what she'd said after that unnerved him. Because if he was honest with himself, she was completely and utterly correct. He was a coward. But, worse than that, he was a failure.

I have to make things right.

And he knew where to start.

Flinging the carriage door open, he bolted out and dashed towards the door. Kate had probably gone back to her room. He would make it up to her and beg her for forgiveness, but he had one other stop to make first.

He didn't even bother knocking, and yanked open the door to the Dowager Duchess's private sitting room. 'Mother!'

'Sebastian?' His mother looked up at him from where she sat by the window. 'Has something happened?'

Sebastian remained quiet. How would he explain this to her?

Rising from her seat, she walked towards him. 'You look troubled. Darling, what's the matter?' She paused. 'Does it have something to do with Kate?'

How the devil had she figured that out?

His mother tsked. 'I thought there was something going on between the two of you.' Tucking her arm into his, she tugged at him. 'Now, come.'

'But I have to—'

She ignored his protests and dragged him out of the room, then led him to the front hall. The footman opened the door as they approached. 'Please have Eames fetch Miss Mason and bring her to the orangery,' she said, as they walked across the threshold.

The young man bowed low. 'Yes, Your Grace.'

Once the footman had left, the Dowager Duchess tightened her grip on his arm. 'Come and walk with me.'

Unsure of what was happening, Sebastian allowed his mother to drag him towards the gardens.

'Now,' she began, 'tell me what's the matter.'

What was it about his mother that he could not say no or lie to her? He let out a breath. 'I've made a muck of things. With Kate.'

And he told her everything—about Kate's plan, their arrangement, his mixed-up feelings about her and his subsequent reaction, along with what had happened in the carriage that morning.

When he'd finished, his mother didn't say a word, but the way her lips quirked and her brows drew together told Sebastian that she was thinking.

She spoke as soon as they entered the orangery. 'If you didn't feel the same way, you would have just told her. But you didn't. Instead you said terrible things to hurt her. Why would you so utterly reject her without thought?'

'I don't feel the same way.' That was his automatic response.

'Don't lie to me, Sebastian. I am not blind. I have watched you two these last few weeks. Now, tell me why you seem intent on driving her away when you clearly have feelings for each other?'

The answer was stuck in his throat, because he had kept the truth from her all these years. But perhaps his silence revealed too much, because her expression fell.

'It's because of what happened between your father and I, isn't it?'

'Mother—'

'No, there's no need to deny it. Not for my sake.' Untangling her arm from his, she walked ahead, stopping in front of a row of hanging orchids. 'Sebastian, I am sorry,' she said, her voice hitching. 'Please forgive me.'

'Forgive *you*?' He was beside her in an instant. 'Mother, no. You did nothing wrong.' His fingers curled into his palms. 'If he were alive, it should be that...that man who should be asking forgiveness.'

Calling that bastard 'Father' always left a bitter taste in his mouth.

His mother's eyes turned vacant, as if the life had been sucked out of them. He remembered that look. It was the same one from five years ago, after she had been revived.

'I think it's time I told you the truth,' she said. 'Years ago...before I met your father... I had an interest in mathematics.' She shook her head. 'No, it was more than an interest. One of my mentors—a distant uncle who'd taken an interest in teaching me—encouraged me to work on a paper to submit to the Académie des Sciences in France.'

He blinked at her. 'Truly?'

'You've always been good with numbers, Sebastian.' She smiled weakly at him. 'Did you think you'd got that from your father?'

'Not with his lack of accounting skills,' he said wryly.

If she had been working on something for the French academy of science, then she really had to have been exceptionally gifted.

'But what happened?'

'What else? I met your father.' Reaching her hand out, she touched one of the orchid buds. 'I was madly in love. And I'd like to think he loved me too.' The delicate bloom was perhaps too fragile, and it fell to the ground. 'When we married, I gave up my work so I could be Duchess, and then I had you... Oh, don't fret, darling. You were the best part of that bargain. And I was happy for a time. We all were. Then your father...' Her lips pressed together tightly. 'I was a fool. The signs were there but I ignored them. Then he died, and with the scandal… I couldn't hide from it any longer. In a moment of weakness, I thought to end it all. The regret. The pain. I—'

'Stop.' A pain sliced through his gut. 'Please. Say no more.'

'But—'

'You don't have to explain further. I understand, Mother. I truly do. And why you had to hide away from me all these years. You couldn't stand the reminder.'

Saying it aloud didn't make things better. It was like an open wound that wouldn't stop bleeding.

Colour drained from her beautiful face. 'You thought that was why I stayed away from you? Because you reminded me of your father and I feared you would eventually turn into him?'

It was more a statement than a question. He knew it to be true.

'But there's more, darling. Something else is bothering you. Tell me. Do not be scared.'

Kate's words haunted him. *'Now, tell me, what are you really afraid of?'*

'I'm your mother. I shan't judge you. Please, Sebastian.'

His mother's soothing words made the agony of years of repressing his own inner turmoil slowly lift. 'I couldn't protect you, Mother.' His throat tightened. 'I'd been so blinded by my love for Father that I ignored you all those years. I couldn't stop him from hurting you. From making you want to take your own life. *I couldn't save you.'*

And that was the truth. Kate had seen it before he had. That all these years he'd been blaming himself because he felt he'd failed his mother.

She enfolded him in her arms. 'There, there… It's not

your fault. It was not your role to protect me. I made my choices. Allowed despair to take over. And I didn't want that to touch you, so I stayed away. That's the real reason. I wanted you to be free of my melancholia, to live your life as you always had without me weighing you down like an anchor. But it seems I only made it worse.'

Sorrow marred her face.

'And that's why you must forgive me. It's because of me you've run yourself ragged these past five years. I'm the reason why you haven't let anyone love you and why you've rejected Kate. Your guilt has made you think yourself unworthy of love. You think you don't deserve her. That you don't deserve happiness.'

'It's true. She'll be better off with someone else,' he said bitterly. 'Someone who won't be a hindrance to her.' As his father had been to his mother.

'Oh, darling, can't you see?' His mother's fingers wrapped around his forearms. 'You are *nothing* like him.'

'You two are like two peas in a pod.' Those had been her very words when he was growing up.

'How do you know that?'

'Tell me this, Sebastian…' The Dowager Duchess pressed her lips together. 'Why do you want to marry Kate? And don't say it's because you've ruined her. There are many lords out there who would have overlooked her lack of virtue for her dowry. And why go into business with her father to build this factory? You don't need the money, or the problems that go along with such a huge venture.'

Sebastian couldn't find any logical explanation except for one. 'Because she wants it. Just as she wants to save her grandfather's legacy.'

'The fact that you care for her hopes and dreams already proves you aren't like your father. No one else can give her that. You deserve her, Sebastian. You deserve to be loved. Don't let the ghost of your father prevent you from pursuing what could be a happy life with the woman you love.'

The woman I love.

'Kate…'

Yes, Kate was the woman he loved.

Slowly, the Dowager Duchess's mouth spread into a smile. 'And you'll tell her, won't you? That you want to marry her because you love her.'

'I will.' His heart plummeted. 'That's assuming she still wants to speak to me and doesn't despise me after this morning.'

By God, he would do anything to make her forgive him. Beg on his knees if he had to. Buy her a hundred factories across England. Because she was the only woman for him from now on.

'Mother, what do I do?'

'Just say what's in your heart. You— Ah!' Her hands clasped together as the telltale *clink* of the door latch told them someone was coming in. 'She's here.'

The thought of seeing her again after this morning set his nerves on edge and built excitement in him at the same time. Clasping his hands behind him, Sebastian began to pace across the tiled floor.

'Your Grace!'

'Eames?'

Sebastian halted. From the grave expression on the butler's face, he knew there was something wrong.

'Where is Miss Mason, Eames?' the Dowager Duchess asked.

The butler wrung his hands together. 'I'm afraid we can't find her.'

'Can't find her?' Sebastian thundered. 'What do you mean, "can't find her"?'

'One of the maids said that she saw Miss Mason on her way to her room, but when Mrs Grover checked it was empty. A footman mentioned he saw her outside, but no one has seen her since.'

Cold, icy talons of fear pricked at Sebastian.

'Tell all the servants to start looking for her. Everywhere. Have Mrs Grover and Kate's maid search her room. I'm going to see her father.'

Sebastian made it to his private study in record time, his mother trailing behind him.

'Arthur!' he roared. 'Where is Kate?'

The old man peered up at him from where he sat behind the desk. 'Kate? How should I know where she is?'

Damn this man! If it didn't have monetary value, he didn't give a whit. 'She's missing.'

'Are you sure?' His mouth twitched underneath his snowy moustache. 'Perhaps she's just wandering about the estate.'

'Your Grace!' Mrs Grover rushed into the study and curtseyed. 'Begging your pardon, b-but…w-we…uh…'

'For heaven's sake, spit it out!' Sebastian snarled.

The housekeeper's lower lip trembled as she handed him a piece of paper. 'This—this was on her bed.'

Snatching the note from her, Sebastian held it up and read through it.

'What is it?' the Dowager Duchess asked.

His jaw tightened. 'Here.'

His mother's brows knitted as she began to read. *'"Cannot live with this lie…forced to marry…leaving to be with Jacob…"'* She gasped. 'Sebastian… I'm so sorry.'

'What does it say, Your Grace?' Arthur asked.

'That she has run away with Mr Malvery.' The Dowager Duchess paled. 'To Gretna Green.'

Sebastian gnashed his teeth. 'No.'

'No?' She tilted her head to the side. 'What do you mean, "no", darling?'

'I mean—' he snatched the paper from her '—Kate did not write this. And she did not run away with Malvery.'

'But how can you be sure?'

'The handwriting is atrocious, for one thing.'

The loops, whirls, and smudges on the page made the note barely legible. Kate was an engineer: that meant she had to have excellent, precise penmanship for drawing up plans and blueprints.

'And half the words are misspelled.'

And deep in his heart he knew that Kate would never betray him like this.

'She could have been in a hurry,' Arthur said.

'Kate hates Malvery,' Sebastian countered. 'Why do you think she chose to marry me? And they can't have been lovers all this time.'

Not when Kate had been a virgin when she'd came to his bed and had spent nearly every night in his arms.

'What do you think happened?' asked Arthur.

'I think Malvery took her.'

'J-Jacob?' Arthur spluttered. 'But why?'

'I don't know why, precisely,' Sebastian growled. 'But when I find him—' *when, not if* '—he will regret trying to take what's mine.'

Chapter Twenty-Three

Kate's hope drained away as the carriage continued its journey. The further they were from Highfield Park, the smaller were her chances of escaping. Even if she did manage to flee when they arrived at the coaching inn it might be too late. No one would believe she hadn't run away with Jacob—not if they read that letter.

Stop it!

If Pap were here, he'd tell her never to give up. *'There's always a solution,'* he'd always said. *'And if you can't find one then you aren't looking hard enough.'*

'What is going on?' Jacob snarled. 'Why are we slowing down?'

Kate had been so deep in her thoughts that she hadn't noticed that the carriage had reduced its speed.

Jacob drew the curtain back. 'Driver! What are you doing? Why are we stopping?'

'Gotta stop for a piss!' the disembodied voice of the driver shouted back.

'You're stopping to—? I demand you keep going! I didn't pay you to dawdle about.'

'Wot am I s'posed to do, then? Piss me pants? Cor, I got more piddle than these horses…might even dribble some into the cab. You don't wanna sit in my stink, do ya?'

'Fine,' Jacob grumbled. 'But be quick about it.'

Kate gathered her thoughts. This was it! Her chance. But what to do...?

'Jacob, I need to...uh...powder my nose as well.'

'What?'

She blew out an exasperated breath. 'I have to...do my business.'

'Hold it in,' he snapped.

'But I can't. Please, Jacob? Or do you want to be locked up in here for the next few hours in my...you know...'

'Oh, all right.' He retrieved the pistol from his coat pocket. 'Move. But stay close, you hear?'

She opened the door and alighted. Scanning the surroundings, she spied a tree just a few feet away. Thankfully the driver was nowhere in sight, so she trudged over, Jacob plodding behind her.

'Do you mind turning your back?' she asked through gritted teeth. 'I need some privacy.'

'No way in hell I'm leaving you out of my sight.' He motioned to the tree with the gun. 'Go.'

Gathering her skirts, she marched behind the tree, turned so her back was to him, and crouched down. *What to do now?* She could only see flat fields all around her. She supposed she could attempt to outrun Jacob, but her skirts would slow her down. If only—

She blinked at something on the ground. Was that...?

'Hurry up!'

'I'm trying!' Reaching down, she ran her hands over the grass until she felt the large, spiky round seeds.

Burrs!

They'd used to grow right outside their house in West

Virginia, where she'd played. The familiar prickles sent a rush of excitement through her. Carefully, she gathered as many of them as she could in her right hand, then stood up and brushed her skirts down.

'All done.'

They headed back to the carriage and as she passed by one of the horses she pretended to trip. 'Oh, dear!' She grasped the bellyband, apologised to the poor animal silently, then shoved the burrs underneath the leather strap.

'Stop stalling.' Jacob pressed the barrel of the gun to her back. 'Go inside!'

Scrambling into the carriage, she settled into her seat, her heart hammering like mad the entire time. *Be patient*, she told herself. *And be ready.*

'Where is that confounded man?' Jacob groused. 'Driver!'

'Right 'ere!' The carriage bounced as the driver returned to his seat. 'Hold yer britches—we'll be off, then.'

Kate heard the driver whistle and they began to move forward. For the first few minutes everything seemed normal as the carriage bounced along the dirt road. *Dear God, please...* If the burrs didn't do their job, then she didn't know what else to do.

The carriage stopped without warning, but since Kate had expected it, she'd held on to her seat the entire time. Jacob, however, lurched forward.

Now!

A buzz of energy propelled her towards Jacob, reaching out to grab the gun. She cried out in triumph when her hand grasped the weapon. Quickly, she aimed it at Jacob, who scrambled to get up on the seat across from her.

'Don't move an inch, Jacob,' she warned.

His little beady eyes grew to the size of silver dollars. 'Do you even know how to use that?'

She pulled back the hammer of the pistol. 'You forget, Jacob. I was raised in a West Virginia coal mining town. Now, put your hands up.'

He did, and the hate-filled expression on his face only made her triumph sweeter.

'Wot's going on 'ere, then?' The driver's outraged shout made Jacob flinch. 'No need for guns, gents! I'll give ya wot ya want.'

Jacob gulped. 'Bandits. We've been set upon by robbers!'

Oh, for heaven's sake! Would this day ever become better for her? 'If you say anything, Jacob, I swear to—'

'Kate! Kate are you in there?'

The familiar baritone nearly made her drop the pistol. 'Sebastian?' Was she dreaming? Hallucinating? 'Sebastian, I'm here!'

The door was flung open and Sebastian's large frame filled the tiny interior as he barrelled inside. He immediately grabbed Jacob by the collar. 'Blackguard!' he growled, then hauled him outside.

Kate un-cocked the gun and leapt out of the carriage, just in time to see Sebastian deliver a blow to Jacob's face. Her cousin's head popped back and he landed on his back, out cold.

'John!' he called out to Mr Lawrence, who stood a few feet behind him, brandishing a shotgun. 'Take care of this bastard.'

'Right away, Your Grace.'

Mr Lawrence put the gun down and walked over to her unconscious cousin. Kneeling, he removed the loop of rope hanging from his shoulder and used it to tie Jacob's wrists together.

Sebastian finally turned to her. 'Are you all right? Did he hurt you? Touch you?'

She was in such a state of shock she blurted out the first thing that came to mind. 'What are you doing here?'

'What am I *doing* here?' he asked incredulously. 'I'm rescuing you! Are you—?' He glanced down at the gun in her hand. 'What are you doing with that?'

'I'm…uh…rescuing myself.'

Their eyes locked, and the look of pure relief on his face nearly had her weeping. She dropped the weapon and careered towards him, just as he opened his arms.

'Kate… Kate…' he murmured into her hair as he held her tight. 'Oh, God. I thought I'd lost you. That I would never see you—'

'That wasn't my letter,' she sobbed. 'Please, believe me.'

'I know… Shh, love… I know you didn't write that note,' he soothed.

Blinking back her tears, she looked at him. 'You do?'

'Of course I do,' he scoffed, then smiled down at her as he cupped her jaw with his warm hands. 'You would know how to spell "elopement".'

She barked out a laugh and then rubbed her cheek against his palm.

'I'm sorry,' he began, his tone remorseful. 'For the way I've been acting. And for the words I said to you this morning. I didn't mean any of them.'

'Then why did you say them?'

'I didn't want you to love me. Because I was afraid, Kate.' He swallowed hard and she could sense the internal battle within him. 'You were right. I was scared—of the truth. I couldn't protect my mother and I've felt so guilty. I didn't see how she was deteriorating. All those years I did nothing. She's brilliant, and beautiful—like you—and all that was eroded over time because I was too blinded by my love for my father. And in the end it nearly destroyed her. Because I couldn't save her from him. I failed her. And that's the real reason I feared turning into my father. Closing myself off to love made me feel I was in control of the situation, and it was the one thing I *could* do since I couldn't go back and change the past. But now I know all that was false.'

'Sebastian…' Her chest squeezed and her throat thickened with emotion she couldn't verbalise.

'Our marriage was supposed to be a business arrangement. But even before you agreed to marry me I already knew then I couldn't let Seagrave or anyone else have you. I deluded myself into thinking it was only because you might be with child. Then I started feeling things I wasn't supposed to.'

'Sebastian…'

He took her hands into his. 'So I stayed away, tried to put a stop to my emotions. But it was like trying to make a waterfall flow upwards.' He let out a huff. 'I tried to push you away. I said those things to you because I didn't want to end up hurting you and destroying your dreams, like my father did to my mother.'

'You couldn't,' she said.

'I know that now. It was my mother who made me see it.' His hands squeezed tight around hers. 'But, Kate, know that I love you. Only you.'

A dizziness came over her. It took her a moment, but Kate eventually remembered to breathe. 'I thought you didn't care for me at all. The night of the engagement ball… I was so overwhelmed by my own emotions. I wanted to tell you, but I was afraid. Afraid that you would change your mind if you had an inkling of how I felt about you. But this morning it just came out, and you said—'

'Shh…' Bringing her hands to his lips, he kissed her knuckles. 'Those were all lies. But if I've hurt you so much that you don't feel the same way any more I understand. I will do anything to be deserving of your love again.'

'There's no need for that. I love you, Sebastian. Only you.'

Strong arms came around her and hauled her to him without reserve, then his mouth came down and laid siege to her lips, so that she had no choice but to surrender. This was not their first kiss, but to Kate it felt like the first of something. That her life from now on would be bigger and better than before she met him.

When he pulled away at last her body felt boneless, and she dared not attempt to stand on her own. Instead, she leaned against him and pressed her cheek to his chest, feeling the solidness of the muscle underneath. 'Can we go home now? Please?'

'Of course, love. You can ride with me.' He nodded at Thunder, who stood patiently by the side of the road. 'Thank you, John,' he called out to his companion.

John bowed his head. 'No trouble at all, Your Grace. I'll haul this bugger into the carriage and take 'im straight to the magistrate.'

'I'd appreciate that, John.'

'Thank you, Mr Lawrence,' she said.

'Very welcome, miss.'

As they walked towards Thunder, she asked, 'How did you know where to find me?'

'It was easy enough. Malvery isn't exactly a sophisticated criminal mastermind. When he saw you run off after we quarrelled he went into the village, looking to hire a coachman. There's really only one coachman for hire in town—Thomas Brown. John overheard them negotiating in the tavern. Later, when he got back to his farm, John saw Brown's carriage heading in this direction.'

She glanced back and smiled at the man, who waved at her as he tossed Jacob into the carriage. 'Thank goodness.'

'Not that you needed my help,' he said wryly. 'Looks like you were doing very well on your own.'

'I didn't exactly have a plan for what to do next.' She smiled sheepishly up at him. 'So I'm glad you came after me.'

Halting, he turned to her, midnight eyes filled with a new emotion she'd never seen before—love.

'I will always come after you, Kate. Just try and get away from me. To quote our favourite Bard, "I'll follow thee and make a heaven of hell, to die upon the love I know—"'

'Oh, bother.' Her eyes rolled heavenwards. 'Not that drivel again.'

Gathering her in his arms, he leaned down close to her ear. 'How about...?'

His description of all the scandalous things he was going to do to her that night and every night for the rest of their lives made her shiver in all the most delicious places.

When he'd finished, he pressed a fiery kiss to that spot below her ear, then asked, 'Well? Was that acceptable?'

Wrapping her arms around his neck, she flashed him a wicked smile. 'That, Your Grace, was pure poetry.'

Epilogue

A few months later...

Kate, Duchess of Mabury, still didn't understand men as well as she did steam engines—and even if she did, she highly doubted her life would be simpler.

Take her husband, for example.

'Sebastian, where exactly are we going?'

'I told you, love, it's a surprise.'

'But why must I be blindfolded?'

He let out a frustrated sound. 'The very nature of a surprise demands one party must be kept in the dark until said surprise is revealed.'

'And so you decided to take that definition in its most literal sense?'

'Just indulge me this once, please, love?'

Kate sank back into the plush seating of the coach. Sebastian had said they were going into London for a night, to attend to some business with his solicitor, but when he'd produced the blindfold halfway through the journey, she'd known something was up.

She crossed her arms over her chest. 'I'll be bored. If you take off my blindfold, I could at least work on my design,' she said, patting the reticule on her lap, which bulged with another half-filled notebook and pencils. Once she was done with that, she would add it to the growing pile in her office at Highfield Park. And soon all those plans would turn into reality, as she finally settled into married life.

The wedding had been pushed through as planned, with no more setbacks, and Jacob was currently sitting in a London prison after his attempted kidnap of Kate. Apparently, Arthur had grown displeased with his cousin's failure to move their expansion along in England, and once Kate had secured a proposal from Sebastian he'd told Jacob he should be heading back to America. Much to Kate's surprise, Arthur had actually shown some remorse that his actions had driven Jacob to desperation, and he'd refused to bail Jacob out and completely washed his hands of him. Thankfully, with Arthur's vast resources and Sebastian's influence, they had been able to keep things hushed.

With all that ugliness behind them, Sebastian had taken her on a six-week-long honeymoon on the continent, where they'd visited his villa in the South of France, and another in Italy he was considering purchasing. Kate had fallen so in love with the gorgeous villa on a lake that Sebastian had bought it on the spot, and they'd extended their honeymoon for another two weeks.

As soon as they'd got back, however, Sebastian had immediately gone to work—not at the estate, but in London, gathering support from other peers in order to obtain approval from Parliament to start acquiring the land they needed to lay down railway lines. At the same time plans to start the construction of the factory were underway, but first they had to find the right location.

'Bored, eh…?' In her mind's eye, she could see him

raise a dark eyebrow mischievously. 'Perhaps I can help, Your Grace.'

'What—? Oh!' She felt her skirts being lifted and a hand wrapping around her ankle. 'Sebastian! We're in a coach.'

'I know,' he said, in that smooth, low baritone that never failed to make her shiver.

'B-but…do we have time?'

'All the time we need, love.'

And thus, for the next hour or so, her husband did, indeed, find a way to alleviate her boredom.

Making love half-undressed while blindfolded proved to be Kate's favourite thing to do in a coach. There was something about the motion of the wheels under them, and the fact that she couldn't see anything—only feel, hear, smell, and taste—that added a thrill to their love-making.

'Can I remove this blasted blindfold now?' she asked, breathless, as she lay on top of a naked Sebastian.

'Not yet, love.' He pressed his lips to her temple. 'But we should set you to rights as we're almost there.'

Kate didn't know how he did it, but Sebastian managed to re-lace her stays, button up her dress, and even smooth her coiffure while she remained blindfolded. He finished just as the coach stopped. Finally, they had reached their destination. Wherever this place was.

'Careful,' he said, as he guided her down from the coach.

Her travelling boots hit solid ground, and she could smell and feel the humidity in the air and hear the shrieks of gulls above them. 'Sebastian, where are we?' She was dying from anticipation.

'One moment.' He guided her forward a few feet before halting. 'Ah, here we are.'

When the blindfold was lifted, the harsh light piercing through her eyelids made her pause before she even attempted to open her eyes. After blinking away the blurriness, she found her vision revealed that they were standing near water, on a large, empty piece of ground.

'Sebastian? What is this? Where are we?'

'We're on the Thames River, a few miles south of London,' he said matter-of-factly. 'But to be more specific we're standing on the site of the future Mason & Wakefield Railway Works.'

She gasped. 'All of this land is ours?'

'Yes—and we'll be ready to break ground as soon as you approve the plans. Do you like it?'

'Of course I do!' She flung herself in his arms. 'Thank you,' she murmured against the side of his neck.

'And a few miles up there—' he nodded upriver '—is where Cornelius will be establishing the DeVries Furnace and Iron Company in London. That way, all the necessary materials can be shipped down here via the Thames.'

'That's fantastic news.'

While Cornelius DeVries hadn't originally planned to open his own forge in England, somehow Arthur and Sebastian had used their combined powers of persuasion and convinced him it would be a wise move. Kate had been thrilled, as had Maddie, because it meant that the DeVrieses would be staying in London for a long time, whether or not the two sisters found English husbands.

'By the way,' Kate began, 'a letter from Mama—your Mama—arrived this morning. She'll soon be finished with packing up her Hertfordshire home and shall be fully moved into the dower house by week's end.'

Sebastian's face lit up. 'Wonderful.'

It was clear that the Dowager Duchess had finally

put the past behind her and found a new purpose in life. After everything had been settled, her new mother-in-law had confessed to Kate that when she'd initially read Miss Merton's letter she had been intrigued by her description of Kate and Maddie and their unusual interest in the sciences, and that was what had prompted her to invite them to Highfield Park. She'd said she saw herself in both the girls, and that was why she'd wanted to help them.

And Kate was confident that if she herself could find love, then Maddie, too, would find someone who truly deserved her. Speaking of which…

'You know what Mama living at Highfield Park means, though, don't you?' she said.

'What?'

'The Season will be here again soon.'

'And so?' Sebastian asked. 'What does that have to do with us?'

'Well…' Kate bit her lip, wondering how to broach the topic with her husband. 'Apparently, after her success in matching me, Mama has decided to continue with her project.'

'Project?'

'Yes. Finding girls like me and bringing them to Highfield Park to find them their own husbands.'

'Oh, dear Lord…' Sebastian massaged his temple. 'That means our peace shall be disturbed.'

Kate laughed. 'But it also means Maddie is coming back.'

'Good,' Sebastian said. 'I like her.'

'And Caroline, too, unfortunately.'

Her husband groaned. 'Why?'

'Sebastian!' Kate admonished. 'It would be unkind to

leave her out. Besides, Mama has explained that finding Caroline a husband will help keep her out of trouble.'

'As long as she stays away from us,' he grumbled. 'Now, come.' He gave her a quick kiss on the nose. 'Let's have a walk around.'

Kate could barely contain her excitement as she and Sebastian toured the site. Sure, it was mostly bare for now, but she could see the potential. When they paused near the edge of the water she closed her eyes and pictured her factory. Yes, *hers*.

It's really coming true, Pap.

And she knew that if her grandfather were here, he would be the first to celebrate with her.

'Lord, you're exquisite when you do that.'

She chuckled and turned to Sebastian. 'Do what, exactly?'

Those onyx eyes darkened with promise. 'When you stand there thinking. Dreaming. Breathing.'

Reaching out, he drew her closer, his arms wrapping around as he lowered his head, his mouth capturing hers in a kiss that left her breathless.

'You know,' he said as he pulled back, 'you never did answer my question.'

'I—I beg your pardon?' Her knees wobbled, and she had to brace herself against him or risk melting into a puddle. 'What question?'

The corner of his mouth inched up. 'Do you believe in love?'

'Of course I do, my Pyramus,' she answered without hesitation. Even though she couldn't open it up and take it apart, she knew love existed. The very evidence stood before her. 'And how about you?' she asked. 'Do you still think love is as unsteady as sand?'

Cupping her chin in his hand, he gazed down at her.

'Your love is anything but unsteady, my Thisbe. It is unwavering like stone. Constant as the sunrise…as the rain in the spring and snow in the winter.'

Moisture gathered at the corners of her eyes. 'I am your faithful love, until the end.'

'Until the end,' he agreed, his breath hitching. 'But let's not talk of the end, love.' Slipping an arm around her, he turned her to face the water and the bright blue sky above. 'Because this is just the beginning.'

* * * * *

If you enjoyed this story, be sure to look out for more great books from Paulia Belgado, coming soon!